"Seductive. . . . Lisa Carey's second novel contains as much magic as [*The Mermaids Singing*]." —*Dallas Morning News*

"Lisa Carey is a major talent with brilliantly luminescent writing. Rarely today do we find new writers who can craft characters, scenes, and settings with such a beautiful touch. This soaring, descriptive writing is certainly the best seen in the last quarter-century." —*Bangor News*

"Catherine and Heathcliff enter the twentieth century. . . . [A] powerfully evocative novel." —*Irish Edition*

"Riveting. . . . The setting is stark, romantic, and evocative; the characters are rugged and likable; the tone is dreamy. . . . The subtle, naturalistic way that Carey leads us to accept that a girl who never fit in when alive in nineteenth-century Ireland can find her place as a ghost in twenty-first-century America is remarkable." —*Maine Sunday Telegram*

"Lusciously lyrical, Carey's second novel once again seductively crosses the line between reality and magic. If her first, *The Mermaids Singing*, introduced her as a skillful writer . . . and acquired her a considerable readership, her new book should establish her as a serious presence in the field of quality . . . fiction." —*Publishers Weekly*

About the Author

LISA CAREY received her M.F.A. in creative writing from Vermont College. *In the Country of the Young* is her second novel, following her highly praised debut, *The Mermaids Singing*, which was translated into seven languages and has been optioned for a film. She lived in Ireland for five years and resides in Massachusetts with her dog, Axel.

ALSO BY LISA CAREY

The Mermaids Singing

In
the
Country
of
the
Young

LISA CAREY

Perennial

An Imprint of HarperCollins*Publishers*

A hardcover edition of this book was published in 2000 by William Morrow, an imprint of
HarperCollins Publishers.

First Perennial edition published 2002.

Designed by Claire Vaccaro

Library of Congress Cataloging-in-Publication Data is available.

ISBN 0-06-093774-2

02   03   04   05   06   ❖/RRD   10   9   8   7   6   5   4   3   2   1

FOR MY BROTHER

Love to all of you who heard me say:
Not until the book is finished.

Guide to Pronunciation of Names

Oisin = *Oh-sheen*

Aisling = *Ash-ling*

Darragh = *Dah-rah*

Nieve = *Nee-av*

She is a girl and would not be afraid
to walk the whole world with herself.

LADY GREGORY

Visions and Beliefs in the West of Ireland

PROLOGUE:
THE DEAD

She was only a girl—an unwanted, invisible child, crouched within the beginning of her life—but when she died, it changed everything. The island where she landed now has a history that, if mapped, would look like a crossroads: a time line of unremarkable events intersected by a single, fate-altering tragedy.

She came to them from the sea. In 1848, twenty miles off the coast of Maine, November arrived with the first of the winter's blizzards. A local fisherman, surveying the storm from the warmth of his house, spotted a stain of red amid the horizon of gray and churning sea. He fetched his spyglass and focused it on the image in the turmoil. A flag. A quartered Union Jack, surrounded by red, hoisted within the void of the storm. It was flying upside down.

"Ship in distress," the fisherman bellowed, as if he were giving orders on deck. The cry startled his wife and daughters, and his son, a brave boy of sixteen who had been raised a sailor, jumped up. Father and son went for their jackets and boots and hurried out into the blizzard.

One by one the island fishermen were summoned from their homes. The flag told them that the ship was with the British merchant fleet, as did the size of it, which they glimpsed through the snow, a hulking mass of wood, tipped to its side, shuddering with the battering of water and ice. A cargo ship, most likely blown off course on its way to Canada. The fishermen knew the dangers of the shallow sandbars to the east of their island; this was not the first ship that had run aground, but it was the largest one.

The fishermen set their storm sails and, one at a time, battled their way toward the ship. After hours of effort, one schooner managed to pull up alongside the vessel. The others waited, watching when the sea ebbed enough to let them, the small boat rising above the rails of the ship with each massive wave.

When the schooner finally returned to the harbor, the men waiting on the quay expected to welcome a handful of hardy but storm-tired seamen. Instead, what they dragged, dripping onto the solid planks of the island pier, looked and felt alarmingly like children.

"Over a hundred passengers," the captain shouted to his neighbors, his voice barely reaching above the screams of the storm. "No sign of crew. Vessel breaking apart."

They *were* children. A dozen ghostly, half frozen children slapped dumb by fear. The wives were fetched to gather and warm them, and the men set out to try to save the rest.

The rescue stretched over the two long days of the blizzard, the fishermen making runs when the tide allowed them to sail. As the men navigated ice floes and the swells, which grew with every hour of the storm, the women coaxed a story from the older children, who spoke in broken English, shuddering in blankets by the church hearth.

Theirs was an emigrant ship, on its way to Quebec from Ireland. They had been at sea for eight weeks; many of their parents had died of fever and been dropped over the railings, left behind in the depths of the Atlantic. The island women had heard rumors of the massive exodus from famine-ridden Ireland, and of the "coffin ships," where passengers were stored like cattle in the cramped, airless hold, victims to the contagion of typhoid and cholera. These stories had come home with their husbands from trips to Boston, but the women had believed them exaggerated. Looking at the wasted faces of these children, their little brows set in a permanent poise of horror, the women felt shame chase away their disbelief.

Out at sea, the island men saved 150 souls, 100 of whom were children, lifting them one by one over the railings of the ship and passing them down to the outstretched hands on the decks of the schooners. After shouted exchanges with the few men onboard— where the accents proved difficult to understand—they learned that the crew had abandoned ship and had last been seen trying to make their way to safety in the lifeboat. They were never found.

By the time all of the passengers had been brought ashore, the cargo ship, abused for two days by rough water and wind, was threatening to break apart. Jack Seward, the fisherman who had originally spotted the flag, standing on the massive deck from where he'd been dangling small bodies toward their rescue, heard the moan of timber and felt beneath his feet a shudder, which had a desperate quality, as though the ship were protesting as she fell victim to her final, violent death throes.

"Checking the hold," Jack bellowed down to his son, Daniel, who was waiting in the schooner with the others, to assist his father back down.

"No!" protested the fishermen. They were anxious to sail away from the splintering ship. But Jack had already disappeared, making his way on sturdy sea legs.

Jack forced open the hatch and ducked down the stairs into the hold. The darkness at first was absolute, and when he lost his footing and was immersed in icy water, he thought he'd fallen through a hole into the sea. Then he came to the surface, sputtering, relieved as his feet touched the wood floor below.

What overwhelmed him was the stench. The air down here, though obviously freshened a bit by the influx of seawater, was still unbreathable: he was swimming in a soup of human waste, and the taste in his mouth told him that what he'd spat out was the loose, foul product of illness. He gagged and his waterlogged ears popped in response.

As his eyes adjusted to the grayish light from the hatch door, he began to make out the dimensions of the room. The walls were latticed with crude bunks, burlap sacks of belongings still tied to them, swinging forgotten in the storm.

"Anyone there?" he screamed, for the racket below was at its worst, the shriek of wind and groaning of timber echoing upon itself endlessly.

He sensed a movement of human proportions in the water behind him, and reached toward it. His hand closed on fabric and flesh and he knew, from the absence of resistance, what he had found. A face streamed into the gray light, the dead face of a woman, her eyes frozen open, the lashes and fine hairs above her lip crusted with ice.

Another wave set the boat in motion, and he was thrown backward, bombarded by a dozen more corpses. Jack swam toward the hatch, pushing his way through the dead, who, within the currents, seemed to be performing a violent water dance.

He climbed back up to the deck, and made his way toward the

railings, back to the schooner, his son and home. Had her large eyes not flashed in the darkness like a cat's, Jack Seward might have lived. But he saw her and faltered.

Crouched beneath the railing was a small girl, no older than six or seven, who had wound herself up in dangling ropes until she was fastened to the bow like a tiny ornament. Though it was clear by her stare that she could see Jack, she made no attempt to communicate; absent from her lips were the pleas he'd heard from the other passengers. Slowly, his boots slipping on the hail-strewn deck, he made his way over to her.

"It's all right, darlin'," he said, and began to untangle the fury of knots tied at her middle. She only blinked at him, apparently unable to respond. But when he'd freed her from her net and started to lift her into his arms, she resisted with a strength that surprised him.

"My brother," she said, and Jack thought at first he'd imagined it, for surely her voice was too soft to reach his ears over the cacophony of the storm. But she spoke again: "My brother, where is he?"

There was no time for answering questions. But Jack had a girl, about this size, of his own.

"I've got him," he said. "He's waiting for you on the island." Her eyes grew larger at this, and she allowed him to scoop her up, wincing in a way that made him suspect that those ropes had broken her tiny ribs.

He tried to hold her gently as he struggled back to the safety line leading to his boat. Once there, he dangled her over the rails, and silently asked her forgiveness as he dropped her into the waiting arms of Daniel. His son caught the girl, then yelled something up to him. Though his voice was swept up in the wind, Jack could read his lips enough to know that one of the words had been "Dad," which meant that Daniel was frightened. Normally, while onboard, his son addressed him as "Captain."

Then there was an explosion.

Daniel had seen the wave coming; he had been trying to tell Jack to jump down along with the girl. Daniel watched his father in slow motion as the rails were ripped from his hands, his body flung into the air, thrown away from the ship and into the sea.

Though they searched for hours, they could find no sign of Jack Seward; it was as though the force of that plunge had sent him plummeting to the ocean floor, where he stayed, the sea closing over him like the lid of a coffin. When it became clear that the schooner might soon follow, the other fishermen held the grieving Daniel back from the rigging and made their precarious way home.

The girl Jack Seward had lost his life saving died quietly on the church pew where she had been laid to recover. In the confusion that followed the rescue, with the islanders tending to 150 frostbitten and ill Irish passengers, the girl lay dead for hours before anyone noticed her. It was the minister's wife who finally found her small body, swaddled in blankets, already stiff between her shivering neighbors. The minister's wife asked around, planning to break the news to the girl's family. Information from the other passengers was contradictory—some believed the girl had been traveling alone, others recalled an older brother lost to fever in the middle of the journey. A few could not remember having seen her before at all. She had apparently been so self-sufficient and shy, she had passed eight weeks on the ship as quietly as she had ceased to breathe.

The girl was buried beneath the Seward headstone in the graveyard, occupying half the space that Jack would have if his body had been found. Though they tried, no one could remember her name, so no memory of her was carved on the face of the stone.

The other shipwrecked passengers recovered for a few weeks on the island. Eventually, most of the adults—young men and women caring for their siblings, old couples who had lost both children and grandchildren—decided that they would travel no further. They settled on the island, dividing up the orphans among their already large families, building houses and joining in the local professions of fishing and farming. Thanks to the efforts of the island doctor, who had spent ten years in Boston and learned the value of quarantine, the fever that had killed so many on the passage never spread beyond the passengers. And the islanders, feeling a kinship with those whom they'd rescued, welcomed them into their community.

The island had originally been settled by a group of colonists determined to build an autonomous community on virgin land. Later generations would remark upon their sheer determination with pride. By the time of the Irish shipwreck, however, the island population had been dwindling for years, as the isolation and harsh winters took their toll, and the islanders who hadn't given up and moved away were tired. It seemed the survivors of the wreck, who had come from the western province of Ireland and were used to struggling with bad weather, stubborn land, and life on the fringe of society, had arrived just in time. So the tragedy, ultimately, saved the island from extinction— and even christened it with a new name.

The ship had been called *Tír na nÓg*, an Irish name for a mythical land called "The Country of the Young." It had been common for famine ships to compete for customers by giving the ships romantic, appealing names. A week after the storm, the emigrant ship's name board washed ashore on the island, where it was recovered by one of the passengers, a middle-aged bachelor, Patrick Molloy, who later married Jack Seward's widow and raised his stepchildren with a gentle, unobtrusive kindness. Patrick hung the name board over his door as a reminder of the tragedy which had brought him there.

As the years went by and marriages between the Irish and the locals became more frequent, the accent of the islanders became a strange concoction of rural Maine twang and Connemara lilt, and—especially as the children began to outnumber the adults—the island began to be referred to with a bastardized version of the ship's name: "Tiranogue." The old name, which honored a township in England none of them had ever seen, was eventually discarded.

And though the tale of the shipwreck has become the focal point of the island's history, though it has been passed down and paid homage to as a legend of heroism and survival—even reaching the shores of Ireland and setting the course for future emigrants—when island children first hear this story, from their grandparents or in a schoolroom history lesson, it is not the living they remember. Later, when they are grown, most see the shipwreck with its intended inspiration. But at first telling, all children, with a fear that is that much more powerful because it is newborn in their brains, imagine that nameless girl, who tied herself to life with the knots of a sailor, was saved by a brave man, but died anyway, alone and forgotten, as though it hardly mattered that she was young.

PART ONE

Winter

The boundaries which divide Life from Death,

are at best shadowy and vague.

Who shall say where the one ends,

and the other begins?

EDGAR ALLAN POE

The Premature Burial

1.

In the palm of his hand, beneath ink stains and scars from careless splatters of acid, Oisin MacDara has three life lines.

He has known this since he was twenty-two, when he paid ten dollars on the street in Portland for a palm reading. The young woman who held his hand and traced its lines with a flirtatious stroke that left him half hard did not look like a spiritual adviser. Instead, she could have been one of the female students whom Oisin had seduced during his year of teaching art at the community college. Which was half the reason he'd stopped and put his hand out in the first place.

"Your life line is broken into three," she said. "This is the first part of your life." She pointed to the indented half moon in the curve between his thumb and forefinger. "It's the deepest line: your life as a child." She smiled at him, and the tiny green stone in her nostril rose slightly out of its hole.

"This is the second part of your life," she said, running her thumb over the center of his palm, where a fierce jumble of slices converged, like brambles attacking the skin.

"And this is your last life."

A line so smooth he could have etched it himself, reaching all the way to the pale skin that barely guarded the blue veins of his wrist.

"You are here now," she told him, pointing to the thicket of brambles. She had a Maine accent. She was trying to disguise it, but it leaked into her words, *he-ah* for *here*.

She looked up at Oisin, narrowing her eyes. It occurred to him that he could have sex with this girl. At twenty-two, such opportunities were still new enough to surprise him, and sometimes he forgot to ask himself whether he was interested before his seduction reflex took over. This time, he resisted.

I'll give her a miss, he thought. It was superstition more than anything that made him walk away. He was afraid of jinxing the palm reading, of disrespecting that small psychic moment. For she had recognized what he had always known—that there was a gap, a clear divide between his childhood and his life now. When he was young, he could see (he'd had a gift, a second sight), and in the years that followed, everything, even the tangible world, had seemed indistinct. As though, sometime during puberty, he'd gone blind.

Though his neighbors think he is a cynical, faithless man, Oisin is actually highly superstitious. It's his demeanor that's misleading. He is intensely moody, his eyes seem to search faces for evil motives, and he has a sarcastic, sometimes harsh humor. People tend to assume that he would not be open-minded to the spiritual or supernatural aspects of life. Nobody realizes that Oisin knows more than most about such things.

If he were as cynical as he appeared, he would have tossed the moment aside, denounced it later as a whim and the girl as a New Age student desperate for hash money. But Oisin, who is secretly hopeful above all else, in the twenty years since he had his palm analyzed in Portland, has been waiting for his sight to be returned, and for his last life to begin.

T he haunting begins with an open door and missing tobacco, though Oisin, who has grown lazy from so much waiting, does not recognize it at first.

Oisin has been smoking since he was a teenager, but in the two years since his fortieth birthday, he has rolled his own cigarettes from imported blond tobacco. He rolls them partly because it is cheaper, partly because he enjoys the ritual of creating each smoke, and mostly because he considers it a step toward giving up smoking altogether. Rollies are healthier, he tells himself; pure tobacco, none of the burning agents, glass fragments, or formaldehyde you find in filter cigarettes. This pure tobacco leaves brown streaks where his two front teeth meet, which he scrapes off with a paring knife every few weeks.

This is the second time he has lost the eight-dollar tin that is supposed to last him a month. He's too much of an addict to be careless about where he leaves the tobacco. He has considered the possibility of schizophrenia and imagines that he is experiencing blackouts during which he chain-smokes and then disposes of the evidence. Perhaps he has a second personality that is not getting its fair share of nicotine.

Before beginning the day's work in his studio, he drives to the island quay to buy another tin. Lined along the docks in a sheltered bay are Tiranogue's few businesses: a restaurant with picnic table seating, a pub with fishing nets catching dust on the ceiling, a husband-and-wife-owned store specializing in hardware and Irish sweaters, and a lobster hut rocking perilously on a small float, tended by local girls in bikinis who reapply suntan oil when they're not hoisting submerged traps of shellfish.

Oisin enters the general grocer, which is stocked with everything Moira, the proprietor, imagines an islander might need. In one corner is a soda fountain pharmacy, where locals can have a bowl of chowder while Moira's brother, Michael, fills their prescription. It has the same menu as the restaurant, and often Michael runs next door to fill orders for clam plates, but the locals never enter the restaurant—it is meant for the tourists.

Moira orders Oisin's tobacco specially; all the other islanders smoke one of four popular brands of filter cigarettes. He wants to explain to her that he just keeps losing his supply so she won't start ordering extra tobacco. He can imagine her unease as it slowly goes stale on the shelf. But he's afraid of how this absentmindedness will look, and how rumors of his deteriorating brain will spread. He ends up buying two tins; it seems easier than explaining. He'll hide one from himself and test the sharpness of his errant personality.

Once back in his studio, he cannot work. He'd planned on beginning a new print plate today; the sheet of copper gleams across the table, teasing him. All he can think about are the possible whereabouts of his missing tobacco. He searches the junkyard of the studio but finds only three half-filled lighters. He checks the pockets of his jackets in case he went for a smoke-walk he doesn't remember. Because his attention span is limited, the search for the missing tobacco evolves into an inventory of print materials. There are things missing here, as well; he doesn't remember his ink supply being so low, and where has he left his favorite sketching pencil? He has to make a shopping list for his next trip to the mainland, and the task calms him. Though he is not an organized man, Oisin occasionally spends hours on the simple logistics of life. He always does this when his work is not going well or when he's feeling the fear of beginning a new piece. He sometimes worries that he puts more energy into procrastination than anything else.

He is relieved when the daylight is gone; it has become obvious that his only hope is to begin again tomorrow. He walks the wooded path from his studio to his cottage, and it is only as he rounds a corner, and sees the cracks around his front door glowing with the light from the kitchen, that he remembers.

Last week, on the night of the full moon equinox, Oisin had left his front door open until morning. He has done this every November for almost thirty years, but it's been ages since he truly expected anything to come of it. Now the light in a house that should be dark pulls him toward his door with a combination of thrill and panic. He swings it open, propping it with a tree-trunk stool from the porch. Please please please, he repeats in his mind, and he hopes this begging will serve as an invitation.

He knows what happened to his tobacco. Something has entered his hermitage, something he has anticipated for more than half of his life. Something that most people—if they believed in such things at all—would not welcome with an open door.

These are the things the ghost does for the first week, which Oisin records in his journal—not with words, but with tiny charcoal sketches:

It slams the front door open and shut whenever Oisin is trying to sleep. It pilfers clumps from his tobacco tin and all his matches and lighters. It brings bright red leaves into the house and tucks them under his pillow and inside his wooden box of carving tools. It goes through a stack of his prints in the studio and carpets the floor with them, grouping images by subject: trees together, female figures lined up, horses surrounded on all sides by ocean waves.

And, at night, when Oisin is in bed, he feels a pressing sensation by his feet, a puckering in the blanket as though something, something very small, has settled there to look at him.

Though hauntings are nothing new to Oisin, it has been so long since he experienced one that he is plagued by something he tells himself is excitement, but which is closer to fear. As a boy, Oisin was able to see the spirits which disrupted homes. Now he can only see the disruption. Sometimes he believes that it is not a ghost but his mind finally snapping. Perhaps he has gone mad in a way that disguises itself as a sort of resurrection or awakening.

In his good moods, when he believes, he talks to her.

"Nieve," he will say, rolling up the last crumbs of his tobacco, "lay off the smokes, *le do thoil*." If you please. He has started reciting phrases in a badly accented Irish, a language he has not studied since he was a boy.

"*Is leor sin!*" he explodes, when the door slams so hard that the mugs shake on their hooks in the kitchen. That is enough!

Sometimes, he thinks that the invisible being in the house responds to the Irish. Then he will hear himself as a stranger might, an eccentric alone in his cottage, scolding the thin air in a language most people in the world cannot name. This is when he crawls into bed (Oisin tends to nap whenever he is faced with a serious dilemma) and contemplates antipsychotic drugs or a move to a warmer, more benign climate. Sex would do, he thinks, but if he found a willing partner, wouldn't he feel like he was being watched?

It is only after hours of thoughts like this—during the three A.M. questioning of his life and his sanity—that Oisin actually sees her.

Up in the exposed beams of his cottage ceiling, as though they belong to some crouching, deliberating cat, he sees two eyes watching him from the darkness. Large, shifting eyes that seem to be gulping down everything, that stare at him with both fascination and familiarity. The particularly naked gaze of the young. Though he tells himself otherwise in the morning, Oisin doesn't recognize these eyes. They are luminescent—a color he has never seen before, a color that will not stand still, like melting gold or the sun moving down toward the water.

Though Oisin is wrong about who watches him, he is right about one thing: the eyes belong to a child.

O isin lives in a place where he can hear his neighbors' phones ringing, not because they live crammed close together, but because so much quiet stretches between them.

Tiranogue Island has a population that changes with the seasons; it is packed with day tourists and cottage owners in the warm months and deserted in the winter except for two hundred locals. The only class distinction here is between the islanders, the summer people, and the tourists. The islanders, though in the minority, are the makers of this distinction. Summer people—those who own houses and have returned every season for years—are tolerated, though occasionally ridiculed. Tourists are barely endured and penalized with inflated prices. Oisin does not fit into any of these categories. He is a permanent resident who is not an islander. He has heard himself referred to as a "blow-in," in a good-natured, teasing tone. He suspects that the islanders are easier on him than they are on others "from away," but that they don't trust him as they do one another. It would not be tolerated if he began to call himself a local.

Oisin's end of the island remains quiet even in July and August,

because the woods here are still wild and the west end has no beach—
only a small strip of slimy green rocks peek out at low tide. Oisin's
habit, in the ten years since he bought the one-room cottage and con-
verted studio barn, has been to avoid the east end during the busiest
months. He ignores tourists, but he doesn't buddy up with the locals,
either. Though he came here because he was attracted to the island's
history, the hint of Irish in the accents, the fierce loyalty to home that
reminds him of the neighborhood he grew up in, he remains a loner,
as he has been for most of his life. Aside from trips to buy art supplies, Oisin is always in one of three places: the woods, his cottage, or
his studio. Though lately he is not alone in any of them.

When he walks in the woods now, he hears, behind his own careful footsteps, the sound of someone swishing and kicking through
layers of leaves. The banging continues through the cottage at night.
And today, in his studio, a present has been left for him.

Laid out on the large wooden worktable are pieces of Oisin's best
print paper, covered with thick blotches of dark ink. As Oisin moves
closer, the blotches take shape. Palm prints, half the size of his own,
carefully made so that the lines show through in eggshell white. Unlike Oisin's, the lines in this palm are simple and few. One life line,
one heart line, one head line. They are not branched or broken but
solid. There is no fate line, no creative mark, no slices for children or
wealth or illness. A small, new hand, with limitless possibilities.

Oisin, a shiver moving up his neck, clears the table and tries to
work. He hasn't created a new print in too long, and he has the per-
vasive desperate sound knocking in his brain that is there whenever he
neglects his art. A sound that seems to say: *if you leave it too long it will
be taken from you.*

He wants to find a print he made years ago—which he remembered last night as he sat up listening to the ghost. He searches through

seven portfolio cases before he finds it—a large piece of paper with rough, natural edges. He made it from a copper etching; the image is a simple room in a small house, a large fireplace dominating the back wall, the only furniture a table and mismatched chairs. There are figures crowding the room—separated into two types by their shading. Figures predominantly black, with white lines outlining their features, and figures that are mainly the empty space of the paper, their features inked with the lightest gray. For each pale figure, a black figure hovers close by, watching or imitating body posture or action. At the table, two people squash into each chair, one pale and one dark. By the fireplace, where there burns an orange fire—the only color in the print— a pale boy stands next to a tall, dark man. They are the only two who appear to be aware of each other. The title of the print is written in the bottom corner in Oisin's writing: *Spirit Night*. He looks at it now and hears the words in Irish in his mind. *Oíche na sprideanna.* The night the dead come home. It is his grandmother's house in Ireland—where he hasn't been since he was a boy. A time when he could see two types of people in every room. In this print, the pale people are alive, and the dark ones, who were once so much more real to him, are ghosts.

He wants to do a new print with the figures like this one—himself pale and ghostly, and a girl, dark and real, dominating the room. He makes a few sketches, but after an hour of mostly staring out the window, he gives up and marches away from his studio.

He can't draw her. He is having trouble remembering what she looks like.

In the mornings, when he would normally be beginning work over his second cup of coffee, Oisin looks for her.

Three hundred yards into the woods are two trees layered with an inch of lime green moss. The intricate fur grows up beyond where he can see, disappearing into the branches of surrounding pines. This is a quiet, attractive resting point in acres of pathless forest. It is here that Oisin built a fort when he first moved to the island. Woven in the space between the twin trees is a canopy of pinecones, wire, and branches. Clinging vines grow up toward this roof to create the walls of a miniature house. If you don't look closely enough to see the glint of wire, the house appears to have grown there, perhaps for the purpose of sheltering some small, hibernating being. Oisin is not a big man, and could probably fit inside if he curled his body just the right way. But he has never entered the fort. He built it for someone else.

There has been evidence lately that someone is hiding here. Shuffled pine needles, a long blond hair pinched in the bark. The once empty air holds within it the traces of living breath.

Each time he visits, he kneels by the slivered opening in fern and whispers into the room. "Nieve?" he says, and the desperate, begging tone of this frightens him. "Nieve, are you here?"

There is never a response, and eventually he leaves feeling foolish. A victim of his own imagination.

One morning, as he stands up, he sees a woman's face peering at him from behind a green trunk.

"Hello, MacDara." The face belongs to Deirdre Molloy, Oisin's closest neighbor in the woods of the west end of the island. Her hair is pulled back in a ponytail under a navy blue baseball cap, which makes her face and her large brown eyes look much younger, even girlish.

"I usually don't meet humans this early in the morning," says Deirdre, in the strange accent peculiar to this island. Not the voice

Oisin was expecting. When Deirdre realizes that Oisin is not going to respond, she looks down at the little house.

"This is my favorite of the things you've made," she says, and she runs a finger over the pattern of pinecones on the roof. "It reminds me of a book I used to read to my son—*Peter Pan*. It looks like Wendy's house."

Oisin still hasn't acknowledged Deirdre, has in fact stopped looking at her and is staring down at the opening in the ferns. The islanders are used to Oisin's moods. Sometimes, without warning, he ceases to speak. His silence does not give the impression that he is ignoring people, rather it is like he has just gone away, and is listening to something that only he can hear. His neighbors have learned to wait until Oisin returns to the world before attempting to talk to him. Except for Deirdre, whose approach is just to keep talking, raising her voice the way some people do with foreigners, slicing through Oisin's silence.

"I can't remember the story of Wendy's house, now," Deirdre says. "Either the boys thought Wendy was dead and they were building her a tomb, or she was just sleeping and they were protecting her from the rain."

Occasionally, Deirdre has posed a question to the silent Oisin that he does not answer right away, but days later he will reopen the topic without introduction, as though he'd merely paused in thought. She expects that later on this week, Oisin will pass her on the road and say, "Wendy was only sleeping."

Like many of the unmarried island women, Deirdre has had sex with Oisin. But, unlike most of them, she does not hold a grudge. It was only one night, over three years ago, and occasionally the two of them forget that they have even seen each other naked. Although Oisin forgets more often than Deirdre does.

"See you later," says Deirdre, and she leaves him standing by the knee-high roof, looking confused, like a man who was searching for something in his dreams, and now that he is awake, can't remember what it was he was looking for.

In the gloaming, Oisin has a tendency toward obsessive reflection. He does not think back on his day but mourns the patterns of his life as a whole. When he is lonely, he worries that he has burned too many bridges and wishes there were another body keeping his bed warm, wishes there were a woman he could call who won't hang up on him. New women, whom he generally finds in the summer, require too much preliminary work. And eventually, they, too, end up on the DO NOT CALL list. As if there is a club, a support group, a military barracks of women trained to shoot his charms down at first sight.

Oisin has a reputation for being quite good in bed. Which surprises some women, since he has never been in a relationship that lasted longer than four months. These women tend to think that prolonged intimacy teaches men what they need to know about a woman's body. When it comes to Oisin, they are wrong. Oisin takes women more seriously, every detail of them, than he has ever taken anything, including his art. Which is part of the reason (besides the fact that he believes he has not truly lived for the past twenty-seven years) why he has never been in love. It would be too exhausting for him. As he studies women, he finds more and more that is unfathomable to him, and this makes him afraid. Luckily for Oisin, fear has always been an aphrodisiac.

Which is why, this evening, as he lies on the stale sheets of his bed, watching the kitchen cupboards slam open and closed in a rhythmic performance, Oisin has an erection. It is standing up beneath the blankets over his lap, mocking him. There is nothing he can do about it—he hasn't masturbated in a week for fear of feeling like some pervert in a schoolyard jerking off in front of a child. Even an invisible, irritating ghost-child.

"Hey, Nieve," Oisin calls out to the empty, charged kitchen. "My neighbor asked if I was remodeling the house. She can hear every noise you make, so you'd better quiet it down unless you want the whole island's attention."

It is then that he sees a different sort of movement, something solid, heavier than the flash of eyes. The only light in the room is the candle he left in the window, so all he can make out is a dark shadow against another quality of darkness. He freezes in bed, not breathing, his penis hardening further with the terror. The shadow moves again, a figure about as tall as the countertop, and there is a clinking of glass in the dish drainer.

"Nieve?" Oisin whispers, and the sound of his own voice gives him the courage to move. He drops his feet slowly to the pine boards of the floor, pulling the blanket around his shoulders and draping it in front to hide his bouncing erection. As he walks toward the kitchen, he hears the tap turn on, and the hollow, rushing noise of a glass filling up with water. Away from the candlelight, Oisin's eyes adjust, and the pale twilight reveals the shadow of a small person facing the sink. He stops walking when he hears the next noise. The gulping, gasping noise of a desperately thirsty person guzzling water. The figure drains a large glass, taking only three loud breaths between swallows. The gulping ends and then there is a gentle, charming little sigh. Then a child-sized belch.

Oisin pulls the ceiling light chain.

A girl is there. Dressed in a dirty rag of a dress, turning to look at him with the large, gold eyes that have studied everything from the rafters. Her hair in the overhead light appears dark for an instant, then when she shifts, fair. She is there in vivid detail, down to a mustache of beaded water above her generous mouth. A dead girl, looking more real and more alive than anyone he has ever seen.

She is not the girl—Oisin knows this with an instant, wrenching disappointment—whom he has been waiting for.

2.

When his face peers between the ferns, close enough that she can see lines like roads on a map leading away from his eyes, Aisling thinks he can't possibly be looking for her. Even when she was alive, she was not wanted.

She was aware of being unwanted before she ever learned the word for it. She knew it by the rough, careless touch of the woman who fed her, who handled her small body as though she were smashing it against a hard surface rather than drawing it to her breast. She knew it by the face of the man, the line that appeared like a wound between his eyebrows when she passed into his vision. Her unwantedness was a part of her, as unquestionable as her beauty, which, like her presence, was resented, and which, until she learned the meaning of the word, she believed was a kind of deformity.

When words finally began to grow in her, she learned the names of everything she could, collecting them the way some children collect rocks or shells—at first indiscriminately, in piles; later, choosing the words according to their beauty, their harshness, or simply because they seemed unwanted themselves. But she never found words for the man and woman. The others called them Mammy and Da, but her instinct told her that these words didn't belong on the tongue of the unwanted. When she was forced to refer to them she used pronouns—Himself, Herself—words that could refer to anyone and did not have the intimacy of names.

The others had names that sounded like the qualities of the bearer: Margaret, who slapped. Hannah, who sighed and whose gaze never focused. Aileen with her shrill voice and quick hands, who preferred quarreling to talk. These girls were alien to her—their bodies had less energy, seemed to grow out rather than up, sprouted strange blemishes and dark hairs, and smelled of greasy skin, rather than of the grass, bog, and fire she smelled on herself. When they were not in physical pain, they were in mental anguish, mourning their noses or chins. "I suppose you think you're a beauty, do you not?" they would bark at her. When really, without their comments, she would barely know what she looked like. She sensed that perhaps if she were older, or she were wanted, she would understand these three girls as they understood each other. Though she was their sister (she'd heard herself referred to this way in a spitting voice—*mind your sister*) she didn't feel related to them. She clung only to her brother.

His name was Darragh, the Irish for oak, and this was how he appeared to her—tall, strong, and quiet, the skin of his palms rough and whorled like bark, his umber hair smelling of clean earth. He taught her how to use the words, in Irish and in the English he had learned in school. He was the only one whose eyes held within them anything that she recognized.

Her own name was also unwanted. For a long time she had no name, and to the others it was as if she never received one. When they had to, they called her the baby or simply *Her*. It wasn't until she began to speak, in a careful voice so soft he had to lean forward to hear, that Darragh gave her a name. *Aisling*, he called her, a beautiful, whispery name. Vision, it meant in the Irish, or dream. The title carried within it, along with its irony, an element of danger, as though in calling to her, Darragh was casting a spell upon the others who refused to give her a name.

When Aisling was old enough to envision her place in the world, what she saw was a girl held aloft by the shadow of this boy. Like a wee fairy round an oak tree. He was the only person she belonged to. He was good; he took her because she was unwanted. She accepted this long before it began to hurt her, because it was all she had, this image of herself, a small brightness circling the dark, solid trunk of her brother.

This was all a long time ago, when she still believed she would grow to be a woman, and in doing so, become wanted. It was before the hunger came, the hunger that made everything before it—including her family—seem like a paradise. Before she ever heard the sea screaming in chorus with the wooden walls of a ship. Before she died.

When she was living, there had been a tiny house much like this one. Darragh had carved it for himself, a hole in the damp ground just out of sight from the family home, a roof with a skeleton of hazel sticks and a skin of mud and reeds. The stairway leading down, fashioned out of gray slabs of stone, gave it the illusion of elegance, as did the shelf along the inner wall, where his precious few books and papers nestled. The floor was the dark earth, which Darragh raked in careful patterns nightly, sweeping away invading snails and the indentations of his bare feet. Darragh had lived there alone, removed from the stone room that housed his sisters and parents, safe from the stale air of resentment, until one night, when Aisling was three, he decided she would come with him. "I'm bringing the baby out," he said after dinner, and there was no argument, only a disapproving noise from his mother's throat.

"You'll be named a bog squatter," she had said when he first built his house, one step above a beggar in the hierarchy of the poor. But she hadn't tried to stop him. Instead, she'd moved her blanket up to the feather bed in the loft, and began sleeping nights with the girls, leaving his father alone on the pallet by the hearth.

When Darragh brought Aisling underground that first time, he widened the narrow mattress with another layer of straw, making just enough room for them to lie together if they curved like spoons. In this position, they watched the twilight as it moved across the door above the stairs.

"As long as you're with me," Darragh said quietly—he always spoke softly in the twilight—"you don't have to be invisible."

This was her first indication that Darragh knew about her secret power to disappear. She had a talent for remaining so still that the others could brush by her—close enough so she could smell their breath—and not even know she was there. Occasionally, one of them would walk straight into her and be startled, as though Aisling was some sort of spirit that had materialized in their path. Then recognition would enter their eyes and she would see the expression that made her yearn to disappear in the first place. The expression that said her presence—even the small amount of space which she took up—was resented. So Aisling had learned early on how to tend to herself and at the age of three she could feed the fire, do up buttons and laces, gather water from the well and heat it for her bath. She performed these chores surreptitiously, while the others were preoccupied, moving within the shadows of the house. She never cried and rarely spoke. She became so good at vanishing that, when she was older, she sometimes scared herself, imagining that she would lose the ability to reappear.

Even after she'd moved in with Darragh, she maintained the superstitious habit of not moving, barely even breathing, until she saw or heard her brother nearby. Often Darragh, who rose before dawn for his chores, would peek down into their dark hole and think it empty, until he saw the fluttering of two large eyes, like gold butterflies trapped in a void. Her eyes were the only thing Aisling could not stop from moving. If Darragh forgot to check, she would lie underground for hours, patiently inanimate.

Which is why this evening, as Aisling wakes in the little house that is both familiar and foreign at the same time, she lies in a dead stillness, waiting for the figure of Darragh to tell her it is safe to move. It is the smell of the place—a smell both sharp and sweet—that tells her that, though she is finally awake, she has not come home.

The ceiling of this house is made with thin branches and wire, woven together like the threads of a blanket. The roof would not keep out the rain, she thinks, and it gives her brief pleasure to have a thought that sounds so maturely disapproving. The floor is covered with small green and brown needles, a handful of which tells her the origin of the strange smell. A portion of this floor, sticky with a clear syrup, has attached itself to her hair. There is a small opening in the wall of leaves, through which she can see a sliver of the world, a world of deep, shocking colors. Her world has not been in color for a long time.

Her senses have returned to her slowly, as if she is thawing gradually into life again.

It began with an open door. It was not her first invitation. There was the man from the ship, the man who untied her, who wanted to take her with him, but he was going the wrong way. Later, there were accidental encounters where for a brief instant she was almost seen. But it was this entrance on one particular night that sparked in her an ancient, dormant longing to be recognized. When she had first seen the door, propped open in the twilight, she had thought that it was the sign from Darragh. She found not her brother inside, but a strange, small man. He had been sitting alone in the shadows of sunset, and there had been something about his posture, and the tilt of his head listening toward the door, that had been familiar to her. As though he, too, were waiting for some signal that it was safe to move.

Now, every time she breaches that threshold, she finds something that remains with her when she goes again. First it was smell. Stale smoke and new tobacco. She took the tin of tobacco away with her so she could breathe from it whenever she wanted, conjuring up images of her brother plugging twigs into his pipe with his stained thumb.

Then she began to make sound. Perhaps she'd always had this ability, but her instinct to remain quiet had kept her from discovering it. Now she delights in calling attention to herself. She slams, thumps, pounds. And though the man sometimes protests, his scoldings are more encouragement, she can tell by the tone, than anything else. She collects color in the fiery and gold leaves on the ground outside his door, then hides them among his things like small treasures.

When she sees the stories the man has made out of drawings, she decides to make one herself. But she can't think what to draw—in her mind her own story takes the shape of an empty space—so she presses her palm, dripping with ink, onto the paper. She presses hard, over and over, and with each mark she thinks to herself, I am here, I am here. Afterward, the marks she left frightened her. They were bold, they asked for punishment. She could almost feel the burn of a hand across her cheek. See the look of disgust, as though her very existence were unforgivable. But the man hung her handprints up on his wall, as if, like Darragh's books, they were worthy of display.

She believes it is the man's influence that keeps her coming back here. Every time she slips into his world, he responds with a voice and eyes that can only be described as hungry. He speaks her language. He encourages her disruptions. The fact that he calls her by a strange name means nothing—for her, names are interchangeable. She could be, and has been, called everything and nothing. She will become who he is looking for.

He is not the one she planned to come back to. But he wants her—at least he thinks he does—and his desire has changed everything; after an eternity of being invisible, she longs to be seen.

She thinks at first it is a mob of ghosts. When it passes by her, a large, giggling life, she sees only children. Both boys and girls, she can tell by the varied pitch of the laughter. Despite the girls, she knows it is the eve of November, Spirit Night. The children are walking drunkenly, barely able to see their way through grotesque masks.

Darragh once dressed her as a phantom. He blackened her face with ash, stained two spots red with berry juice, and, using a cloak stolen from their mother, layered her head beneath the shadows. As a girl, Aisling should have been at home with her sisters, preparing food for the holiday, celebrating the beginning of the year by peeling an apple and letting the skin fall in the initial of her future husband.

Instead she crept beside Darragh through the village that night, surrounded by the other boys, ghosts who rapped on doors and ran away cackling with evil laughter.

The boys were always energetic at the start of November. The harvest and the hardest work of the year over, their bellies fuller than usual, they were on a mission to terrify. They dared one another into the graveyard and up to the fairy mound, they pretended to hear the chinking wheels of the *coshtabower*—the death coach—approaching the village. They formed a circle around a pile of dirt with a branch propped upright in the middle, taking turns shaving the sides of the mound with their sticks. The last one to shave before the branch collapsed would be the first of them to die. That night, it was Darragh. The other boys squirmed with excitement and looked at him cautiously.

But Darragh smiled.

"I now have the power to choose who follows me to death," he said, and his face, whitened with flour, chilled even Aisling. Though none of them had heard this rule before, they ran home, checking behind their costumed shoulders with panicked regularity.

Aisling had shyly shaved the mound at her turn with no understanding of what death meant. Later, she asked Darragh.

"Is it not bad?" she said to him. "The other boys were scared of it."

"Not at all," Darragh said. "It's the same as day turning to night. Your life is like the day, and after death comes, it's all different—not worse or better, just different—because, as at night, the world no longer looks the same. It's why twilight is the holy time, when day and night come together, and the living and the dead can meet one another on the road."

Aisling was relieved. When Darragh died, they would still have the twilight, which was when he came in from the fields, and they ate their potatoes and buttermilk in the room beneath the earth, and he held her as she watched the stars being lit like candles, one by one above their door.

Here also, there is a twilight, and a Spirit Night. There are moments, as opposed to before—where time had been blurred, and there is ground under her feet.

She is cold. She wonders how she could have forgotten the cold, and the desperate feeling where nothing matters beyond the attempt to drive it away. Like hunger, which can escalate to a pain similar to being chewed at from the inside, but which now is only a mild longing. It's the thirst that is making her dizzy; it is so bad that she thinks it must have been there all along, that last feeling she remembers before all sensation stopped.

She limps toward the open door. Her feet, the bottoms of which were once as thick and brown as leather, are now on fire. She has come back with new, delicate skin on the soles, which is scraped and bleeding because she has been walking as carelessly as she used to over the brambles in the forest. There is a candle in his window, flickering an invitation to the dead.

Inside the cabin is dark, but she can make out the figure of the man in his bed. She feels as if she is slipping, one moment she can see her own hand, the next she is gone. She slams the small doors on the walls of his kitchen to get his attention. When he speaks to her his voice is like kindling at the start of the fire, and she feels herself reappear. She reaches for the shining knob that she's seen him turn to make water run straight into the house.

She cannot decipher his words, but she doesn't care because there is water licking the inside of a glass, and then it is in her mouth; she can feel it penetrating every pore of her, soothing the dryness and making her even more thirsty, as if it takes the water to make her realize how truly thirsty she is. Then she hears that name that isn't hers again. The man is standing before her, he has turned on the light, and she sees in his eyes that she is fully there.

She also sees that he would like to scold her. She is the wrong girl, and he is disappointed—she can tell by the drooping of his eyebrows. She has a brief desire to disappear again, but knows she has no choice but to plunge forward.

"I'm able to read," she says in Irish. He blinks at her. "I'm able to sew and cook for myself, I run faster than any boy my size and some of the larger ones, and I am quite beautiful, which some say is a curse, but Darragh says there's not much truth to that." She stops when he holds up his hand and takes one step back.

"My Irish," he says, "is not that good."

She repeats herself in the English that Darragh had taught her. When she is halfway through, the man sits at the kitchen table as if he is suddenly too tired to stand. When she tells him of her beauty she sees a smile threatening his mouth.

"Well," he says. "Em, good for you." She knows he hasn't really been listening. She remembers that adults prefer to talk about themselves.

"Who is Nieve?" she asks, and this works. There is a reaction there: sadness, anger, and the relief at having been heard.

"Nieve was my sister," he says.

"Is she dead?" Aisling asks.

He nods.

"Will I be your sister now?" she says, and he looks at her, and despite what he says next she knows she has gotten somewhere.

"You can't be," he says.

There is a small opening there, hidden between the rigid planks of his dashed hope. She settles in the chair across from him, saying nothing.

And, though neither of them notices right away, in these first few minutes the gloaming has receded, and she has already begun to change.

3.

Oisin is terrified. His fear has become too much for his penis, which has fallen flaccid against his thigh. He is not afraid because this girl is a ghost, nor, ultimately, is his fear bound up in the disappointment that she is not Nieve. What frightens him is the tone of her voice. When she asked about Nieve, the words seemed to spring from a well of jealousy, as if she were a woman betrayed. And she recited her attributes, as though trying to sell herself as a bargain. It's the same tone he has heard from lovers, who, no matter how proud they once seemed, humiliate themselves in an attempt to keep him from slipping away.

Though he knows little about children, he knows enough to realize a responsibility has been dropped in his lap. You can't just feed a hungry dog once, because the dog will rely on the false hope you offered and starve to death.

Though he was the one who invited her in, Oisin suddenly wants to be alone again. But she has settled her small body into his other kitchen chair with a determination that makes him see that, even if he ripped the seat out from under her and battered her with it, she would smile through it all and tell him she can count to one hundred.

She is still watching. Oisin, back when he could see ghosts, grew used to following their lead. Spirits always wanted something, and were never shy about asking for it. It occurs to him that this ghost, though her eyes are boiling with want, does not know how or even what to ask for.

Perhaps she is not a ghost at all; she no longer looks like one. Her skin is dull and dirty, she has brought inside with her the smell of damp leaves and cold air, and the faint, slightly moldy—but not unpleasant—odor of a child's exertion. The way his sister once smelled when they undressed for their bath.

Without warning, Oisin grabs for the girl's arm. His fingers close around a thin wrist, dipped with the cool night air, but warm underneath, solid, pulsing with channels of blood. She stiffens, pulls away, then, as though deciding this is rude, moves her arm back toward his retreating hand.

"You're real." It comes out of Oisin like an accusation. And the girl, who seems used to being blamed, arranges her expression accordingly: meek guilt stained with thinly disguised pride.

Later, when daylight has just begun blueing the sky, Oisin bathes her feet. For hours she has been bearing the pain silently, and it would have remained a secret, had he not seen the ovals of blood she left behind her on the pale floor. The soles of her feet are crowded with scratches and deeper wounds—some still bleeding, others swollen and beginning to gather pus.

Oisin fills a plastic basin with warm water and kneels by her chair, guiding each of her feet in with a gentle plop. Dirt and blood slowly discolor the water, and he swishes it gently around her ankles. Then he empties the basin, refills it and begins to wash her feet with liquid disinfectant, which lathers and seethes, staining her skin an orangey brown. She makes no sound and barely flinches as he dabs Neosporin and stretches large Band-Aids over the heels and balls of her feet. Oisin, who often cuts himself while working, performs these ministrations with cool efficiency and no attempt to comfort her. All he feels is the impatience at having to be thorough, the way he does when he must interrupt important work to attend to his own wound.

It isn't until he is finished, as he clears away the wrappers, bloody cotton, and the sudsy orange water, that he is taken aback by the smallness of her feet. He elevates them on the chair next to her, cushioned with a towel. It occurs to him that she is probably the only child he has ever touched so intimately. Oisin is not the type of man that people encourage to hold babies. He is uncomfortable around children, and most children, sensing this, steer clear of him.

For the first time since he filled the basin, he looks at the girl's face. Her forehead is beaded with sweat from the effort of trying not to whimper. Her gold eyes dart to his face, and he guesses by the stiffness of her posture that she is as surprised by—and as lost within— this intimacy as he is.

Oisin has isolated himself for so long, and so well, that occasionally, the most basic interaction with another human being leaves him with an embarrassing sense of pride. Because he avoids affection beyond occasional sex, he is relieved when these moments of contact come upon him accidentally and he manages to respond to them like a normal man. So, after Oisin has bandaged this girl's feet, his ego inflates a bit; he briefly imagines himself to be the generous, kindhearted sort of person that children are drawn to. And when she

tucks herself into his bed, he doesn't have the nerve to protest, because it would shatter this new image of himself.

This is how the girl is able to carve a space for herself in his
home, and, before he even understands what she's doing, she is
wedged in so tightly that it becomes impossible to pry her out.

For the first week, Oisin swings between feelings of magnanimous
charity and resentful irritation. When she is sleeping, which she
seems to do a lot, he can almost hear the voice of his grandmother,
praising him for being the admirable sort of man who would take in
an orphaned child. (This had been a common practice when Oisin
was growing up; his parents and grandparents were often taking abandoned children or poor cousins in and raising them along with their
own.)

But when she is awake, though she is quiet and unobtrusive, she
violates his peaceful cocoon. She stares at him, fixes upon him with
gulping gold eyes, as though she is trying to press his image within
her, the way he transfers an etching to paper when he makes a print.
He finds himself wishing she were still only a ghost. All ghosts had
ever asked from him was recognition. But this girl, though she says
nothing, requires more, though he can only guess at what it is. Guid-
ance? Definition? Sometimes, when he is sketching, he forgets she is
there, and when she appears again in front of him, he is furious at the
intrusion.

Oisin has patterned his life around being alone. The few friends
he had once, from college, gave up on him years ago, taking personally his tendency to cancel plans, never return phone calls, or disappear for hours when he was a guest in their home. None of them
seemed to understand that he preferred to be alone, that his solitary

lifestyle was not just a way to bide his time until he found the right woman to share his life. He has no intention of sharing his life, his time, or his home with anything except his art. Thanks to an inheritance from a grandfather he never met, he hasn't had a job in ten years, so he doesn't even have office acquaintances.

He used to wonder if his introversion had evolved to facilitate his art—so that every ounce of energy he possessed could be channeled into creation, which even under perfect conditions is the most draining thing he does. Or, on the flip side, maybe he became an artist to justify his naturally antisocial personality. But he no longer ponders this chicken-or-egg dilemma. His infrequent desire for human contact is satisfied by affairs with women he inevitably disappoints. There has never been any toothbrush but his in the bathroom, he has never come across foreign garments in his neglected laundry, there was no object in his life that wasn't purely his.

Until this girl arrived, smearing her presence over everything he owns. Long blond hairs fasten themselves to his sweaters with surprising durability, the milk disappears in a steady leak from the refrigerator, his body has been excommunicated to the outer edges of the mattress by sprawling young limbs, he is awakened at night not by his own insomnia but by the whimpering of a nightmare that belongs to her.

Even his schedule—his decisions about the pieces of time in each day—is no longer his own. When he was a boy, he never expected adults to entertain him; then again, he'd had Nieve. But this girl studies him to see what they should do next. Oisin has begun to announce every move he makes, hoping she'll take the hint and develop her own routine. His voice, self-conscious and slightly childish in his once quiet house, now follows him with the same consistency that she does.

"Time to get up," he says in the mornings, though she is usually already awake, waiting for him. "Getting dressed now. Breakfast. Studio." All he needs are sneakers and a cardigan and he could pass for Mr. Rogers. For the first time in years, he wishes he had a television; he would park her in front of it without the slightest remorse, if it would stop her from watching him.

When he varies his schedule—if he oversleeps, quits work early, forgets to eat lunch, even if he pees first before putting on the kettle in the morning—he feels her discomfort as strongly as if she has screamed in protest. Any departure from routine makes her panic.

How did this happen, Oisin's metamorphosis from introvert artist to makeshift guardian? Why does he suddenly, without asking for it, own this responsibility?

He has learned next to nothing from his interrogations. He knows her name, Aisling, and remembers that in Irish it means vision. Her soft voice has the accent of the west of Ireland, and before she adapts to match his speech, it has an old-fashioned ring to it. This, along with her unfamiliarity with the appliances in his house (she tried placing the kettle directly on his fireplace until he showed her how to turn on the gas stove), makes him suspect she has not been alive for a long time. His questions about her parents are answered with a soft, unregretful "they're dead." When he asks her why she is here, with him, on this island, she merely shrugs. Occasionally, when she is sleeping, she calls out in a voice that is louder than her waking voice, for someone named Darragh. With her eyes open, she denies the knowledge of any such person.

For the first few days, Oisin believed that only he could see her. Then, while she shadowed him on a walk along the beach, quietly stepping into each of his sandy footprints, they came upon a local fisherman, tying his dinghy above the high-tide mark.

"New admirer, Oisin?" the man said, winking at Aisling, his face softening at the sight of a child. "You're a pretty vision," he said, and Aisling, though she struggled not to, smiled at him.

Oisin, confused, horrified, only nodded at the man and quickened his pace. It had not occurred to him that he would have to explain her. For a moment, he thought he'd been fooled, perhaps she was just an island child who had run away from home, and his longing for the return of his second sight had sent him leaping to ridiculous conclusions.

He went to Deirdre's house under the guise of borrowing children's books, but with the intention of testing his sanity.

"My niece is staying with me," he said, and Deirdre nodded.

"I've seen her," she said. Oisin was relieved. If Aisling was a missing island child, Deirdre would have recognized her. He noted the hint of surprise under Deirdre's politeness. Obviously, she did not expect him to be the type to take in children.

The books had helped to lessen the pressure of Aisling's gaze. She devoured them, reading for hours, finishing whole books in one afternoon. She still insisted on occupying the same room as Oisin at all times, following him from studio to home and back again. If he turned around suddenly to retrieve a forgotten tool, he crashed into her. Even when he told her to sit still, in a tone that sounded like one of those frazzled mothers he's seen snapping orders to their children on the ferry, Aisling looked up from her book periodically, to make sure he was there.

Oisin, who spent years reading about the occult after his own second sight deserted him, searched his memory for some explanation. He remembered stories of returning souls who had appeared to die but had actually been snatched away by fairies. Occasionally they managed to return, surprising the relatives who had mourned them for a decade. Perhaps Aisling was one of these souls.

Or, he thought, maybe she'd returned on a mission, as spirits with unfinished business were known to do. Oisin had seen dead mothers return to breast-feed their babies, men delay their eternal rest because of an unpaid debt.

Either way, he told himself that this girl was with him temporarily. He could give up his privacy for a while, if it meant that he could exercise the long dormant talent of second sight. Perhaps this odd, intense little girl was only the beginning, a precursor to the return of Nieve, for whom he has been waiting for more than half his life.

This is how he resigns himself to Aisling's presence until the feeling that something else is wrong begins to eat into the little sleep he is managing at night. He notices something that causes everything he thought he knew about the dead and the living to fall apart, and he is left with nothing on which to begin again.

She is growing, and not at the normal rate of a living child.

4.

When Oisin was a boy, his mind burrowed in the comfort of opposites: A person was either a twin or not a twin. One either possessed second sight, or they were half blind. It was his twin sister, Nieve, that made Oisin special. But, beginning the winter he was seven, it was the ghosts that made him separate.

Most of Oisin's childhood was spent in the ground floor of a three-family, porch-circled house in South Boston. Southie was a peninsula poking into Boston Harbor, an insulated, almost entirely Irish neighborhood. Oisin's father was a dock laborer when he had to be and a fisherman when he could be. When he found work on a boat, he was away from home for months at a time.

Oisin and Nieve had a habit of waking before dawn to spend time with their father. They loved rising while it was still night, brewing the coffee their father took with sweet cream, shuffling around in slippers and robes with no rush to get dressed. After their father left, they had hours alone before their mother woke. They came to think of these as precious hours, while the stars faded and the dawn spilled across the sky like blue ink.

Even when their father was not there, they rose at five A.M. They were forbidden to run around and wake their mother, so the twins spent the mornings in their bedroom, their heads touching at the foot ends of their identical beds, telling each other travel stories. Since they had discovered there were worlds outside the one they inhabited with their parents, the twins had imagined escape. Their walls were papered with maps, and, pasted between lines of latitude and longitude, were pictures they'd cut from *National Geographic*. They had a story for every exotic place they'd ever heard of, and it was in the first few hours of the day, with one parent gone and the other asleep, that these places seemed almost attainable.

Oisin's sighting occurred on one such morning in December. Though it would be remembered as his first, he had always been aware of silent, unobtrusive people who lurked in corners. Their neighborhood was a social one, and their house buzzed at all times with friends and family, so it had never really occurred to Oisin that there was a class of people that only he could see.

His father hadn't left yet, and the three of them were at the breakfast table, sipping coffee and cocoa in the dark. (Declan MacDara hated the glare of lamplight that early, so their mornings were blindly organized.) It was quiet except for the twins' gulps and gasping (they both forgot to breathe while drinking, and often sounded as though they were drowning in their cocoa). When Oisin began mumbling answers to a battery of questions—*Uh-huh, Nope, I think so, Of course not*—Declan stared, but Nieve didn't seem to notice. She had heard Oisin mumble like this before.

Then Oisin stood up and hurried into the hall. When he returned a minute later, the kitchen was filled with a cold wind that seemed to have followed him into the room. When Declan investigated the draft, he discovered the front door unlatched and propped open with winter boots. Snow had already formed a tiny hillock on the carpet. Declan closed the door, turning the bolt that was too high for Oisin to reach.

"Has the *Globe* arrived?" he said to his son, although it was too early even for the paperboy.

"Granddad's going for his walk," Oisin said, blowing steam from his mug. "He told me to leave the door open. He hates keys."

Nieve stopped drinking her cocoa and looked at Oisin, then her father. Declan's father lived in Ireland; they hadn't seen him since their visit the summer before.

"Is this one of your games?" Declan said, looking to Nieve for help. Nieve shrugged, and Oisin only squinted at him and sighed, as if to say that any explanation would be lost on his father. This was the way Declan and Oisin often looked at each other. Declan seemed to find his son unfathomable and slightly threatening. He preferred Nieve and always had, just as his wife, Sara, preferred Oisin.

The phone call came seven hours later. Oisin's grandfather had fallen dead from a stroke at the same time they'd been sitting down to their morning ritual. Declan, who had a superstitious side he rarely shared, told his wife about the incident at breakfast. Sara took her son aside in the evening.

"Daddy says you pretended to see Granddad this morning."

Oisin shrugged.

"He wasn't really here, you do know that?"

"Sure," he said.

"Because Granddad died last night, Oisin. We won't be able to visit him anymore; he's in Heaven with God now."

"Okay," Oisin said. He dismissed his mother's explanation of death immediately, and wouldn't understand or believe it for many years. No one who died stopped existing for him or went anywhere that he couldn't find them.

The next morning, when Oisin and Nieve were alone in their bedroom, they whispered while their grieving parents slept.

"Are you sure you didn't see him?" Oisin asked.

"I swear," Nieve said. "What did he look like?" she asked, though Oisin had already told her a dozen times. "Was he white and ghostly—could you see furniture through him?"

"No," Oisin said, and again he tried to explain. Oisin had never seen anything as vivid, as real-looking as the ghost of his grandfather. He had been brighter in color than anything in that room, and his skin looked different, as if you could see that it was made up of millions of smaller pieces, each of them possessing more energy than any person could. His grandfather had glowed—but not in an untouchable way. His glowing had included Oisin. Since he had seen him, Oisin had realized that his parents, his friends, even Nieve, all looked shadowy and insubstantial in comparison.

"I know what it means," Nieve said. "You have second sight. I read about it in a book at Nana's. It's like being a prophet or something. It means God wants you to be special."

"That doesn't make any sense," Oisin said. "If it's so special, you would have it."

Oisin believed in the mystery of twins: no matter how similar they seem at first, one is always better. Better looking, smarter, more talented, taller. For as long as Oisin could remember, Nieve had been the better one. This was the way he liked it. His sister in the spotlight, and him—her favorite—cozy within her shadow.

Nieve took after her mother, flawless skin and hair so thick and blond it was like a waterfall of sunlight. She was always slightly taller than Oisin, the way their mother was taller than their father, with long legs and delicate, almost fragile-looking ankles. Nieve's eyes, though, were her own, and no one could figure out where she had gotten them. They were so dark in her fair face that the effect was startling, as though she were possessed by the soul of another, tribal sort of woman.

Oisin was awkward enough to attract sympathetic sighs from adults. His hair was a shocking orange, and it was uncontrollable, a field of brittle cowlicks. In the sun he often burned violently and was left with large, irregular-shaped freckles. He was allergic to sleep; the sandman's morning crust refused to release from his eyelids and left them swollen, raw, and slightly sticky at all times. Because of this, the peculiar and striking blue of his eyes was rarely noticed. He was told that he looked more Irish than his own father, than any of his relatives in Ireland, and he grew up thinking that to look Irish was not an asset.

"Where do you think Granddad was going?" Nieve said. Their faces were so close he could feel her breath. Years before, Oisin had tried to regulate his breathing with hers, inhaling everything Nieve let out.

"He didn't say." Oisin frowned. "Heaven, probably."

Nieve snorted. "If he can go anywhere, he should pick someplace more interesting than Heaven."

Oisin nodded his agreement. This was their third year of Catholic school and the nuns made Heaven sound like an eternal mass—complete with stiff clothing and off-pitch voices chasing the tones of an organ.

"Well, I hope he doesn't come back tomorrow," Nieve said, as though the spirit of their grandfather were an irritating neighborhood boy. "Because I want to go to Africa. The lion cubs should be learning to hunt by now."

"Okay," Oisin said, though secretly he hoped to see the ghost again.

Nieve sighed. "Do you think we'll ever really go anywhere?" she said.

"We go to Ireland every summer," Oisin said.

"I meant somewhere exciting," Nieve said.

When Oisin and Nieve started kindergarten, they were put into different classrooms, one down the hall from the other. It took three days of Oisin's uninterrupted screaming to bring them back together. Though they had planned the protest beforehand, and Oisin—with his raw eyes and high pitch—had been chosen as the better crier, the desire to not be separated was sincere enough. When they weren't together, they were uncomfortable, preoccupied with worry over when they'd be reunited. The nuns gave in and told Oisin and Nieve's parents they'd adjust better as a team.

"That's what they want you to think," their mother had sneered.

Their parents had always tried to separate them. Oisin and Nieve had never worn a matching sailor suit and sailor dress: their Sears portraits—toddlers plumply arranged on sheepskin—were taken individually. Never, in their own home, were they referred to as "the twins."

Their father, who had grown up in the shadow of his own twin brother, was trying to be helpful. But their mother seemed simply to find their closeness offensive, and discouraged it. When she saw them in the morning, squeezed into one twin bed, her face pinched as though she were tasting something sour. "It's not natural," she said more than once, "for siblings to be so fond of each other."

Oisin and Nieve's parents seemed odd to them. If children learn about relationships from the interactions of their mother and father, then what Oisin and Nieve learned was this: Life can bring the most unlikely people together, not necessarily in the name of love. Oisin and Nieve grew up believing that they existed because of an accident; an accident that neither of their parents seemed to remember fondly. Later, they learned that their family's conception had been not an accident, but a mistake.

Oisin's mother was originally from the South, where—she told her children—people were nicer, the air was warmer, and the soil was red. She met their father when she was in her first year of college at Radcliffe, in Cambridge. Declan was an illegal Irish immigrant, working as a dock laborer with his twin brother, Malachy (Malachy, handsome and humorous, was the better one). Their mother met their father at a bar, and, within two months, married him and was disinherited by her rich, Southern, Protestant family.

Whenever this story was told, mostly to Nieve, who asked for it again and again, there was no mention, by either of their parents, of love. The children tried to add elements, but the story never changed.

"Was it love at first sight, Daddy?" Nieve would ask. "Is that why she gave up everything to be with you?"

"Oh, I don't remember, Nieve," their father would say, and he would stare meanly at the space above their heads. "It was a long time ago."

When Nieve was small, she thought her mother's abandonment by her family was romantic. Oisin was frightened by it. He worried that strangers would arrive one day from the South, red dirt on their boots, and take his mother away.

When Nieve asked their mother the same questions, Sara said it was none of her business.

"Of course it's my business," Nieve would growl to Oisin later. "They made me. The least they can do is tell me why."

Oisin discouraged Nieve from such questioning. He had a feeling, even when he was a little boy, that the real story was not a nice one. He didn't care as much as Nieve did; his parents' relationship was not something that interested him. They barely spoke to each other. Oisin thought that love between a man and woman was nothing like what he felt for Nieve, who filled every empty space within him.

Oisin and Nieve rarely fought, and even when they did, they kept it to themselves instead of running to their parents for interference. They did not compete for attention, despite their parents' obvious preferences. Sara babied Oisin, Declan spoiled Nieve. Each parent thought of one of the twins as their own. This could have made Oisin and Nieve resent each other, but since neither of them trusted their parents, it only brought them closer. Though they allowed Sara and Declan to think otherwise, they belonged only to each other.

Oisin and Nieve didn't just imagine escape, they practiced it. Together they tested the boundaries of their neighborhood to see how far they could go and for how long, before their parents reeled them in. They measured adventures by city blocks, though it was hard to lose themselves on lanes where everyone knew them. Whenever they thought they'd ventured furthest from their front stoop, their excitement was dashed by the long-voweled greeting of a housewife. It was impossible to pretend they were rowing the Nile when Mrs. Kennedy told them she could hear Sara calling them for dinner.

The spring after their grandfather died, the twins got as far as Castle Island. They sleuthed their way downhill, then followed the sea promenade, weaving among families on their Sunday strolls, until they rounded the point and came upon the old military fort that guarded Boston Harbor. Unfortunately, one of the tour guides was a distant cousin of their father, and they were dragged home at their moment of greatest glory. Their mother, who was only angry that she hadn't noticed their absence, punished them in the only way she knew how: by separating them. She closed Nieve in the bathroom with cleaning instructions, and locked Oisin in their bedroom. Sara escaped upstairs for cocktails with the neighbors.

Nieve and Oisin had long ago discovered that if they opened the windows of bedroom and bathroom, they could lean out and talk to each other from their separate prisons. That day, as Nieve struggled with the swollen window, she heard Oisin's voice, speaking to someone else.

"Ossie!" she hissed, when she'd forced enough space to lean out. His voice stopped abruptly, his orange head poked out the other window. "Who are you talking to?" she said.

Perhaps because Nieve was using a condescending tone that made him defensive, Oisin hesitated before answering her. It was that split second, when he first held himself away, that he would remember as the beginning of his betrayal of Nieve.

"It's only Granddad," he said.

Nieve's eyes narrowed, considering him. When she spoke again, her voice was full of forced cheer.

"Ask him to tell the story of our names," she said. It was their favorite Irish story, recited every summer by their grandfather in front of a glowing turf fire.

"But you can't hear him," Oisin said. Nieve squinted again, and Oisin felt a pinch of shame, as if he had insulted her.

So Oisin told the story, pausing between sentences for the prompting of his grandfather's disembodied voice.

"There is a land under the sea," Oisin said, trying to sound like a man. "It is called Tír na nÓg, the Country of the Young, because age and death have not found it. Only one man who has gone there has ever returned, and that man is Oisin, leader of the tribe of the Fianna.

"The Call of Oisin came about in this way. There was a time in Ireland, a time before Saint Patrick, when magic was everywhere and men lived with nature. The Fianna had many horses and hounds and spent their time hunting and playing chess. They were happy, brave, and content in a way it is not possible to be in the world today. One day, when Oisin and his comrades were riding along the shore, they came upon the most beautiful woman they had ever seen, riding bareback on a gleaming white horse. The woman had gold hair and lips like sweet red wine. She wore a dark cloak of silk that was covered in red and gold stars, and a crown of rubies nestled in her curls.

" 'I am Nieve Chinn Oir,' she told them, which means 'Nieve of the Golden Head.' 'I am in love with you, Oisin, and wish to take you to Tír na nÓg, where my father is king, where you will never grow old or discouraged, and where no one ever dies.'

"Oisin, who was no fool, fell instantly in love with Nieve, and was flattered that she had chosen him. He took her hand and said: 'Why you should love a man as common as me, I shall never know. It is you who are the shining one, you who are the sweetest and the comeliest, you who are my star and my choice above all the women in the world.' "

This was the part where Nieve always sighed, as though the young hunter were saying the words in her ear.

" 'If you come with me, you may never return to your home or your people,' Nieve warned Oisin.

" 'Nothing but yourself matters to me now,' Oisin said, and without a second look he was on her horse and they were gone, to the Country of the Young under the sea.

"Tír na nÓg was everything Nieve had promised and more, and Oisin lived there happily for three hundred years. But one day he became homesick and asked permission to visit Ireland. Nieve sent him on her magic horse, but warned him that he must not step down from it or all his years would immediately come upon him.

" 'You will be disappointed, Oisin,' she said. 'Ireland is not the land you remember.'

"So Oisin rose from the sea to Ireland and searched everywhere, but could not find any of the Fianna. The country seemed full of strangers and sadness. Then he saw something in the sand—which looked like a piece of armor from a Fianna warrior—and he forgot Nieve's warning and jumped off the horse.

"In an instant, three hundred years fell on him, and he wrinkled and shrank, lost his hair and his teeth, and became the oldest man alive. When Saint Patrick found him, he was blind as a bat and keening for all he had lost. They say the saint tried to convert him—these were the days when everyone was getting religion—but I don't think it worked, because Oisin believed in things even a saint couldn't understand. Oisin died soon after that, and they say the sea raged that night, as if the Country of the Young were mourning beneath the water."

Oisin and Nieve's grandfather used to seem as sad as they did whenever he finished this story. Nieve had a habit, during the telling of it, of chanting softly—"Don't get off the horse, don't get off the horse." And when the Oisin in the story jumped to the ground, Nieve always thumped her brother with her fist, as though he were the one who had made such a tragic mistake.

But that evening, as twilight reached them at their window perches, Nieve was quiet as Oisin reached the end. Finally she broke the silence with a sigh.

"Every time I hear it," she whispered. "I think he won't leave her. Every time."

"Why?" Oisin asked. To him, the most exciting part of the story was the gory bit. Imagining that shrinking face gave him a fearful thrill.

"Oisin," Nieve said softly, "don't be a *boy*."

5.

The girl is Oisin's illegitimate child; this is what the islanders decide. It fits perfectly with the conflicting images they've had of
him over the years: hermit, ladies' man, talented artist, overgrown boy.
There is no trace left of the awkward child he once was; now he is
one of those men, a lover once told him in disgust, who gets better
looking with each new wrinkle. Men like Oisin father unwanted children. It explains why he seems to be trying to hide the girl, why when
they do see her, in the shops or along the beach, she refuses to look
at them, like a child that has been taught to be ashamed. The sight of
this shy, beautiful girl has aroused the protective instinct of a number
of the islanders, as though a soft spot for orphans is a hereditary trait
handed down with the island's history.

But Deirdre Molloy corrects them.

"She's his niece," she tells a group of women during their afternoon tea in the pub. "She's seven years old, visiting from Ireland. Her
mother is ill, so she's been sent away until things improve."

The women are silent for a minute, leaking disappointment at this less mischievous explanation, as well as jealousy of Deirdre's inside information.

"Where'd you hear that?" Moira says.

Deirdre hides her amusement. Her cousin Moira has had a crush on Oisin for years and begrudges Deirdre their brief affair.

"MacDara told me," says Deirdre. She has always called Oisin by his last name; his first—because of the way it slides on her tongue— feels too intimate.

"And you believe him?" Moira adds.

"Why shouldn't I? It's not as if he cares what we think of him." None of them can argue with this. Though they know few facts about Oisin's history, his decade on the island has revealed plenty about his personality.

Though there's no fun in it, Deirdre's explanation makes sense. Almost all the islanders have relatives in Ireland who occasionally visit, and there are always European tourists in the summer, who are encouraged to tour Tiranogue Island by their guidebooks. In the seven generations since the tragedy, the island has become almost exclusively Irish American. The accent is unique, Maine and Connemara jostling for space in the same sentences, the island telephone book is dominated by entries under *O* and *Mc*, the Protestant church was refurbished into a community center because everyone on the island is now either a Catholic or a lapsed Catholic. The island pub, like those in Ireland, allows children and dogs at any time of the day, and there is a group of traditional musicians who play there on summer weekends. The primary school offers fiddle rather than violin lessons; the library has a separate section for Irish literature. Many islanders believe there is only a negligible difference between their home and Ireland itself, and those who have taken holidays to

Europe are confused and a bit insulted when the Irish call them
Yanks.

"I don't like the idea of that girl being hidden away up there,"
Moira says. The other women grunt their agreement. Deirdre laughs,
stirring her tea loudly.

"It's not as if he's locking her in," she says. "Besides, my son is
'out there,' too."

"That's different," Moira says. "Gabe's in school. It's all fine for
Oisin to bury himself away, but it's not fair for a little girl. She should
have other children to play with." Moira gestures with her mug to the
open window, where they can see a few of the island boys racing their
mountain bikes over the ramp in front of the grocery store. There is
a pause in the conversation as mothers lean their heads out to order
their children to stop.

"Perhaps someone should talk to him," says Maggie. "We could
all take turns having the girl for dinner, or invite her to the school's
Christmas party."

"I think we should just leave them alone," says Deirdre.

"The poor thing's going to be miserable out there with nothing
to do," Maggie says.

"She's not," replies Deirdre. "She's happy enough. She likes Mac-
Dara. I think she's as much of a hermit as he is."

The women silently agree to postpone the subject for when
Deirdre is not there. Deirdre can see their furtive looks, the simulta-
neous sips of tea. They take nothing she says regarding Oisin Mac-
Dara seriously. They think, because she slept with him, that her
objectivity is impaired. On this island, certain things are never forgotten, but stamped on you permanently like your height on your
driver's license. For three years, Deirdre has been lumped in with the
other women who've had sex with Oisin. And though she harbors no

angry feelings toward him, nor any secret plans to bed him in the future, everyone assumes she does, because Oisin has a reputation for breaking hearts. Deirdre finds this extremely frustrating, but she knows better than to try to defend herself.

Last month, Oisin came to Deirdre's house to borrow some children's books. Deirdre led him to one of the built-in bookcases that dominate her house; every available wall, crawl space—even the stairwell—is covered with tightly packed shelves. Oisin stared blankly at the selection of thin, spine-cracked books. It was clear he didn't know where to begin.

"What's her reading level?" Deirdre asked, and Oisin blushed. He obviously had no idea.

"What grade is she in?" Deirdre tried. Oisin cleared his throat.

"I'm not sure. She's seven. She seems fairly bright."

"Take a sampling, then," Deirdre said, seeing the relief in Oisin's face as she made the decision for him. "Some picture books, a few first readers, and some of the classics—you can read them to her if she can't manage them on her own." Deirdre piled volumes in Oisin's arms.

"*Charlotte's Web, The Secret Garden*, here's the first Narnia book, and take *The Little Princess* and *Anne of Green Gables*; they were mine and I can't get Gabe to touch them because of the girly covers."

Oisin looked appalled—perhaps at the thought of the time it would take to read so many books aloud.

"You're welcome to any others," Deirdre added. "Which were your favorites?"

"I don't really remember," Oisin said.

"Surely you read something when you were a boy. Jack London, maybe?"

"Only for school," Oisin said. "I was always drawing."

"Of course you were," Deirdre mumbled, and felt Oisin's eyes on her. She avoided looking at him and began pulling out more titles.

"*Danny the Champion of the World. A Wrinkle in Time. Bridge to Terabithia.*" She tossed the paperbacks onto Oisin's pile. "God, I read constantly as a child. My mother used to take books away from me and force me to play outside. Now I have to take them away from myself, or I'd never get a thing done."

Oisin, she could see, was barely listening to her. She scolded herself for babbling. They had agreed long ago that they didn't want to know much about each other, that their one night together would be just a physical insulation against loneliness. And here she was, going on about herself like they were on a date. She didn't want to share anything with Oisin, but this was the only time he had ever been in her house, and it was discombobulating her mind.

"I think that's enough," Oisin said, balancing piles beneath his arms. "I'll bring them back when she's done."

"She's welcome to come over and pick them out herself," Deirdre said.

Oisin seemed torn between gratitude and panic.

"Either way," Deirdre added.

He only smiled at her, forcing the skin around his mouth to move. Oisin, except during moments of seduction, is not a smiling man.

"Here," Deirdre said, "take *Peter Pan*, too. You may like it yourself." Her joke was lost on him. Oisin, at times, has reminded her more of her ten-year-old son than of a grown man. It's the look in his eyes—in the rich blue that attracts so many women; there is a self-absorption there, combined with a naïveté, as though he doesn't know people are searching his eyes in the first place.

A week later, Deirdre walked toward Oisin's cabin to see how the girl was getting on. She found them both in the studio, Oisin sketching at a stained wooden table, and the girl, who answered the door furtively, holding *Tuck Everlasting* in her hand, her forefinger saving her place.

"Well, hello," Oisin said, obviously startled. He didn't ask her in, and she wasn't sure if this was purposeful or his normal forgetfulness concerning manners.

"I was just passing by," Deirdre said, conscious of how her voice echoed in the high-ceilinged room. "I wanted to see if you liked the books. If you need any more."

Oisin looked at the girl, and Deirdre saw that they shared an unwillingness to answer questions.

"I've almost read them all," the girl said, and she spoke so softly that it took a pause for Deirdre to decipher her words.

"You can borrow as many as you like," Deirdre said. "Your uncle can bring you by my house."

The girl looked at Oisin quickly, then back at Deirdre. Her eyes were an unusually light color and they flashed in a way that gave the impression that she had a lot to say, despite her timid voice.

"I'll come on my own," she whispered, and Deirdre recognized jealousy at once. This girl didn't want to share Oisin; Gabriel acted this way when Deirdre occasionally dated. Though she knew it was perfectly normal, there was something creepy about the intensity of this girl. And how Oisin, immersed again in his sketching, didn't seem to notice, or care, that he had such a loyal little admirer. Deirdre left them behind in the studio, but she couldn't shake the overwhelming sensation that something was wrong.

Deirdre doesn't tell the women in the pub about these meetings or about her intuition. She has convinced herself that there is nothing to tell. Oisin, everyone knows, is an odd man, and this girl seems to fit in with his oddness. Deirdre suspects that she would not have an easy time with the island children, who have grown up together and tend to be clannish and a bit hard on outsiders. She would be teased, and Deirdre, who remembers how cruel girls can be, would end up appointing Gabe to watch out for her.

Apart from this, Deirdre has always had an instinct to preserve Oisin's privacy. Deirdre is an island girl, and she chose to remain here even after her parents and her husband died. She believes that a close-knit community, though it can be suffocating for some adults, is the perfect place to raise children. Gabe is happy here, and she can take it for granted, most of the time, that everyone keeps an eye on him. If she or her son has a problem, there are countless numbers of people they can go to. Not all single mothers, she knows, have it so easy. When Brian died four years ago, she was not left alone; the whole island supported her. She loves her job teaching English at the high school; she gets an odd satisfaction feeding her passion for literature to teenagers who are so hungry for life, even while they're having such trouble with it. She is the favorite teacher of many island boys and girls. Even so, Deirdre occasionally wishes for anonymity, for a night out with strange, promising faces, for a life where no one knows or cares what she does. She protects Oisin's privacy because she envies him his secrets, his autonomy. She still remembers, though she refused to share the details with her friends, making love to him. How, when he touched her, he managed to make it feel intimate and casual at the same time, how she had been able to open herself up for a few hours, and afterward walk away without the feeling of vulnerability and loss she had sometimes experienced with Brian. Oisin, whom she thinks of as an emotional miser, is surprisingly generous and fervid in bed. She was relieved that he neither asked for nor offered any confirmation of their feelings; he took nothing away from her when they made love.

And because she is grateful for this, she tries to return the favor, tries to keep her curious neighbors from honing in too closely on Oisin's life.

Which is why she tells no one about the odd air in the studio that day, or about the times she has seen them since, walking in the woods or reading books on the rocks of the beach. It would be too hard to explain. That every time she sees this girl—with her long hair that changes color with the light, and eyes that appear to see more than most children—something about her seems to have changed. She knows this feeling from Gabe, who, every few years, grows into himself more. But with Oisin's girl, the impressions are too quick and overwhelming. It is as though every time Aisling passes by, what Deirdre sees is actually a completely different child.

6.

It takes Oisin a month to figure it out.

One morning in December, after a normal, wordless break-fast, Aisling turns from the sink to find Oisin looking at her with the same combination of wonder and betrayal he had worn at their first meeting.

"You're growing," he says.

His eyes flick up and down, she can almost feel them, like hands searching her roughly for an explanation.

"You're clothes don't fit," he says. Scolding.

Her first week, he had bought a pair of children's overalls from the local store to replace the filthy, ragged dress she'd arrived in. She has worn them every day with a red Tiranogue T-shirt, an old cardigan of his draped over them like a robe. He had bought the wrong size overalls, and they'd hung off her at first, but now they are pulling at her crotch, and the hem is hovering above her ankles.

Aisling had learned early on that she should not tell everything, not even to Darragh. Keeping secrets was once as useful to her as silence. No one could blame her for what they did not know was there.

She grows at night. She can feel it beginning in the twilight with an aching heat that starts in her spine and spreads outward to every muscle of her limbs. While Oisin is sleeping, she tries not to cry out with the pain. She once played on fences, swinging by her arms until she could not stand the strain anymore. Now every inch of her feels like this, and relief doesn't come until she finally drops off into exhausted sleep. In the morning there are always notable differences. Everything about her is longer. Her hair is so thick it pulls heavily at her scalp. Her fingers have a better grip on things, and she is almost able to keep up with Oisin's strides in the woods. She can see farther now; distances she never noticed are appearing in front of her eyes. Often she wakes up in the morning with her arms reaching above her head, as though she is trying to lessen the pressure of her growth by giving in to it.

Even her thoughts are longer. She finds herself planning ahead, imagining how much she will grow by next week, next month. A day used to seem an eternity to her, now a week can go by without her noticing. She has begun to write things down, in her own invented shorthand, a diary of blunt facts, because she suspects she will forget the details as quickly as she notices them.

During the day, when Oisin is working, she spends her time inspecting herself, noting down changes, and reading the books he borrowed from that woman. She reads quickly and sometimes feels, taking in page after page, as if she is eating the words. She was like this before. Darragh had tried to teach her to read as he did—carefully, reverently. But she always raced through the books, skimming in search of important passages. She doesn't think of reading as entertainment; she is reading for research, reading to learn how to live. Most of what she learned in her old life is of no use to her here. There are no animals to tend, no sisters to avoid. She spends more time in the presence of Oisin than she has ever spent with anyone, including Darragh. She reads with the hope that the books may tell her how to behave, how to speak, who to be. She is re-creating herself in the interest of safety. Oisin, she believes, will keep her if she appears to be as normal and as useful as possible.

"Are you, or are you not growing?" Oisin snaps, and she flinches, shifting uncomfortably on her bare feet.

"I am," she says in her barely audible voice.

Oisin, as if he was secretly hoping it was all a trick of his imagination, lowers himself with a thump into his armchair.

"How long is this going to go on?" he says. She thinks now is not the time to answer that.

Oisin is angry. He has an urge to slap her, she can see it, and even though she knows he never would—he is not a hitting man—she can imagine this action perfectly: his arm flying at her, the unforgivable sound his callused palm would make on her face.

"This is unacceptable," says Oisin. He stands and begins to pace. "You can't just . . . *grow up* here."

"Why not?" she whispers.

"Because it's not that easy," Oisin says. "Someone would have to raise you, and there's no one to do that."

"Can you not do it?" she says.

"No!"

"Why?"

"Because I have work to do!" Oisin yells. Then his face changes, as if he feels this sounds flimsy. "Look," he tries. "If I had any desire to raise kids, I'd have had my own by now. You can't just come in here and pick me for a father and proceed to grow up. I have to want you first."

"You invited me," she says.

"I didn't. . . ." He begins to say that she wasn't the one he meant to invite, but he stops.

"I can't," he says instead.

"You can, of course," she says lightly. "I'll not trouble you. I'm able to tend to myself."

"I'm barely a fit neighbor, let alone a guardian," says Oisin. "The very idea of you approaching puberty makes me tempted to call Social Services. You'd be better off with someone besides me."

Aisling, not sure what he means, does not ask what puberty is, or Social Services. Instead, she says, "Perhaps. But there is no one else."

Oisin sits down again, looking exhausted. He covers his ears with his scarred palms, not wanting to hear any more. Though he is much older, his face reminds Aisling of Darragh. During the cutting of the turf in spring, it was Aisling's job to bring tea out to Darragh and his father at the bog. She would stagger across the fields with the heavy basket, and, though he must have expected her, Darragh always seemed startled. From the time he first glimpsed her until she stood in front of him, offering up his lunch, his face would be in a battle. As though he couldn't decide whether to hit her or gather her up in his arms. His goodness always won out, and he would touch her hair lightly and let her stay while he ate, offering her sips of amber tea from his tin mug.

She sees the same thing now in Oisin's eyes: a goodness winning out over selfishness. She'd hoped for more; that Oisin would want her rather than keep her out of obligation. But this obligation is familiar; she knows what to do with it. Like a limited amount of food, she knows how to make it last so it is enough, for now.

H er growing is not the only thing she has been hiding from Oisin. She has not told him of her family, for fear that if he knows the story, he will see her the way they did. He knows her language; he may know the words that label her as the one to blame for everything.

Her first life had been ruled by the seasons. In spring there was planting. Summer, with a twilight that lasted until the late hours, was a patient time; if you were still enough, you could hear the crops growing. Fall, with the harvest, was the busiest, and along with the work brought an air of celebration. And winter was endless, when you fed meagerly on what you had stored, and waited for it all to start again.

Among the papers which Darragh kept on the shelf of the underground house was a map of Ireland he had made when he was still in school. The classroom hadn't any paints or inks, but had an abundance of donated glue, and so the four provinces were represented by materials Darragh had gathered and pasted into the penciled outline of Ireland. When Aisling had first seen it, she had thought it was a map of the seasons. Spring was at the top, green grasses and gold reeds woven like a Saint Brigid's cross, but snipped at the edges to fit into the boundaries of the northernmost province. Summer was the east, the crushed pink of fuschia pasted to a bed of sand. Autumn was the soil from the potato beds, dark, still moist under its protective husk of glue. And winter—which she later discovered was the western province where they lived—was represented by chips of slate. The chips were so thin they seemed like gray-blue paper, and lichen, stiff as frost, peeked between them in the same way it grew, stubbornly, from the hard rocks on their land.

When she told Darragh that she saw the year in his map, he nodded as if the idea were reasonable, then proceeded to tell her of the four parts of Ireland. Ireland, he said, is larger than you know, but also smaller—when seen on a map of the world—than you'd imagine. Darragh's voice had a different tone when he took out his books and papers, a tone she thought must be teacherly, though she'd never met a teacher.

"Why did you stop going to school?" Aisling said once. Darragh had winced, covering up the reaction with a shrug.

"I'd learned everything," he said. "Everything a farmer needs, anyway. Reading, writing, sums, the borders and crops of the countries of the world." Then his eyes, as if peeking over the edge of his sorrow, brightened. "Had I been born a prince," he whispered, and Aisling saw it in a flash, Darragh's face, royal and serious beneath a circle of jewels, "I would have studied other maps. Philosophy, the map of the mind. Astronomy, the map of the stars. The map of time, which is history, and of God himself, theology."

Then he straightened up as he did when preparing himself for a scolding.

"I was only allowed to stay so long because Da has no English. It was easier to send me than to learn it himself."

"When was it you were in school?" Aisling said. Darragh put away his ream of papers quickly.

"Before you were born," he said.

Long before she knew why, Aisling had always suspected that her birth coincided with the beginning of some dark time for Darragh. It was the same with the others; her sisters spoke fondly of times "before the girl," as if the coming of Aisling was a border that separated two halves of their lives. Her parents had not exchanged words for as long as she could remember, but the skeleton of their former connection still rattled between them, like a third person, living stubbornly within the silence. If it was necessary for them to communicate, they did so through Darragh or her sisters. The house where they lived had only one room, and in it the woman cooked and served the man his breakfast and dinner every day, each pretending the other was not there. In the summer, when the farm required more work, the man was gone most of the day and they ignored each other effortlessly. But after the harvest—after the wheat and best potatoes had been sold at the fair, and the remaining pig had been brought inside again to live in a pen by the fire—their silence acquired a vengeance that was palpable. Resentment sucked the oxygen from the tiny room and left everyone within it gasping for air.

Aisling's birthday came at the worst of it. Often the others ignored it altogether, and she preferred it this way. Though the calendar meant nothing to her, she knew her birthday came every year along with the first chill in the air, the digging of potatoes, and the filling of pits. Her birthday always came at the end of the old year which began in November. *Samhain*. When darkness came early and the land began its rest. And when, for only one day, there was money.

With the money came the arguments, translated by the children, so that the man and woman never actually had to speak to each other.

On returning from the fair, where everything they'd grown had been traded in for these precious bits of metal, Aisling's father would sit at the table and arrange coins into piles of descending diameter. He would count in an audible murmur, and recount so often that he would inevitably make a mistake, which would excite him into counting again. Sometimes, when he wasn't looking, Darragh would let Aisling hold a coin. They were heavy and layered with grime, and smelled of unwashed clothing, sweat, and a sharp metal that clung to her hands and transformed to a taste in her mouth.

After he finished his counting, the man would move to the fire to smoke and brood. Then the woman would attack the piles, knocking the coins haphazardly onto the floor and kneeling over them. She could count faster than him, and silently, and she did it only once. It looked like more money the way she did it, as though better coins might be hiding beneath the top layer of the pile.

The sisters hovered in the background, waiting for a coin to be tossed their way, though as far as Aisling could remember, that had never happened. The sisters spent money only in their outspoken fantasies. Eventually, the counting would end in words that scattered the girls and made Darragh's face go hard.

"There isn't enough," the woman would begin, directing her words to Darragh. He would then turn and repeat the words to his father, with slight alterations, as though he were trying to re-create a message he had heard long ago. The rest followed like a well-rehearsed dialogue. Where had the money gone? Was he drinking away the rent again? The woman would assail him, Darragh repeating her accusations, until the man lost his patience and struck back.

"Tell your woman that we'd have enough to live on if I weren't obliged to feed her *páiste gréine.*"

It was something he said every year, and it always ended the argument, because Darragh refused to repeat it. He would take Aisling from the house and, with the girls hiding in the loft, the man and woman would have no one left to speak for them.

Before Aisling even knew the words, she understood that they referred to her by the glances that came with them. Somehow, she was responsible for the lack of coins. For one year, after she had begun to speak, she thought they were calling her the "sun child," because she

learned the words, taken separately, to mean this. She thought it referred to her hair, which had streaks of gold in it and was envied by
the brown-haired sisters. Perhaps, she thought, it was more expensive
to take care of a golden-haired child than a regular one. Perhaps the
sun in her hair left the others chilled in shadow.

When she was five, she was told what it meant by a yellow-haired
boy in the village. She had used the nickname on him and he'd been
angry; he'd spat at the ground by her bare feet. It wasn't her fault, she'd
said, that his hair was that color.

"That's not what it means, you fool," the boy had said. "It means
you've no father. You were never baptized, and when you die, it won't
be the normal graveyard you're buried in, but across the field with the
suicides."

She'd dismissed the boy as stupid; it was plain that she had a father,
even if he was a bad one. And though she wasn't wanted, she surely
wasn't so evil that she'd have to be buried outside of consecrated ground.

But after the next harvest, when her father spat those words again,
Aisling went to Darragh's dictionary, a present from his teacher when
he was still in school. Darragh had taught her to read with it. What
she found in the book were more words that she did not understand:
illegitimate, bastard. What they sounded like were names given to
something that was unnatural or not whole. As if she were a
changeling; something evil the fairies left behind in a crib after stealing a human baby. And though this frightened her, it was better than
the explanation she eventually persuaded out of Darragh.

What she noticed first in Oisin's house was the money. It
was everywhere. On table surfaces, between the cushions of couch and chair, in a pottery crock alongside the containers

of sugar and coffee; there were more forgotten coins in this house than she'd ever seen piled on her parents' floor. Under the guise of straightening up, she'd collected all she could find; taken together they filled the kitchen container to the brim. The coins were not the same as the ones she remembered; they were smaller and lighter and had miniature heads in raised profile on their surfaces. Foreign coins. But they smelled the same—filthy, as though they had passed across an infinite number of unwashed hands. She poured them on the floor and arranged them the way her father would have, in teetering piles according to size. Oisin came out of the shower to find her surrounded by tiny columns of silver and gold, and he looked at her for an explanation.

"I was counting them for you," she said.

"Keep them," he said, and though she was shocked, she didn't dare argue. She hauled the container over to the bed she'd set up for herself: a rectangle of pillows in the corner, positioned so she could see the whole room. (She'd moved because Oisin didn't like sleeping with her; she knew by the stiffness that struck him the moment he lay down.) She wedged the crock between the pillows and the wall, so that when she slept, the cool pottery pressed reassurance into the small of her back.

It was only a matter of days before she discovered why Oisin had parted so easily with his fortune. At the island shop, she watched him pay for a paper box of milk and a plucked, decapitated chicken with a number of softly worn bills from his wallet. The shop lady had given him back bills and coins, and he'd dropped the gold coins into a small dish beside the register. She knew by the casual way he did this that the money she'd hoarded was almost worthless. It was bills she needed. But no one left bills lying around.

Then four of her top teeth fell out. They were pushed out by thicker, whiter teeth, their bottom edges uneven like tiny saws. She laid her old teeth out in a line across the palm of her hand; once they were out of her mouth, they looked too fragile to survive biting. Oisin came up behind her.

"Put them under your pillow," he said.

"To ward off evil spirits?" Aisling whispered.

Oisin smiled. "For the tooth fairy," he said. "She'll take them and leave you money."

"How much money?" Aisling asked.

That night she tied her teeth in a bit of blue tissue paper she'd found in Oisin's studio. She didn't want to lay them naked under her pillow; over the day they'd browned and shrunk until they looked like tiny corpses. She dreamed that the fairy who collected her teeth was building a sculpture from them, in the form of a young woman she thought must be herself, grown up.

Just before she woke, she was wondering if there would ever be enough teeth for the job. Her eyes opened on Oisin, who was leaning over her, his hand pressing gently under the edge of her pillow. She pretended to roll over in her sleep, moving her head to make it easier for him to slide his hand underneath. She felt him pull away the package and replace something else with a tiny push. After he'd gone back to bed, she slid her hand under and felt warm, wrinkled paper. In the morning, the bill was damp and molded into the curve of her palm. Oisin put such enthusiasm in pretending to be surprised that she didn't let on that she knew the secret.

By the end of the month, she had eleven dollars. Some mornings she found crisp bills folded into shapes: a bird, a flower, a tiny fox. The last teeth to go were the back ones; in her impatience she discovered she could use her fingernail like a lever at the gum line, prying her tooth free with a painless, satisfying rip. She was disappointed when Oisin told her the new teeth would not fall out as well. She kept her bills folded and pressed beneath her crock of coins. She thought it was enough money, and recounted it daily. When Oisin asked if she'd like to spend it, she shook her head so violently that he never asked again.

The money was not for herself. She was saving it, for when the rent came due again, when she believed that Oisin, like her father, would have squandered everything he was meant to save. Along with the stories and words she collected from books, she was gathering the money as a cushion against the future. Just as her body was lengthening, growing away from the label that had poisoned her life, even before her birth.

Most of what she learned about this phrase, *páiste gréine*, was from what Darragh did not say. His explanation was a shifting of the truth; he left out the parts that would hurt her. She filled in the rest from listening at mass and from the mutterings of the people in the house. The man who belonged to Darragh and the sisters was not her father. She was alive because of a sin her mother committed with a man no one had seen since. She was more than unwanted; she was the cause of everything that was bad in that house. It was because of her that there was a lack of money, because of her that the man and the woman never spoke, it was her fault that the sisters were cruel and unhappy. Her fault that Darragh was not able to go to school, was forced to look after her, had to dig a hole in the boggy ground in order to find some peace. It was all because of her and there was nothing she could do to fix it. All she could do was continue on as she had been, trying to be invisible, trying not to get in the way of those who were pained at the sight of her. And she woke each day hoping the inevitable had not yet occurred: that Darragh would not be looking at her with similar blame in his eyes. She expected it, and dreaded that it would come before she was old enough to survive without him.

It is much like the dread she feels in Oisin's house now: that one day he will find the strength to reject her. So she is growing rapidly, hoping that if she can reach a certain age, she will no longer be a burden. She believes there is an age where she will be wanted, or if not, at least she'll be able to choose to be alone.

7.

$\mathcal{E}$very summer, Oisin's father would sublet their house to new immigrants and take his family to Ireland, where his siblings ran the local pub in a small Galway village. Declan thought himself lucky—most Irish immigrants made it home only once in ten years. By exhausting whatever savings he'd accumulated each winter, Declan never had to give up home.

The summer after their grandfather died, Oisin, to the horror of his parents, stepped over his nana's threshold and announced: "I saw Granddad in Boston the day he died." Oisin's mother never got a chance to blame his overactive imagination, since the room was full of women who believed in such things.

"It is from your grandfather, God rest him, that you got the second sight," Oisin's nana said that first night.

"I'm glad I have eyes like Granddad," Oisin said. Oisin's grandfather had been a gentle man with laughing eyes, eyes unlike his father's, which were resentful and brooding.

"It's a gift, Oisin," his nana said. "I can't say it's a blessing—your grandfather didn't always think so. He saw a lot of things not meant for human eyes—many of them ugly things. I hope what you see is always as harmless as the soul of your grandfather, but I doubt it will be."

"Do I have a gift, Nana?" Nieve said.

Their grandmother, as though she'd forgotten Nieve was there, blinked twice. She smiled and touched the girl's cheek.

"Is being beautiful not enough of a gift for you?" she said.

Nieve frowned. "Of course not," she said. When the roomful of adults began to laugh, Oisin saw rage flicker in her eyes.

O isin was not skilled at the transition from America to Ireland. Six hours on a plane and the world turned upside down. Words changed their meaning, sentences reversed themselves, he had to fight to make himself understood. From the airport on, American voices, which he hadn't noticed before, sounded loud and intrusive. Fries were chips, chips were crisps, "yes" and "no" were not complete answers, "you're welcome" was a greeting. Fags meant cigarettes rather than some sexual thing he hadn't quite figured out. In Galway, you had to thank people repeatedly. You were expected to refuse what you were offered three times before accepting, had to offer what you had three times even if it meant you had nothing left for yourself. Oisin always spent his first week draped in a clumsy blush, straining to decipher the low voices, pausing before he spoke, translating in his mind what his mouth wanted to say.

Nieve found it easier. She was a natural actress and could disguise her Boston accent. Her Irish voice was soft and lilting, and strangers often thought she was from a "posh" section of Dublin. She remembered what everything was called and assimilated without a snag, but was quicker to defend America than Oisin was. "America's the grandest place on earth," she would say to any child who called her a Yank, "and you just lost your chance to visit me there."

"Southie is supposed to be a little Ireland," Nieve once said to Oisin. "But that's only pretend. All that's the same is there's a lot of beer."

In Boston, the twins played on concrete, but their Irish summers were ruled by nature. Their uncle Malachy built them a fort from tree branches and pinecones, a little hut stretched between two trees covered in an electric-green moss.

"A home between twin trees," their uncle said when he showed them the fort. "For my twins."

Uncle Malachy, their father's twin, lived next door to their grandmother. He was taller and more handsome than their father, with a face that hardly ever scowled. He was married to a woman named Rose, and though they had no children, she often looked like she was pregnant, something Oisin and Nieve were told never to ask about. Malachy was a musician—he played the fiddle in the pub every night, whether people were there to listen or not. He made a chime to hang on the branch above their fort, which played delicate music in the wind.

Besides Malachy, Oisin, and Declan, the rest of the MacDaras were women. Declan and Malachy had four sisters—three in Ireland, and one who had emigrated to Australia but still wrote home weekly. All of them were remarkably beautiful—it was said that the missing sister was the best-looking of them all—with dark hair and their mother's blue eyes. Oisin and Nieve called them "The

Aunts," and often spoke and thought of them as one large, multi-limbed woman. Aunts Fiona and Dervla lived within speaking distance of their mother, and Emer was still at home. They worked together, running a small tourist shop next to their brother's pub, where they sold their own line of beauty products in addition to more traditional Irish souvenirs. They even smelled the same, because they all wore one musky perfume they'd invented themselves. It was called Rún—Irish for "mystery" or "secret"—and was sold in American catalogues alongside Aran sweaters and Connemara marble.

Fiona and Dervla had husbands, but these men were quiet and stayed in the background. At family dinners, Oisin often felt that the husbands, as well as his father, Malachy, and himself, appeared a bit dimmer next to the bright light of all those women. As dim as other people appeared to Oisin, compared with the ghost of his grandfather.

Oisin and Nieve spent most of their time in and around that fort and the woods that stretched for miles behind their grandmother's house. Mostly Nieve wanted to play the princess from Tír na nÓg, a game in which she had the majority of the lines. She had a cape made from an old shawl of her grandmother's, sewn sloppily with red calico stars. Oisin made slingshots so he could play the hunter, though Nieve would not let him actually shoot at anything.

In the twilight, which stretched on for hours, Oisin would often see his grandfather, leaning against a tree packing his pipe, or watching through the small window as his wife prepared dinner in the kitchen. Each time he appeared, Nieve would stiffen, and breathlessly whisper: "He's here, isn't he?"

"Can you see him?" Oisin asked the first time this happened.

"No," Nieve said, shrugging. "I can just tell that you see him."

And Oisin felt, with a small, vivid pain, that he had done something to disappoint her.

One afternoon while playing around the fort, Oisin was in a particularly foul mood; it had begun that morning when Nieve spent her breakfast ignoring him and talking to the Aunts. Now they were playing Tir na nÓg, and when they came to the part of the story where Oisin was supposed to get down on his knees (Nieve had added that detail) and profess his love to the princess, he only stood there and glared at his sister.

"You're not playing right," Nieve said from her perch on a low-hanging branch that served as the magic horse.

"This part is stupid," Oisin said. "Once I go away with you I'm doomed to come back, go blind, and die. I don't think Oisin would want to leave Ireland anyway, just because of some stupid girl he's never seen before."

"He's in love with me," Nieve yelled. "I am all he wants in the world. He can't help himself!"

"People don't fall in love like that," Oisin scoffed, though he'd be the first to admit he knew nothing about love.

"They do," Nieve said, her face steaming with anger. "Love makes you do crazy things. I know much more about it than you ever will."

"How do you know so much?" Oisin said.

"Because I'm a woman," Nieve said calmly. Oisin was quiet. He knew there must be dozens of reasons why Nieve was wrong about this, but he couldn't think of any. The truth was, Oisin—at eight—already suspected that women knew things that no one bothered to explain to men. The Aunts, his mother, Nana, all seemed to have secrets. So he played the game Nieve's way, got down on his knees and said, "It is you who are the shining one."

Nieve didn't reply. She merely looked down at him with a little gratitude, a lot of superiority, and a hint of sorrow.

That was the summer that Oisin grew almost as tall as Nieve, before she grew too and left him reaching the bridge of her nose again. It was the summer that Nana began teaching them Irish with urgency and anger at herself for not beginning sooner. Mornings in the house were filled with small voices running through their lessons.

"*Táim i mo chónai*—I live; *chonaic mé*—I saw; *ní fhaca mé*—I did not see; *táin i mo thost*—I am silent."

Nieve, Nana said, had the ear for Irish. But Oisin's vocabulary drills resulted in much sighing from the women.

Despite this, Oisin would have remembered it a happy summer, if not for the banshee.

It began the night Oisin wakened Nieve from a deep sleep.

"Nieve! What's wrong?" he whispered, concern in his voice. When she didn't reply, he thumped her on the back.

"Cut it out," Nieve spat; she was often mean-spirited when someone woke her from a deep sleep.

"You're having a bad dream," Oisin said.

"I am not," Nieve said, pulling the quilt toward her side of the bed.

"You were crying, Nee," Oisin said.

"I wasn't," she said. "Go back to sleep, Ossie."

And very suddenly, like an unfamiliar voice hissing a threat into his brain, Oisin was afraid.

"Nieve," he whispered. "You don't hear that?"

"Hear what?" she whispered.

"Somebody's crying," Oisin said.

He stood up and went over to the small loft window, lifting the lever to tilt the bottom of the glass pane outward. The crying rushed into the room with the damp night air. It was a female sound, a slow, labored whimpering—exhausted, as though the crier had been going on for hours. When Oisin heard a woman cry, he had a few automatic reactions: If it was his mother, he felt guilty; if it was Nieve, he felt like crying himself. Never before had the sound of crying made him cold and terrified.

"Ossie," Nieve said, "you're scaring me. Stop it." She was sitting up in bed, looking at him as though she couldn't decide whether to giggle or scream.

"Do you think it's Nana?" Oisin said. "It doesn't sound like Nana."

"Oisin, stop it. Nobody's crying," Nieve said. She came over to him and laced her fingers with his.

"I'm scared, Nieve," Oisin said, and for a moment, in the darkness, he thought he sounded older, as if he were imitating the voice of their father.

"Go back to sleep," Nieve said. She pulled him over and eased him onto his back, returning his portion of the quilt. She crawled in beside him and manipulated his arm so that it was around her and her head was firmly pressed against his shoulder.

And, lulled by the familiar smell of his sister's hair, woods and sea salt and baby shampoo—and her real warmth pressing into him—Oisin could finally hear what was wrong with that crying. Periodically, in between the gasps of drawn-out grief, came a giggle. A cruel, knowing burst of amusement, as though the crier were taunting itself. The voice moved smoothly from mourning to delight and back again. Oisin lay awake all night, listening until he was crying himself, until the cries and the laughter mingled with his fear and became one white wail that swelled his brain, until he was silently begging for someone, anyone, to stop it.

Nieve told their grandmother about Oisin's odd dream at breakfast.

"It wasn't a dream," Oisin said. "I heard somebody crying. Nieve only thinks I was dreaming because she couldn't hear it."

Oisin, though he had never seen his grandmother afraid, recognized her fear instantly. She tried to hide it, turning back to the stove, but her movements were rigid and the fright came off her in waves that slapped against Oisin's chest.

"You're not to go looking for the crying woman, Oisin," their grandmother said softly. "If you hear her again, stay in the house. Do you understand me?" She wasn't looking at the children, and there was a burning smell erupting from the porridge.

"Yes, Nana," Oisin said. She gave them some porridge, turned the stove off and left the house by the back door, taking the path to Malachy's. The children ate their breakfast quietly, and though Nieve tried to get his attention, Oisin refused to look at her.

The invisible weeping continued for three nights. Oisin lay frightened and rigid until dawn, and slept until midday while the family tiptoed beneath his loft. There was much whispering among the women. Oisin's grandmother and the Aunts wandered about with grim, knowing faces, did not scold or tease him for his sleeping the morning away, and touched him occasionally, surreptitiously, as though they shared a sad secret.

He'd had no intention of investigating, not until the cry changed and began—in its desperation and insistence—to call to him. He imagined the voice was promising that if he confronted it, it would stop.

He was standing barefoot—pajama ankles soaked from the damp grass—in his uncle Malachy's yard when Nieve found him.

"Oisin?" Nieve said, moving carefully toward him. "What are you doing out here? Nana said . . ."

"She's still crying, Nieve," Oisin said. "She won't stop crying."

Suddenly Nieve looked angry. She turned as if to face the woman only Oisin could see.

"Stop it," she barked, as though standing up to a bully at school. "Leave him alone."

"She's not after me, Nieve," Oisin said calmly.

A light came on inside Malachy's house and Oisin heard the latch on his door. Malachy, struggling into his jacket, ran past them without a glance, down the path to their grandmother's house.

"He's getting Nana," Nieve said. "We're gonna be in trouble, Ossie." She tried to pull him home but he wouldn't budge.

"Oisin." Nieve sighed. "If she's not after you, why are you so scared of somebody crying?"

Oisin looked at his sister. In comparison with the shrieking woman behind her, Nieve looked insubstantial, as though one carefully aimed breath would blow her to dust in the air. He could never explain this to his sister, she would never see it, and this thought frightened him almost as much as the woman that moved toward him, passing through Nieve as though she weren't there.

The ghost was more blood than anything else. Blood so dark it drooled like ink over her porcelain face, ran in rivulets from the ends of her hair, soaking the fabric of her dress until her nipples strained against it, large and black, like two mauled beetles. Her crying was no longer a metered whimper, but a tearless scream, which changed periodically into a delighted but cruel laugh. While she cried, she was smiling; while she laughed, she looked anguished and tears diluted the black blood on her cheeks to red.

Oisin heard Nieve scream, "Nana!" The ghost laughed again, as though Nieve's fear were the most amusing thing yet.

As Oisin's grandmother, Malachy, and Aunt Emer came scurrying out of the woods, the crying woman receded, squelching on bloody feet toward the road.

"What in the name of Christ?" Oisin's grandmother said, stumbling as she almost ran straight into him.

"She's not crying anymore, Nana," he said. He could not bring his voice above a graveled whisper. "It's only a baby crying now."

Malachy made a noise in his throat somewhere between a sob and a moan, and ran for his door. Oisin's grandmother made the sign of the cross quickly.

"Take the twins back to the house," she said to Emer. "And bring your sisters."

Oisin cried for twenty-four hours. He was kept in bed in the loft with cold cloths over his eyes, which had developed an infection overnight. One was closed tightly with pus, the other only open a slit, and the tears still managed to pour out of them, though he cried silently. Nieve stayed with him, telling their travel stories and picking yellow crust from his eyelashes.

By the time his grandmother came up the loft ladder to talk to him, Oisin had already overheard much of the family's mournful whispering. Rose and Malachy's baby had died. Born too soon.

"Let us talk awhile, Nieve," their grandmother said.

"He needs me here," Nieve said, not moving from her chair by his side. "He's only a boy." Oisin had heard this phrase all his life, from his Aunts, his teachers, his parents. Lately he had begun to suspect that it wasn't his youth they pitied.

"Just for a minute," his grandmother cooed. She nudged Nieve out of the chair and toward the ladder.

"I'll get you some soup, Oisin," Nieve said cheerily before climbing downstairs.

His grandmother took the seat beside him. If he forced his better eye open he could make her out, stiff posture and her fingers twisting her wedding band, a habit she had when she felt impatient. He knew she expected him to question her.

"Is it because of me," Oisin whispered. "That Rose's baby died?"

"No," his grandmother said. "That baby wasn't strong enough to live."

"Why was that lady there?" Oisin said.

"She is a banshee. A spirit that attends families and warns them when a member is about to die. Sometimes the banshee is a loving guardian who cries in grief. Other times, she's malicious, mocking human pain. Your grandfather saw Rose's banshee when her other babies died. She's a terrible one, he told me that much."

"Did she take the baby?" Oisin said.

"Of course not. She's harmless, Oisin, a resentful spirit reveling in the sorrow of the living. She has no power to do anything but frighten. That baby is in Heaven with your grandfather."

"How do you know that?" Oisin was starting to cry again.

"Do you think you're the only one who knows things, Oisin? I may not have second sight, but there are things I'm sure about nonetheless."

Oisin, the tears pouring down now, salt stinging his raw eyes, turned away from his grandmother. He heard her stand and move the chair back against the wall.

"You can stay in that bed tonight, Oisin," she said. "But tomorrow morning you'll be down for breakfast."

Oisin only cried harder at this, his shoulders shaking beneath the quilt. How could she be so heartless? If she knew anything at all, she should know that he was incapable of going back down there, of opening his eyes, of throwing himself back into a world where women screamed and bled beside you while the rest of the living had breakfast, oblivious.

She turned and said something then, before climbing back downstairs, something that Oisin, when he was older, would remember with a feeling of hopeless exhaustion.

"It's wrong to spend your life afraid, Oisin," she said. "No matter what you see."

PART TWO

Spring

I like men who have a future,

and women who have a past.

OSCAR WILDE

The Picture of Dorian Gray

8.

isling?" Oisin says, and she stops obediently, turning toward him, the sun from the studio skylight setting her face on fire.

"Why are you dressed like that?" he says. He was trying to work but he can't stop looking at her. It's the middle of January, the ground is buried under layers of snow and ice, and the girl of seven who moved in three months ago is now taller than Deirdre's ten-year-old son. It is not her height that strikes him today, though he is always awed by the changes that rush through her; she is beginning to look more like a lanky teenager than the little girl whose feet he bandaged in November. What alarms him is that she seems to have given herself what he thinks is meant to be a makeover, but in a reversed, disastrous direction.

Her hair, normally a different shade depending which angle you look from—gold, chestnut, auburn, or dark umber—has been pinched into two tight, crooked braids. She usually stands straight, but now she is so slouchy it looks almost painful. And, strangest of all, she has sprouted glasses above her nose: black-rimmed, buggy spectacles, so big the stems are angled so they can fit behind her ears. Oisin recognizes them as an old pair of his reading glasses and feels a twinge of guilt. Had she been having trouble seeing and not said anything? But when he looks again, he realizes that the glasses are actually impairing her vision—she is squinting from behind them. Oisin thinks of a former girlfriend who liked to wear his shirts and spray herself with his cologne. Has Aisling developed, along with long legs, a crush on him? He has an urge to check his top drawer for missing pairs of boxer shorts.

"Why are you wearing my glasses?" he asks, and Aisling lowers the black rims, trying to focus on him.

"I'm trying to look *awkward*," she says simply. She walks back to her corner, where she now has an armchair, a stack of books she's borrowed from Deirdre, and a plastic planter cradling the green bud of an amaryllis.

Oisin puts his pencil down reluctantly. He knows that by the time they finish talking, his inspiration toward work will have slipped away. But curiosity has already distracted him.

"Why would you want to look awkward?" he says.

She regards him as though she is trying to determine whether his interest is sincere. He holds his breath whenever she does this, waiting for the verdict. She folds his glasses and arranges her face, mimicking the serious, condescending expression of an adult explaining something to a child.

"It's in these books, you see," she says. Her voice sounds like a tiny flute. As with most Irish children he's known, her speech is oddly formal, like a girl dressed so well for church you hardly notice the scrapes on her knees.

"The ones called herons," she starts.

"Heroines," Oisin says.

"Right, so." She looks irritated at his interruption. "The *heroines* always wear glasses or have too-red hair or they're pale and skinny. They'll be beauties when they grow up, but in the beginning they're awkward. And smart and talented and kind as well. Pretty girls are mean and stupid and selfish. They've no *character*."

"Let me see if I've got this right," Oisin says. "You're afraid you're too good-looking?"

Aisling only blinks at him, irritated, as though he has oversimplified her dilemma.

"You're reading too much," Oisin says. "If you're starting to think those books are anything like real life."

"Were you a handsome boy or an awkward one?" Aisling dares.

"Awkward, but . . ."

"There!" Aisling cries out, stamping her foot.

"I'm hardly Prince Charming now," Oisin says. Aisling nods sadly, and Oisin needs to cough before he continues. "Most people waste half their lives wishing they were beautiful," he says. "Wearing my glasses is not going to make you more interesting."

"But do they make me look *unattractive*?" Aisling says, pronouncing this new word with obvious pleasure.

Oisin is experiencing déjà vu. How many times has he been asked this question? Do I look fat, old, tired? Women are always asking him for reassurance, as though he were qualified at all to make them feel better about themselves.

"Not really," he says timidly. Aisling sighs, handing the glasses over. She returns to reading, the book propped open on her slim thighs, halfheartedly untwisting her braids.

Oisin returns to his worktable, his mouth twitching as he suppresses a smile. This is what consumes him now, what keeps him up at night and makes him sometimes boorish with his little guest: He can't even remember the last time he paid close attention to anyone's mind but his own. Now he finds he needs—needs with a passion that distracts him from everything else—to know what is going on in Aisling's head. He resents the fact that she fascinates him in the silliest, most everyday ways. He has become like an insufferable new parent, who can go on for hours analyzing meaningless baby talk. He even finds himself wanting to tell someone the things she says that make him laugh (though he tries to hide it behind a scowl). But he has no one to tell.

She seems most concerned with appearing normal. She studies him closely and imitates the simplest gestures: the way he brushes his teeth or kicks off his boots; she has even begun to pinch the bridge of her nose and look pained, as if she is developing one of his anxious headaches. It alternately amuses and worries him.

This happens too often. One minute he will be working fairly well on a new print, then he is interrupted, worrying about the personality development of a dead girl. He throws his pencil down, pulls at the roots of his hair.

"You'll have to go," he says sharply. Aisling doesn't even look up from her book. "I'm sorry, but you can't stay here anymore. This isn't working out."

Silence. Aisling is not concerned. He says this to her at least once a week. All it means is that she will be quiet and invisible for a while. Until he forgets and shows interest in her again.

He thinks of Christmas as his turning point—the place where he lost the path back to his normal life. Once he got over the shock of her growing (you don't get over that sort of thing, you absorb it out of necessity, like bad air, and try not to think about what it is doing to you) he was able to salvage his solitary life. He kept working and, for hours at a time, forgot completely about the girl in the corner who was changing like a flower filmed in time-lapse photography. He found a space for her and shoved her in it, compartmentalizing in the same way he has the women in his life. He learned this trick as a boy, when, if he wanted to concentrate, he had to block out the voices of pleading ghosts. He can, from years of practice, make the person standing in front of him disappear, fade into their surroundings. Though they might continue to speak, he hears nothing. He goes inside himself and shuts the door.

He often thinks of the public toilets in Ireland, with the latch that revolves from ENGAGED to VACANT. Not until Aisling has he been bothered by the knocking.

Oisin does not celebrate Christmas. He makes a point of working as if it's any other day; he avoids shopping in Portland between Thanksgiving and New Year's. He thinks of it as a holiday for children and easily pleased grown-ups. He was not prepared to spend Christmas with a child. Or to enjoy it.

The first week of December, while they were driving slowly along the island road at dusk, Aisling looked out her window and saw a house on a hill, electric lights dancing in the bushes, the vague shapes of people milling around inside. Laughter and glassy clinks punctuated the deep singing of Bing Crosby.

"What are they celebrating?" she said. Oisin put the car into third gear, speeding forward.

"Christmas," he mumbled. The word made her squint—a foreign phrase.

"*Nollaig,*" he said in Irish. He felt the tiny childish shiver as the word passed through her. She was a girl; Christmas was still a hopeful word.

For days she bombarded him with questions about what Americans do for Christmas. Though she had fallen for the tooth fairy, the story of Santa Claus left a cynical tilt to her eyebrows. He was relieved. He didn't want to have to go to the mall and choose toys until he was blind from boredom. But, oddly, he wanted to do something.

He bought a tree and metal stand from Moira's shop, telling himself it would distract Aisling so he could work. But when he watched her step forward and put her face between the branches, inhaling deeply, he resigned himself to losing a whole day collecting pinecones and stringing cranberries to decorate the branches.

Once he started, he couldn't stop. Everything he did for her caused a reaction, and her reactions—a smile, the little catch of breath—made him want to give again.

They made snowmen in front of the studio, wrapping them in all the scarves and ties he'd received from girlfriends over the years. He bought a plastic sled, a variety of sappy Christmas albums, candles that smelled like winter spice. An Advent calendar (half price two weeks into December) with tiny cardboard cupboards and a piece of penny candy for each day. He borrowed a video monitor from the high school and they watched *It's a Wonderful Life*. Aisling seemed to enjoy it, spent days ringing the bell on the tree, trying to conjure up angel's wings. The film left Oisin depressed. He hadn't seen it since he was a boy, when he had still believed he would grow up to be an admirable man like George Bailey. The following day, he got a haircut in an attempt to look less like the moody hermit he saw in the mirror.

On Christmas Eve he roasted a huge turkey, cooked potatoes, stuffing, and three kinds of squash, served salad and rolls and cranberry sauce sliced from the can. He watched Aisling eating; she consumed everything as though it was the last food she would ever see.

"Were you hungry before?" he asked gently. "At home?"

Aisling just kept eating. A few minutes passed and Oisin gave up waiting for an answer. After they were finished, he brought out the bread pudding and pumpkin ice cream. He'd already forgotten his question, when she answered in a firm, emotionless voice.

"Once we were so hungry we ate a dog," she said. Her eyes kept him from asking any more.

They sat by the blinking tree and he gave her a present to break the tension. It was a board game—Sorry—that he'd seen at the shop and vaguely remembered enjoying as a kid. They played six straight games; Aisling was quick to learn the rules, but panicked whenever it appeared he might beat her. Though Oisin is normally a merciless competitor at games, he let her win five rounds. And just that small gesture, which coincided with a loosening sensation in the center of his chest, made him feel like a trustworthy, safe, giving man. A guardian.

Just before bed, Aisling took one of the red dinner candles, asked for matches, and brought it to the window. Oisin, his heart beating hard, asked her what she was doing.

"On the Eve of Christmas," she said, "you're meant to leave a candle burning in the window to guide the dead ones home."

"I know," Oisin said hoarsely. She struck a match with tentative care and lit the wick.

"Who's it for?" Oisin said, and Aisling looked at him, considering whether she should answer.

"My brother," she said finally. This admission seemed to exhaust her; and she went straight over to the bed she had made in the corner and climbed under the covers.

Oisin finished tidying the kitchen, changed into his pajamas in the bathroom, turned out the lights and, before climbing into bed, lit the other candle, placing it next to Aisling's in the window. Just before he fell asleep, he heard her voice, and knew she'd been awake, watching him.

"Is that one for Nieve?" she said.

"Mmm" was all he could say.

"My brother told me that no prayer goes unanswered on Christmas Eve," she said. In the pause that followed, he imagined her making a wish.

"He was wrong," she said instead.

Despite this, for the first time in decades, as he settled his face deep in the pillow, Oisin felt that particular combination of thrill and sadness that once had defined Christmas Eve for him. The idea that one night, illuminated with lights, scented with balsam and heavy with time, contained so much more possibility than every other night of the year.

Now it's February, and his days are so full of her, he rarely makes it into the studio. So he ought to know something is wrong when she doesn't eat her dinner.

She's been napping half the afternoon on the new twin bed he ordered from Bangor, which is also odd, since normally she has an abundance of energy: she never seems to have the overwhelming urge to lie down like Oisin does when his work is nagging at him. But he has been so busy fretting over the fact that he's not working—a consuming process that eats up more energy than working would—that it is almost midnight before he realizes Aisling is sick.

He is sketching randomly at the kitchen table when he hears Aisling vomiting in the bathroom. He recalls that there is something he is supposed to do—he remembers that he once gathered Nieve's hair behind her neck while she was sick—but he is startled into immobility. He has never seen a ghost fall ill before. While he is trying to decide whether to get up and knock, he hears the toilet flush and Aisling opens the door, looking weak, her face the color of flour. The sour odor of vomit wafts past him as she walks to her bed.

"Are you all right?" he says quietly, but she is busy burrowing herself under every extra blanket in the house. He walks over to her and sees that she is shivering so hard her new teeth are clacking together. On instinct, he reaches a palm out to feel her forehead, an image of Nieve's small hand flashing across his memory. Aisling feels warm, but he hasn't touched her since that first night and has no idea what her normal temperature should be. The only thermometer he owns is the one he stabs into roasting meat.

"You may have a fever," he says, inflecting the phrase like a question, as though he needs her input to be sure. But she bursts into loud sobs. He has never seen her cry, and it occurs to him how odd that is: don't little girls cry all the time?

"It is the fever," she moans. "I'm dying again." Heat rashes have appeared like red maps on her cheeks.

"You can't die from a fever," Oisin says. But he is having trouble swallowing. He doesn't know what normal children die from, let alone those who come back from the dead. He goes to get the bottle of aspirin, but finds instructions to consult a doctor for children under twelve. She's been growing fast, but he can't tell if she's the equivalent of twelve yet. Like an item on a grocery list he has forgotten, he pictures the pharmacy shelf he has often passed by, devoted to medicine for children. The amount of things he doesn't know suddenly seem to condense in a massive, dangerous form. He wants to yell at Aisling;

he warned her he couldn't handle this, he doesn't even have the common sense to keep baby aspirin in the bathroom cabinet.

But she has fallen asleep. The maps on her cheeks appear to throb
and deepen in color as she thrashes her head on the pillow. Is it his
imagination, or does her breathing seem labored? Oisin pulls a chair
to her bedside; he knows enough to keep watch, though he's not sure
what he's watching for. While she sleeps, he draws her over and over
in miniature, as if this will have some curative effect. Pencils and
sketchpads have always been the only tools he needed. Why has it
taken him this long to realize how useless they really are?

By three A.M., Aisling is delirious, and Oisin is in a panic. She is
calling him Darragh, and she seems to think he is the one who is sick.
This has been giving Oisin hints for how to help her.

"This is the last of the water, Darragh," she mumbles, and Oisin
tips a glass to her lips. When she asks Darragh if he is cold, Oisin
covers her with the blankets she kicked off moments before in sweaty
frustration.

In the last hour, Oisin has recalled every alarming medical story
he has ever heard. That too high a fever can actually boil the brain.
That meningitis seems to be on the upsweep again. It has the same
symptoms as the flu but requires a needle in the spine for diagnosis.
He wonders if she has eaten those poisonous red mushrooms that
look like ears, until he remembers that they are out of season. It is the
truth that he's most afraid of: he has no idea what's wrong and no way
to make her better. There is a local doctor, but Oisin is afraid to call
him. The last his neighbors knew, he had a first-grader staying with
him. There is no way a doctor would miss the fact that this girl is
quickly approaching puberty.

Aisling, who has been vomiting regularly into a pot by her bed,
now has the dry heaves, her body convulsing repeatedly until Oisin

feels like he is the one being turned inside out. When the reflex stops he helps her lie back down, wiping her mouth with a kitchen towel. She grips his arm, pinching him with her nails, and pulls him so he is looking closely at her eyes, the gold almost lost behind a milky, feverish film.

"Make sure I'm dead before you let them drop me overboard." She says this in an odd voice, not her own, as though she is trying to explain something horrible to a small child.

That's when Oisin goes for his jacket and, without a word, slams out the front door.

He has forgotten his flashlight, but the moon and the snow guide his way down the wooded path. He jogs as quickly as the icy ground allows, and for an instant, he is running past his own tears on the streets of South Boston, his voice croaking out for his mother, his legs unbearably heavy because his jeans are adhered to his thighs with blood.

When Deirdre opens the door to his pounding, she is already pulling her coat on over her pajamas. She does not look alarmed, only ready, like a woman used to emergencies; she waits for Oisin to speak. He catches his breath, trying not to sound like a frightened little boy. But there doesn't seem to be any other voice left in him.

"Please," he says finally. "I can't do this by myself."

9.

The first time Gabe was ever seriously sick, Deirdre panicked. At four months, he came down with the croup and woke in the middle of the night fighting for breath; his cough sounded like the barking of an alarmed seal. Deirdre's parents were vacationing in Florida, and the local doctor was on the mainland for the night, so there was no one to turn to. She brought Gabe into the bathroom and rubbed his back as she let the hot shower swallow them in steam. All she could think of were eighteenth-century British novels, in which babies were always dying of croup and women of consumption brought on by broken hearts. Her husband, Brian, also terrified, kept flipping through Dr. Spock and adjusting the shower spray, in what Deirdre had always called his operating-manual mode: the masculine need to stay active and useful in a crisis. Gabe swung between looking lost and miserable and, after rib-shaking coughs, smiling and bouncing, trying to entertain his worried parents. In the morning, when they brought him to the mainland emergency room, the doctor said he was fine, no need for a steroid shot. He'd seen worse cases of croup.

"But he still seems as if he's about to stop breathing," Deirdre said, and the doctor grinned, winking at Brian.

"Nothing like a mother's love for her son," he said, and Deirdre left the examination room in a huff.

Deirdre recognizes herself in the look on Oisin's face: an odd combination of guilt and accusation mingled with terror. He has run to her house, and he pushes his explanation out between gasps. When he gets to *Aisling* and *fever*, she tells him to wait. In the upstairs bathroom she pockets a forehead-strip thermometer and Children's Tylenol. She checks to see that Gabe is sleeping, writes him a quick note. She follows Oisin down the wooded path, jogging to keep up. Though on the short side, Oisin has the loping walk of a long-legged man.

She knows the instant she sees the girl that something is very wrong, something besides the fever. The girl in bed both is and isn't the same one she met three months ago. But her instincts push this thought to the back of her mind, and she steps forward with the thermometer.

When the red bar smears steadily up to the 105-degree mark, she orders Oisin to fill the bathtub with cold water and all the ice he can find. As she slips off Aisling's nightgown and lowers her into the tub, she can see the girl cringe with something more than cold. There is a look in her eyes that reminds Deirdre of Gabe when he was six, just after Brian died. As though she is trying to fold in on herself and blot out the world by refusing to respond to it. Her body under the water has a slight curve to the hips, her nipples are swollen in her still girlish chest. Deirdre swirls the water around, murmuring motherly words and shushes of comfort. When her fever is down to 101 degrees, Deirdre gives her the Tylenol and puts her back to bed.

Oisin is sitting at the kitchen table, looking young—both beaten and hopeful. Deirdre motions for him, and while he kneels by Aisling's bed, whispering his good nights, Deirdre boils water for coffee in the kitchen. By the time Oisin shuffles back to her, she has washed all the dishes in his sink and is setting two mugs, sugar, and milk on the table.

"Sit down, MacDara," she says. "And tell me why your seven-year-old niece is turning into a teenager."

D eirdre is not a stranger to the idea of ghosts. Her mother used to encounter "presences." On vacations, Mrs. Molloy would often change rooms after being kept awake by noises that Deirdre and her father couldn't hear. There had been a ghost in her childhood home, a small woman whom Mrs. Molloy often found sleeping in their beds. And there were houses on the island she refused to enter because of a dark sensation that made it difficult for her to breathe. Deirdre had grown up thinking that all mothers had such visions. When she was a teenager, she accused her mother of everything from lying to lunacy. By the time she was in her twenties, she had settled on acceptance tinged by skepticism. But after her father, then her mother, then Brian died, she preferred to think it possible that they were still present, if invisible. When Gabe was four, the year after his grandmother died, he woke Deirdre up a number of times with the complaint that there was a lady in his room. Brian called it bad dreams, but Deirdre found herself imagining her mother sitting guard at Gabe's bedside, the way she had once watched as Deirdre fell asleep.

But an open mind toward the spiritual realm was no preparation for what Oisin is telling her now. A child back from the dead, growing up in the house of the most unnurturing man she has ever met.

Oisin has left her to digest his story; he's sitting by Aisling with a deliberating hand on her forehead. Not for the first time, Deirdre wonders if Oisin is more than just eccentric. Perhaps he is psychotic, kidnapping blond girls of all ages, murdering them, and posing them in his studio. She can see the quote in the Portland paper: PEDOPHILE AND SERIAL KILLER CONVICTED. NEIGHBORS SAY: "WE THOUGHT HE WAS AN ARTIST."

She shakes the thought off as ridiculous. Oisin is not a bad man, just an odd one. Deirdre has seen the eyes of abused children at school, and Aisling does not have that look. And, though she cannot explain how, she knows this is the same girl she met before. The child has a beauty that is unique. And Deirdre remembers that she's had odd feelings all along, that she suspected without voicing it that Aisling was changing in a way that was alarming only in its pace.

Oisin disappears into the bathroom. Deirdre runs possible explanations through her mind in the same way she flips through the old card catalogue at school. Some children grow in such leaps they're left stretched and thin and bone-tired. Girls mature faster than boys, they enter high school towering and rawly feminine next to the boys, who look like fearful little brothers. Isn't there a disease where children have the body of an eighty-year-old by the time they're ten? Nothing clicks the answer tab in her mind. The only explanation that makes sense is Oisin's insensible one, which she cannot allow herself to believe.

"You think I'm crazy, don't you?" Oisin says. He has made more coffee, sets a fresh cup in front of her, and she stiffens as he leans just barely too close.

"I haven't decided yet," she says.

Oisin's smile is resigned, like that of a man who wished for something he didn't really expect to get.

"Do you want my help?" Deirdre asks. In all the years she's known Oisin they have never asked anything of each other.

"You could leave the baby aspirin," he says.

Deirdre rolls her eyes at his attempt to trivialize the situation. She takes a deep breath.

"Why don't I bring Gabe over sometime," she says gently.

"What for?" Oisin says.

"Because she needs to meet other children. Or she'll end up a female version of you."

"God forbid," Oisin says. Then he smiles.

Deirdre stays until the morning is bright, checking Aisling's fever periodically. When the strip reads normal, she gives Oisin some instructions and her phone number (she can feel both of them tripping over that—we've had sex but never exchanged phone numbers). Oisin steps outside to say good-bye, leaving the door open a crack in case Aisling makes a noise. Like a father, she thinks, and has a familiar prick of longing for Brian. She starts up the path but turns back with a question. Oisin looks tired and dangerously handsome under blue sky.

"How old do you think she is going to get?" she asks him, her voice full of the hushed fear she used to feel when her mother spoke of ghosts.

"I don't know," he says. But he looks startled, as if it is the first time this question has confronted him.

Deirdre is aware that most mothers think too much of their sons, which is why she tries not to brag about her own. People would think she was biased if she told them Gabe was a genius. She often feels inexperienced and slightly slow around her only child. He learned to read at three and was beating her at Scrabble and chess by the time he was seven. He has wise, steady, green-blue eyes which she often finds herself looking to for answers. And she always tells him the truth, because he was beyond child-sparing lies by the time he was two.

When she tells him about Aisling, she sees none of her own doubt, but only fascination in his marsh-colored eyes.

"Don't even think about it," she says, when he opens his mouth with an excited question. Gabe is going through a dissecting phase; he's been reading a medical school anatomy textbook before going to sleep at night. She can see him imagining the wonders to be found in slicing open a growing ghost.

"You don't believe him," Gabe says.

She rarely has to say what she is thinking to her son. He simply knows. "I do and I don't," she says. "I believe that he believes it."

"Not everything follows the rules of science," Gabe says. "Try to have an open mind."

Deirdre smiles. "Think like a child," she says.

"Exactly," Gabe replies.

This had been one of Brian's sayings. After he died, they packaged his words of wisdom like sentimental objects revisited in grief. Deirdre is often amused and slightly sad when she imagines how Brian would laugh at the sage he has become in his absence.

"I told Oisin you'd spend some time with her," she says.

"Sure." Gabe shrugs, but she can see that he's excited. She sometimes worries that he doesn't enjoy his friends. He is popular and outgoing at school (he was blessed with Brian's athletic ability, which distracts the other boys from his perfect grades), but Deirdre believes it is an effort for him to act like one of the crowd. She has seen him spend hours in the yard with boys his age, wrestling, trading foul jokes, and participating in farting contests, but he often comes inside looking exhausted. It is only after an evening surfing the Internet for physics articles that he seems to brighten up again.

"I'll need a new notebook," Gabe says, and Deirdre is suddenly grateful to Oisin and his strange girl. For her son is never as happy as when he has something to study.

They call by Oisin's three days later. Aisling opens the door wearing island shop overalls—a larger size than the ones she had three months ago, but still too small for her. Deirdre makes a mental note to pass along to Oisin the catalogues of children's clothes that clog her mailbox.

"How are you feeling?" Gabe asks Aisling after Deirdre introduces them. She can see his fingers twitching for a pen; she made him promise he wouldn't take notes in front of the girl.

"All right," Aisling says. She looks suspicious but curious, as though she'll risk anything to relieve her boredom.

Gabe teaches her to play Scrabble. Their two figures are still hunched and murmuring over the kitchen table when Deirdre comes back hours later. She recognizes the teasing banter of children who are already at ease in their fondness for each other.

"How'd it go?" she whispers to Oisin, who is wearing an apron. He's looking more domestic every time she sees him.

"Okay, I guess," he says. She smells something savory wafting from the kitchen. "I was in my studio, but I don't think they've moved since you left. It's amazing; last month she couldn't bear to lose at a game, she would cheat out of desperation. Now she's got a poker face and strategy."

He stops abruptly, looking embarrassed, perhaps at the gushing-parent tone in his voice. They stand in awkward silence for a moment on either side of the open door.

"Sorry," he blurts out, moving aside. "I haven't asked you in."

While Oisin excuses himself to go stir something, Deirdre loosens her scarf and looks around the room. She'd been so busy questioning him about Aisling last time, she'd forgotten to think back to her one long night in this house. Three years ago it had been deeply messy, layered with the sort of clutter and dust that accumulate over time. It had given the impression that Oisin didn't spend much time there, as if he only ever came in to eat and sleep. Now there are plants on the windowsills, the rug has been vacuumed, and the room has the pleasant smell of one that is lived in. Deirdre has a brief flashback to the odor of sputtering candles and Oisin's mouth, darkened by red wine and hours of kissing her. She shakes it away.

"Gabriel," she says. "Let's get going."

"Just let us finish this game," Gabe says, and he doesn't look up. She was sure he'd be desperate to come home after two hours of Scrabble with a girl his age. She walks to the table and looks at the game board.

"What's this supposed to be?" she says. The Scrabble board is filled with unrecognizable words: consonants that don't belong next to each other—*mh, bh, dh*—are married with vowels into nonsense.

"We're playing in Irish," Gabe says. "Aisling's teaching me. She's winning, of course, but I'm starting to catch on."

No doubt, Deirdre thinks. Gabe already knows French and Spanish and has sent away for a tape of conversational Japanese.

"Would you like to stay for dinner?" Aisling says, and Gabe has accepted before Deirdre can open her mouth. She looks at Oisin, who shrugs.

"There's plenty of food if you grab for it quick."

"It smells delicious," Deirdre says, trying to catch Gabe's eye and indicate her irritation, but he is rearranging his tiles.

"I didn't know you could cook," she adds, and Oisin looks confused for a minute.

"Why would you?" he replies. He says it so guilelessly.

Oisin serves them a soup that has layers of flavor: the sweetness of orange when Deirdre's lips touch the spoon, then the sting of chili peppers when she swallows. They have chicken baked with prunes and capers, wild rice that tastes like a bed of mushrooms. Aisling eats more than any child Deirdre's ever seen. Even Gabe, whose stomach has been bottomless lately, looks amazed.

After dinner, Deirdre helps Oisin with the dishes while the children sit by the fire conjugating Irish verbs. Listening to Gabe repeating Irish words reminds her of a record her father used to play when she was a child. She turns to say this to Oisin, but stops when she sees his face. His eyes are on them, but he is seeing something else.

"Do you have any siblings?" Oisin says. He goes back to drying the plate he'd forgotten in his hand.

Deirdre shakes her head. "Spoiled only child. My mother couldn't have any more after me."

"I had a twin," Oisin says softly. "A twin sister." But he has walked away to the bathroom before she can ask what happened to her.

It is ten o'clock by the time she convinces Gabe to leave. Aisling flashes her a rare, beautiful smile while Deirdre is putting on her coat. When Deirdre takes her hand in good-bye, something odd happens. Something that makes her believe everything Oisin has told her.

While the pressure of Aisling's palm is there, Deirdre can smell Brian. It is not cologne or maleness or the smell of pine needles that usually makes her miss him. It is what she dug through the laundry basket for on the day of his funeral: Brian's particular, intimate odor in all its complexity, as if she has just pressed her nose into the slight hollow in his chest. When Aisling lets go, it is gone.

Walking home, Gabe is quiet, but she can almost hear the whirring of his brain.

"I think she came on that ship Granddad told me about," he says finally. One of Brian's father's favorite tales is about how the Irish first came to the Yankee island one hundred and fifty years before.

"That's an idea," Deirdre says. But she is still dizzy from that handshake and not ready to think of anything else.

As she is tucking Gabe into bed, performing the nightly rituals that help to curb his worry-fueled insomnia, he reaches out and touches her cheekbone. She is surprised when he catches a tear.

"Did she give you Daddy?" he says, his eyes deeply green in the shadows of the room. Deirdre nods.

"Me too," he says. He falls asleep faster and easier than he has in all the years since they lost Brian.

10.

Aisling doesn't know why Oisin has stopped working, but it disappoints her. His art has a process that reminds her of farming. Each print is born from a long series of labors; at every step the threat of failure looms anew. A finished print seems as satisfying to him as a season's harvest, and Oisin is able, briefly, to allow himself to relax.

Aisling has watched him pass eight hours in his studio rolling cigarettes and stacking them in a pyramid, as though preparing for a time where he won't be able to spare a minute for such details. But if he works consistently, one black-and-white print takes a little over a week. He spends the first day or two sketching plans, the way her father, in the winter months, used to plot the land for the seeding in spring. Oisin's drawing days end with a floor covered in rejected slips of paper, which he drops without crumpling, letting them waft like birds across the open room. Aisling once tried to be helpful by gathering up all the abandoned pages. Oisin looked up when she was finished, alarmed.

"Put them back," he pleaded. "How am I supposed to know if I've done any work at all?"

So Aisling flung the drawings back onto the floor. Oisin, even with his graying hair, was prone to what she thought of as childish behavior. Aisling had had similar rituals when she was alive. She had assumed adulthood came when you left such uncertainties behind. But then she remembers her father counting and recounting coins, and her mother's superstitions, and wonders now if she'll ever be free of reassuring childhood rituals.

Once Oisin has a sketch he's satisfied with (though you'd never know it from his constant scowl), he cuts a square from the long slats of copper that lean against one wall. He dips one side of the metal into a tray of hot wax (the studio at this point smells like a room full of sputtering candles). When the wax dries from a clear liquid to a whitish film, Oisin spends three or four days drawing on it. With sharp tools, which Aisling has been forbidden to touch, he carves away at the wax until the sunburned color of the metal begins to peek through. He is copying his sketch, but with the image flipped backward, as though he is looking at their reflection in a mirror. Often he tests himself with the dusty mirror on the wall, holding the sketch up to it while carving a few lines. Sometimes he rips the wax off and starts the process all over again. Aisling, while listening to the soft slicing and Oisin's chorus of frustrated and satisfied grunts, thinks of Darragh on his knees, folding seeds into moist, cold soil, seriously, as though his demeanor alone will make them grow.

When Oisin is done carving, the sheet metal looks like a field of snow in the morning, punctuated by animal tracks. He fills a shallow bin with chemicals that burp up tiny pillows of noxious smoke. (He usually wears a heavy apron and snaps on yellow gloves, but sometimes he forgets, in his excitement, and has to spend the rest of the

night dabbing aloe on his raw and blistered patches of skin.) He
slides the metal carefully into this bin and waits with a timer while
the pool crackles and bubbles. Oisin explained to her that the chemicals eat away at the exposed bits of copper. So when he removes the
sheet and heats away the wax, his drawing has transformed into tex-
ture. He now has a print plate that he can layer with ink, cover with
paper and squeeze through what looks like a laundry press. What
comes out in the end is a more complicated version of the drawing
he did days before.

At first Aisling did not know why he bothered with so many
steps, when to her the resulting print looked the same as if he'd drawn
it in heavy ink. But after looking at dozens of his prints, she thinks
she understands why he creates these images so laboriously. Though
the etchings are flat, they seem to suggest within them all the layering
that went into their creation. She thinks if you could look backward
through time, and see the changes stacked up against one another, that
it would look like one of Oisin's prints. It would appear solid, but
would actually be constantly shifting, details catching your eye like
small voices crying for your attention.

Each day, when Aisling settles herself in the corner of the studio,
she hangs one of Oisin's prints on the wall next to her chair. At first,
expecting them to tell her something about this new world, his images
only confused her. They could have come from her world. The titles
are written in a strange but recognizable Irish, a dialect different from
her own. He has made a print for each of Darragh's seasons: Samhain,
Imbolc, Beltaine, and Lammas, each one depicting the same pair of
trees: lush and thick, shedding, sharp, empty branches, then peppered
with buds. There is a print titled *The Call of Oisin*, where a beautiful
woman in a cloak of stars sits on a horse by the rough edge of the
sea. Another print shows two children playing in the twilight, inked

in a shimmery blue-black. *Le Dúchán na Hoiche: At Night Fall.* She can hear the words in Darragh's voice, first a harmless phrase, then later, *dúchán,* meaning darkness, used to describe the evil that came to them from the ground.

Many of Oisin's prints are cluttered with figures, as though depicting a strange, mournful party. The figures fall into two categories: dark bodies etched with light, pale bodies scarred with darkness. She can't remember when she realized that the dark figures were ghosts. But now she is used to seeing the few living figures scrambling for the odd spaces left between the dead.

Oisin's repeating characters are mostly women. A large older woman who wears an apron and a tiny sparkling point in the corner of her eye. A voluptuous woman who is always lurking, watching something outside the barriers of the print. A girl the age of Aisling's own sisters, with a fiddle under her chin and dark bruises around her eyes. All the women, though etched with their own characteristics, have the similarities that come with families, and sometimes seem so interchangeable to Aisling that she imagines they are the same woman. One of Oisin's prints, the Goddess Brigid, is a head with three female faces—a girl, a woman, and an ancient lady whose wrinkles make her face look more substantial than the other two. Aisling likes to imagine that she herself is aging like this, trying on the bodies of older girls as though they were costumes. So she begins to collect reflections of herself, with the same ferocity she once collected coins.

She never paid attention to the bathroom mirror until the night she was tall enough to see a bit of her forehead reflected above the sink. She emptied the basket of Oisin's laundry, turned it over, and climbed up to study herself. She stayed in the bathroom until Oisin tapped on the door, memorizing her features. She had only ever seen her reflection a handful of times in her life, but she remembers a darker, thinner, more turned-in version of herself, like a flower closed against the cold. She is not sure she looks older, but she certainly appears brighter, which she attributes to all the extra washing (since Oisin showers every day, she does it as well, though once bathing was something saved for Saturdays). Now, along with the charcoal slashes Oisin makes on the doorjamb to record her growth each week, Aisling pays the mirror a visit every day for another form of measurement. If she looks at herself long enough she sees hints of people she thought she'd never see again. Her mother is there in the high slope of her forehead, her sister Margaret in the lobes of her ears. There is a tear-shaped birthmark on the skin of her neck that once belonged to Hannah. And Darragh's lashes frame the eyes that take it all in.

She begins to put on new personalities like costumes, making herself look like the characters she reads about. She changes the hair in her reflection so she looks mature, then girlish, then severe and serious. Each day that she notices a change in herself, she saves the old version in a box in her mind. She sees herself in stages similar to Oisin's prints, each step a preparation for the real person she will become. One day, when she is a woman, she will lay the versions out and trace her transformation through all the girls she has seen in the mirror.

Since she began looking at herself, she has had moments where she forgets her determination to be invisible. She talks to Oisin with a free, quick voice she once only used in the darkness with Darragh. The words will be out of her mouth before she even realizes she is speaking, and she often stops in the middle of an idea, remembering the stinging slap that used to come when she opened her mouth to her parents. Though sometimes Oisin barely notices her, often he seems to like it when she talks to him. His eyes widen and she often

detects the hint of a smile he is trying to hide. And then, occasionally, there is that feeling she had from Darragh, like a hand from his
mind, a small touch that works as a recognition. Like somebody whispering her name in a chant until, magically, just like when she walked
through Oisin's open door, she reappears.

When he is cooking her dinner, or when she catches him watching her in the studio, she believes that she is more than just a burden
to this grumpy man. That perhaps he has begun to *want* her there. He
gave her loads of presents for Christmas (in her old life, she was lucky
to get an apple). Her favorite gift was a bulb and a small clay pot to
plant it in. The bulb has begun to push out two snakelike stalks,
smooth green fingers that are taller every morning when she enters the
studio. The growth reminds her that this is life, not death, that she is
watching now.

Oisin's moods do not bother her. She believes that, like Darragh's,
his sense of obligation to her will always win out over his resentment.
She feels unexpectedly at home in the corners of his world. Though,
sometimes, even his house seems smaller than the mansion she once
thought it, just like the clothes and girls she has abandoned.

Though it would be a year before she understood it, death arrived on
their land with a smell. Aisling noticed it before the others; it interrupted her dreams. She woke in the middle of the night gasping and
choking as though large hands were pressing on her throat. Her gagging woke Darragh, who reached out to feel her forehead.

"Are you ill?" he said. Aisling had her breath back, but when she
inhaled through her nose, she started choking again.

"Do you not smell that?" she whispered. The odor had permeated
her mouth and her saliva had a cloying, rotten taste to it.

"It's only the rain, Aisling," Darragh said, turning away from her. "Go back to sleep."

Aisling lay back down and kept quiet. She had lived with the same palette of smells her whole life. She could recognize the odor of coming rain as well as her brother could; the sweetness in the air melted into the sour smell of the earth, as though the ground were opening its sleep-layered mouth in thirst. This odor, which choked, was not familiar to her, it came from a place she did not recognize. Not human or animal waste, not the salty decay on the beach, not the sour turning of milk. It was larger than any of these things, but similar, a rotten smell. As though the world itself had gone bad.

In the morning she went to see Darragh in the fields. When she'd rounded the hill, she could see another man standing in the field with her father. She knelt down and crawled in the tall reeds until she was close enough to hear them.

"It's only out of the kindness of a neighbor that I'm telling you this," the man said. It was Mr. Meagher from the farm to the north. He, like most of the villagers, was not fond of Aisling's family.

"It's hit every other parish in the west," Meagher said. "It's only a matter of time before it visits us. They're recommending we dig up the crop right away, to save at least a bit of the harvest."

"Is it the government telling us that?" Aisling's father said. His voice sounded cruel no matter what words he chose. "I'm not digging up my field in the middle of August. The potatoes won't be full-size for three months yet."

"There'll be nothing but rot if you wait three months," Meagher said. "Don't come begging to me when your family's starving." Meagher, after spitting just to the side of her father's boots, turned and walked away.

"Will we not dig a few up, Da?" Darragh said, in the solicitous voice he used with their father. "Just to be sure."

"They stay in the ground." His father grunted. The remains of a cigarette clung moistly to his brown lips.

"One of the beds is all I'm saying," Darragh tried, but his father silenced him with one look.

"Are you giving me advice, now?" he said in a mocking tone that Aisling associated with a flying fist.

"No, Da," Darragh said quietly.

"I'd take advice from a woman sooner than you," their father said. This was something he said often, and meant as an insult, though it made no sense to Aisling. Their father often deferred to his wife, through Darragh or the girls; their mother was clearly the smarter of the two.

Aisling lay flat on the ground while her father and then Darragh wandered heavily away. She knew better than to show herself to Darragh just then. Whenever he was ridiculed or beaten by their father he often ended up looking at Aisling as if his newest bruise, along with everything else, was her fault.

Aisling stayed in the field until the sun passed midday. The shifting rays highlighted the stalks above her, and she saw something white, delicate, and foreign clinging to the undersides of the leaves. It reminded her of the one time she'd seen snow, a weightless, crystallized whiteness. But when she touched it, it didn't melt, but stretched between her fingers like a disturbed spider's web. Even after she dipped her hands in the stream, the smell lingered. The odor that had woken her the night before now seemed to be coming from her palms, as though she were the one decaying from the inside out.

Darragh explained it to her at bedtime. There was a disease on the potatoes, a blight spreading to every field in the country. They were calling it *dúchán*, because it rotted the potatoes to blackness.

"Da's a fool," he whispered. "If we don't dig now we'll lose the whole crop."

"What will we eat if we lose the potatoes?" Aisling said. Darragh tried to lighten his voice when he saw her gold eyes twitching with fear.

"We won't starve, Aisling," he said. "The landlord will have to make allowances for us to keep the other crops."

Aisling knew he was lying. She had never heard of anyone, no matter how hungry, keeping the wheat, the oats, or the livestock. Not with permission anyway. There had been one farmer last year who had pilfered from his own harvest to feed his children. The bailiff had evicted him and set his house on fire.

She went to sleep with the smell in the back of her throat. The family already begrudged her every meal; if the food were to disappear, she felt sure she would be the first to starve.

For three days Darragh paced the fields like a soldier, peering under leaves to check for white fuzz, an early sign of disease. If he found it, he would wipe it away gently with a damp cloth, murmuring quietly, as he did whenever Aisling was bedridden with a cold. Watching him like this, Aisling was sure the crop would thrive. With his noble, kind face, she felt sure, the plants could not bear to disappoint him. Periodically, Darragh dug up one or two stalks, searching for soft spots on the vegetables. He would rebury the roots afterwards, disguising his digging with old soil. Each day news came to them of another field stricken by the blight. Darragh was encouraged by the wind, which for days had been blowing easterly from the sea. He thought perhaps their fields, the closest to the shore, might be saved. Especially if he dug the instant he saw any early signs.

But it only took the few hours they were sleeping for the whole crop to die. At dawn, Aisling woke to the smell worse than ever before, as though the source of it had finally split open to reveal a far more potent center. For once, she moved without Darragh there to encourage her. She ran to the fields and found her whole family hunched and digging in the soil. The rows of plants were black and damp, as though they'd been doused after a fire. Aisling walked closer to see over her sister Margaret's shoulder. Margaret's fingers were searching for the familiar lumps of the potatoes, but were only squeezing through a mush darker than soil. Margaret was crying, her face contorted by overwhelming odor and grief. Aisling, forgetting herself, put a hand on her sister's shoulder. Margaret shook her off so violently that Aisling landed on her bottom in dirt littered with foul remains.

"You've cursed us, you filthy bastard," Margaret hissed. "You won't see me starve for your sins. I'd rather eat you first."

Though it was a ridiculous thing to say, Aisling looked at Margaret's brown, sharp teeth, and imagined the sound they would make biting into her. She got up and ran from the field, hiding alone underground until the moon was out, when Darragh came home smelling of rotted earth, his fingers torn and bleeding from searching all day for even one edible plant. He fell into bed and before dropping into exhausted sleep, he put a filthy, gentle hand on her head.

"This hasn't to do with you," he said, indicating that he had overheard Margaret that morning. Aisling, though grateful for his words and the warmth that came from his palm, was not comforted. She could hear his voice asking a cruel question. *Why* was a word that seeped from Darragh no matter how hard he tried to hide it. Why me, why now, why this. And Aisling was fearfully aware that her name—the name only Darragh had bothered to give her—was the answer.

After the night she had the flu, Aisling began having nightmares. Gone are the deep, redemptive sleeps of the first months of this new life. In one dream, Darragh has shrunk so much from the fever that she can carry him in the pocket of her sweater. But there is a hole in her pocket, and she keeps losing him, and she must feel around in the dark hold of the ship before he gets squashed. Sometimes, when she finds him, it is not Darragh, but Oisin who crouches in the palm of her hand.

She dreams that Oisin is ill, lying on her small bed, and when she wipes his face with a cloth, the flesh goes black and caves in like a wet hole in soil. She dreams of walking the beaches of her home, frantically searching for Oisin, whom she has seen disappear beneath cold silver waves. She wakes most nights at three A.M., the same time that Oisin is brooding, awake in his own bed, and she crawls in beside him. She arises sweat-soaked and nervous in the mornings, and needs to check that Oisin is in sight with obsessive regularity. She has trouble breathing if he drives to the shop alone or leaves for a walk before she wakes in the morning.

One day, while chopping onions for soup, he cuts his thumb, and the sight of him bleeding makes her cry with deep, stormy sobs. How could she have forgotten the things that can happen to people?

Gabe now comes to play board games with her a few times a week. She has seen the way he looks at his mother when she comes to collect him—as though a pinch has been released behind his eyes. So, while they play Othello, white and black discs competing with encroaching lines, she asks Gabe's advice.

"How do I keep him alive?" she says.

Gabe does not laugh at her the way she suspects Oisin would.

"Knock on wood three times whenever you imagine something bad happening to him. Don't let him drive after drinking wine. And make him quit smoking. Cancer."

Later, when they are alone, Aisling stands in front of Oisin trying to look severe.

"Don't you know that smoking makes you die young?" she says.

Oisin sighs. "Wonderful," he says. He seems to think this funny, but she notices that he is smoking less each day.

In March, when it should be spring, there is still frozen snow on the ground, which squeaks with mocking cold under her boots. She wakes on the night of Saint Patrick's Day from a nightmare in which Oisin repeatedly wraps himself in a sheet and leaps from a boat deck into a storming sea. She lies still, fearful she might have screamed out loud, but she can hear Oisin breathing regularly across the room. The moon is full; the cottage blooms with dusty light.

She turns toward the wall, where she has pinned her favorite of Oisin's prints. A leafless tree stretches its limbs like thin, multijointed arms across the paper. Hanging crouched from the branches, taking up every inch, are the dark figures of ghosts. They all look down toward a kneeling boy, so faint you can see the bark of the tree showing through his chest. The boy has been digging with his hands, a hole in the earth in front of him, a pile of rocky soil at his side. In back of the tree are slabs and crosses of slate, rows retreating backward into the distance, an endless graveyard. The boy is so focused on his digging that he doesn't seem to notice his audience in the tree, or the girl who stands just to the right of his hunched shoulders. She is older than Aisling but not yet grown up, with the night sky reflected in the smooth surface of her hair.

When Aisling first found this print, pressed between two pieces of cardboard and nestled in a leather sleeve, she knew that this was the girl Oisin was looking for. Unlike the other figures, she is a combination of light and darkness, the dead and the living both etched in her delicate face. In an effort to imitate the smooth, unrippled hair of this girl, Aisling combed oil through her hair. She does not look old enough yet to pretend to be the girl in the print. But she feels like her. Because this girl's presence throbs on the page, waiting for Oisin to notice her.

Lying in her bed, sleep threatening to recapture her eyes, Aisling, for the first time since she arrived, is no longer hungry. Hunger, like growth, has its stages, and, in the past three months, she has reexperienced every level, from a stomach left not quite full, to the pain that feels like being chewed from the inside out. It hasn't mattered that she eats more in one sitting than she used to eat in a week; the emptiness is bigger than anything she fills herself with. But now it is gone and she feels not as if she has finally eaten enough, but as if she no longer needs to eat at all. Just before she falls back to sleep, she hears Darragh's voice coming weakly out of foul-smelling darkness.

"You eat it, Aisling. The hunger's gone off me."

"Don't leave me behind." She thinks this plea is in her mind, but she must have said it aloud, because a voice answers her.

"I didn't," says Oisin. "I won't."

11.

As a boy, all of Oisin's fear, along with his love, was tied in a complicated knot to his sister. He did not fear her death so much as the idea of anything that might separate them. Coma was a word that stopped his heart—that image of Nieve, tubed and unreachable. When the local police chief came to their school to talk about safety and strangers, Oisin began to keep an eye out for kidnappers. He had recurrent nightmares in which Nieve was trapped in a place he could not reach—in a maze, behind a wall of fire, sucked away in gel-like darkness. His worst fear, the one that clutched like a claw at his throat, was of his own death. He was terrified he would die first, and she would not be able to find him. He would become one of the lonely ghosts that came to him for comfort, because those they had loved could not hear their voices.

By the time he was ten, Oisin had an impressive résumé of ghost sightings, ranging from angelic to ghastly. He had woken to find the road running past his nana's house thronged with a procession of ghosts, limping along in a mournful mass, exhausted, as though they had been marching that way for an eternity. He had been visited in his bedroom in Boston by men looking for their wives, mothers looking for their babies, beggars looking for money. Once, there was a mapmaker who had been dead for centuries, sitting at the desk where Oisin did his homework, muttering and wearing down the points of all his pencils. "It's a map of the new world," he'd told Oisin, "and I'll never have it done in time." He'd sent Oisin away for matches to relight his eternally snuffed-out candle.

Oisin was likely to get out of bed for a glass of water and walk into a room full of immigrants sleeping head to toe on the kitchen floor, their bodies forming a crossword puzzle he had to hop and shuffle through. At times, exhausted from their journeys, the immigrants would ignore him beyond the occasional hungry look. Other times he was kept awake all night, told stories of long ship journeys in broken English, played haunting Russian tunes on an old accordion, or made to share stale bread with Italian mothers who thought he was another orphan. Nieve would find him in the mornings, half asleep at the table, murmuring polite words to an empty room. Oisin went to school in a daze, circles under his eyes, baffling his teachers. They believed he was smart but lazy; they didn't realize he was simply too tired to memorize his multiplication tables. The only thing he was able to do with any enthusiasm was draw. His teachers would lose patience with him and send him to a corner alone, and he would wear down crayons layering large pieces of white paper with intense colors. He drew portraits of whoever had visited him the night before, and while he was drawing he felt revived. But he was disappointed whenever he finished; his drawings looked like people when they were meant to be ghosts.

Though he never cried after the first banshee, and though he kept most of his sightings to himself, his family always knew when he'd seen something that scared him, because, like the first time, it would leave him temporarily blind. A raging eye infection would send him to bed for days, where Nieve would tend to him with warm compresses, picking away gently at the loosened crust with her fingernails. She feigned fevers and stayed home from school with him, exchanging travel stories and playing him music, blaring the volume on her plastic, 45 rpm record player. While Oisin lay supine beneath a steaming facecloth, Nieve would dance across their bedroom, belting out lyrics about love along with the tinny speakers. Sometimes she would change the words and sing about Oisin and the ghosts, whom she made out to be grumbling and harmless. Usually after a few verses, she would get a smile out of her brother, the cloth over his eyes wrinkling in reflection of his grin.

For the twins' tenth birthday, their uncle Malachy sent them what they thought of as their first grown-up presents. To Oisin, he mailed a tin of one hundred chalk pastels, the expensive, professional kind, with colors never imagined by crayons. On the journey from Ireland, they'd been so battered that when Oisin opened the box, he found only a jumble of colored chips and brilliant dust. Oisin was not disappointed; he thought if they had survived the trip, they might have been too perfect to use. He wedged colored slivers under his fingernails and drew away. But even pastels couldn't capture his ghosts.

To Nieve, Malachy wrote a note that he heard she'd expressed an interest in music (what her father had written was that the girl was obsessed with modern American rubbish). Her gift was an amber Irish fiddle, and the promise of lessons in the summer. Nieve was so delighted with the gift that for the rest of the school year she played it almost constantly. By the time Malachy could give her lessons, she'd already taught herself enough to follow him on simple tunes.

"I believe this girl's got the ear," Malachy said. Nieve had walked around stroking her ears for so long after that, her mother said you'd think she'd been deaf and had just learned to hear.

"It's almost like that, Mother," Nieve replied.

Her mother frowned. "All that practicing is forming a callus on your neck," she rebuked. Everything they said to each other hinted at fiercer, unspoken words.

When Oisin was up late with ghosts, it was Nieve who witnessed the real-life melodramas of their parents. Oisin would be listening to an immigrant tale and be suddenly distracted by the yelling of his mother. He wandered between these fights as if they were a vague background that did not interest him. Compared to his ghosts, his parents and their hard words were shadows. Nieve paced the house as if her presence could keep the fights under control—though her parents barely noticed her. If she came home late from a friend's house, she would interrogate Oisin for updates.

"What were they fighting about?" she'd say, and Oisin would not be able to remember. Every row seemed the same to him, his mother pouring words onto his flinching father, who only fought back on the days just before he was due to leave for sea.

"They were drinking," he would say, but Nieve was never satisfied with this explanation. She was far more interested in their parents' relationship than Oisin was. And while Nieve was concerned with the drinking (she often poured most of a bottle of gin down the bathroom sink and diluted the rest with water), Oisin accepted it as an inevitable character in their lives, like a third, ill-suited sibling.

Everyone drank; this was a fact that Oisin barely thought about. Adults drank and they changed and you avoided them as much as possible while they were at it. Nieve was the one who had taught him this in the first place.

When they were still very young, their parents would have cocktail parties, and the laughter and clinking of glassware would lull the twins to sleep. They were not supposed to be up, but occasionally, if it was late, they could sneak out when the atmosphere was jovial enough that they wouldn't be scolded. Oisin had blurred memories of standing by his mother's glimmering legs, watching as she laughed in a wild, unrecognizable way, feeling her hand playing heavily with his hair. There was something on those evenings that hinted at danger in his mother, whenever he saw the odd swaying of her body. As though she were on the verge of losing her balance, but, by some miracle, always stayed on her feet.

Oisin was seven when he learned to separate his drinking mother from the reliable one. He woke in the late night sweating and flooded with nausea. The odd sensations made him reluctant to move, and when the hot, fluttery feeling that warned him he was going to vomit came, he had no time to move from his bed. He threw up repeatedly all over the front of his bedcovers, and by the time he could breathe again, he was crying. He found his way to the living room, half blinded by his tears. A party was in its final stages, and there were only about ten guests left. Oisin found his mother slumped on the sofa, her short skirt hiked up so that the gauze triangle at the crotch of her nylons was visible. There was a man next to her, a man who worked with his father, and he was half lying on her shoulder, whispering solemnly in her ear.

"Mama," Oisin said, and he had to say it twice more before Sara, with difficulty, could focus on him. Her eyes didn't seem to be working correctly, and eventually she slapped her hand hard on his shoulder, as if he were the one weaving.

"This," she said, her voice thick until she burped and set it free a bit more, "is the only man for me." The man at her shoulder mumbled and went closer to her ear to say something, and Oisin saw a flash of his yellowed tongue as it scraped his mother's earlobe. He felt a new wave of nausea.

"Mama," he said, "I threw up." The man wrinkled his nose as the smell of Oisin reached him. He shifted away from Sara as though she were responsible.

"Whoops," his mother blurted out, with a giggle that soon spread to the man. Suddenly they were both laughing, their necks lolling around on the back of the couch. Oisin backed away.

"It's okay, Ossie," a voice said behind him, and he was led from the room by his sister's decisive, gentle hands. Nieve brought him to the bathroom, peeled off his damp pajamas, and set him in a warm tub. She washed him gently and then fetched a huge blue towel, rubbing his hair dry in the frenzied way they both preferred. If you hummed along, the vibrations came out in your voice. She gave him new pajamas and she brought him back to her own bed and its cool, clean sheets. In the dark, with her quick, efficient movements, Oisin imagined that this was not his twin sister, but the ghost of some motherly woman, making everything all right.

"Throwing up is worse than anything," she said, tucking him within the coolness. She even sounded older. "I always think I'm going to die."

Oisin wanted to say that no, it wasn't the worst, that throwing up was not half as bad as the revolting look on their mother's face when she slurred the word "whoops."

"What's wrong with Mama?" he said instead. It occurred to him that his mother was also ill, that it was some sort of flu that made her so flushed and unrecognizable.

"She's just drunk," Nieve said, crawling into bed with him. She was calm, dismissive; her voice had the same tone as his nana's when she examined a cut and said, "That's not as grave as it looks." This was not an emergency, it was something he needed to get used to.

He learned to ignore it. He avoided his drunk mother when he could, suffered her when he had to, but always distinguished her from the mother that was returned to him in the morning, pale but recognizable. The sharp difference between the two of them made this fairly easy to do. When his father was away at sea, she would often drink alone, slowly at dinner and speeding up as the twins got into bed (for the rest of his life, the smell of gin would remind Oisin to brush his teeth). When Oisin's ghosts kept him up, he would encounter a sloppy, maudlin version of his mother late at night. This woman would pull him on her lap, hug him until his breath was gone, and run her fingers, with their brightly colored nails, over his body in a way that made him grateful no one was watching. Sometimes she kissed him slowly on the mouth, her tongue poking at his clamped lips as though she were tasting him. Then there would be a quiz.

"Who do you love best?"

"Mama."

He separated his answers the way he separated his drunk mother from his safe mother. He said, "Mama"; he thought, You're not my mother, and I love Nieve best.

Eventually he barely listened to the questions because they were always the same.

"If I die, who will look out for me?" his mother would slur.

"I will."

He would endure this ritual, his ghosts calling him in the background, until his mother let go of him to pour herself another gin.

"Go play with the dead, Oisin," she would say, "I'll see you to-morrow." Tomorrow was the key word, because that's when she'd be-come his real mother again, and he could forget about this one until the next time.

Though he never told Nieve about his mother's scenes (to discuss it would remind him of what he found so easy to forget), he would occasionally be at breakfast and see his sister gazing with a suspicious, slightly frightened expression at his mother. It occurred to him that Nieve must have seen something similar, or even worse, in the middle of the night. And that she had forgotten what she taught him in the beginning—to find a safe place and put it away.

One night, years later, Oisin woke to voices so cruel, he thought ghosts were dredging up a 200-year-old feud in his living room. He left the bedroom without stopping to find his slippers, bouncing along on the balls of his feet to avoid resting too long on the icy floor. He found not spirits but his mother and sister, upright and tan-gled together in an awkward embrace, weaving so much that at first he thought they were dancing. But Nieve was trying to help his mother walk. He could have helped—actually pictured himself stepping for-ward and steadying his mother from the other side. But he couldn't move. There was something about the jellied movements of his mother and the balancing act of his sister that was so grotesque, he could not bear to join in. This is wrong, he thought, as he watched Nieve try to untangle her hair from under his mother's arm. This is not how things are meant to be.

Then his mother pitched backward, sliding out of Nieve's grip. Her head met the coffee table with a crack, and Oisin looked away. It was like watching a clumsy child in gym class, whose accident makes you laugh even as you blush with empathy.

"Bitch," his mother said, her tongue sounding wooden in her mouth. She waved Nieve's hands away, trying to roll herself upright.

"Don't touch me," she sneered. Then her voice became young and mocking. "Mama come to bed, Mama, Mama, Mama." She struggled to stand, weaving in Nieve's direction.

"Just the sound of you," she said, trying to focus on Nieve's face, "makes me nauseous. Self-righteous little bitch, dragging your father and brother around by their cocks. You know what you'll be when you stop giving them hard-ons?" His mother began to giggle, allowing Nieve to grab her again and lead her toward the hall. "Nothing!" she sang out. "Nothing nothing nothing." Laughing so hard she did not see Oisin through her tears and spasms, allowing Nieve to drag her to bed.

Oisin waited up for his sister, listening to the thumps, gagging, laughter, and then tears that came from his parents' room across the hall. When she finally came back, she slipped into her own bed quietly, as if she hoped that Oisin was asleep. Oisin was quiet for a while, listening to her breathing, which kept catching in a way she was trying to hide.

"Nieve?" he said finally, unable to think of a question that did not sound as ridiculous as the scene he just witnessed. He wanted to know if they always hated each other like that, and how it was that he never noticed.

"She's just drunk," Nieve said. The words did not have the same dismissive comfort they'd once had. Was drink that powerful, that it could create a monster out of a mother?

"But, Nee," Oisin began.

"It's okay," Nieve said.

She was lying. It was the first outright lie she'd ever told him, and he did not know how to react to it. Should he accuse her, demand confession? Or stay silent and act as though he believed her?

In the end, as always, he followed her lead and pretended to sleep. After that, he no longer seized up with fear over comas or his sister's kidnapping. He already knew, though he was an adult before he understood it, that there were subtler forces at work. It wouldn't take a disaster to set him and Nieve on different paths.

12.

Gabe Molloy is a collector of death. He keeps his research in color-coordinated notebooks—articles, textbook diagrams, even poetry, which he cuts to size with a razor blade and secures with a glue stick, until the notebook swells like a fan with an overload of information. He has a dissection lab set up in his room, where he slices and draws the dead animals he finds in the woods. He is able to answer any question about the workings of the human body, knows step by step the breakdown of systems involved in every form of death. His favorite book is *Frankenstein;* his goldfish is named Lazarus XIV (the previous thirteen did not live up to the name). According to Oisin, Gabe is considered a genius by most of the islanders. When she sees Gabe, the word that comes to Aisling's mind—in English now, like all her thoughts—is not smart, but scared.

Gabe is scared in a different way than Aisling. It's not people he's afraid of, and he doesn't feel threatened by being young. He is afraid of death, which is why he studies it. He knows how people die, but what he wants to find out is why. He sometimes reminds her of Darragh, who, until the very end, thought that staying optimistic and organized would save them.

Gabe now has a notebook dedicated to her; a hardcover spiralbound swirled in silver, which makes her dizzy if she looks at it too long. She endures his interviews, revealing details she would rather forget, because Oisin is always listening. It is easier to answer Gabe's blunt questions than to try to tell Oisin who she was. She is afraid of telling him too much. Oisin has become more often sweet than surly, but there are still those moments when she turns to him bursting with joy and she finds his old self, vacant and uninterested or even slightly annoyed. She feels as though a door has been slammed, clouting her with frigid wind, and each time it happens it takes a bit longer for her to recover. She needs to fold away and rebuild her strength before speaking to him again. Oddly, he often recovers before her, seems confused and hurt by her prolonged silence.

So she answers Gabe's questions, and while he notes down details, she watches Oisin's reaction. He pretends not to listen, but tenses his shoulders and breathes like an eavesdropper—not at all, then with far too much enthusiasm.

"Who died first?"

"Himself took it first and was the quickest. Then Hannah, then Aileen, then Margaret, then Herself. Darragh died on the ship."

"What was the first symptom of the sickness?"

"A bad smell."

"What's the last thing you remember before you died?"

"A lady asking me my name, and me too thirsty to tell it."

When Gabe first hears her story, he searches his attic and finds the weathered wood board carved with the words *Tír na nÓg*. He gives it to Aisling and she can only nod.

"My ancestors came on this ship," he says. "With you."

She cannot answer Gabe's questions about where and who she has been for all this time. Now that she is used to her physical self again, the memories of before are vague. She can only remember a sleepiness, and her determination to stay invisible. A century and a half seems to have passed in an instant, as if it were only last year that she watched the land and then her family rot away, until the very air she breathed was heavy with the stench of death.

When the poor started to die in large numbers, after the potatoes failed for the second year in a row, they began dumping the bodies in mass graves, transporting them in reusable coffins—wooden boxes with trapdoors fitted in the bottom. A twist of the catch and bodies were disposed of with a sickening slide and thud. Whole families were transferred in the same wooden box, piled on top of one another, generations filling the pits to their brims.

"Don't let them put me in one of those boxes," Aisling said to Darragh one night in the underground room, where they had chosen to remain though the house was now empty.

"There's no need for that talk," Darragh said, holding her tightly against the xylophone of his ribs. "I've a plan."

Her brother was never without a plan. The first winter they'd had to survive without the potatoes and, as if by a curse, the herring deserted the coast as well. It was Darragh who collected seaweed and pounded limpets off the rocks in the harbor, and boiled them into a thin, salty soup. Darragh decided to slaughter the pig, even though they needed it to sell for the next rent payment. Aisling held the bucket when he slit the squealing gray throat, and she was so hungry even the steaming blood looked appetizing. He killed a few rabbits by waiting motionless outside the entrance to their dune lairs. He sold off the turf, weighing the importance of food against the luxury of warmth. Aisling had to sew blankets into ponchos for wearing over their thin clothes. When the public works began, Darragh spent long days building roads through Connemara, and came home with corn-meal or the occasional egg, which they split between the two of them. Aisling was his priority in the doling out of food, though the rest of the family was not aware of this. Had they known, Aisling was sure one of her sisters would have killed her for the egg.

Darragh was a font of optimism and temporary solutions. Like his father and many others, he believed the blight would only last one season, so he focused only on how they would survive until the next harvest. By the time the crop failed again, there was nothing left. No livestock, no grain, and no money to pay the rent to the landlord, who was still collecting as though nothing had changed. The hunger and debt alone might have caused Darragh panic, if he had not been dis-tracted by everyone around them beginning to die.

When the fever reached their house, Aisling knew it first. She could smell it. She passed by Himself on the way to the bog, and though she was so quiet he didn't notice her, the odor off him made it as difficult to breathe as if he'd kicked her in the stomach. It was the same smell that came from the ruined crops, as though inside he was as black and slimy as the remains of their fields. An hour later he was bedridden with cramps, explosive vomiting, and a face al-ready blue with death, though he hung on for three more days. The women of the house, though there was no love lost when he was alive, fell apart when he died. They turned to Darragh with shrunken, hungry faces, begging for help even as their eyes sparked with blame.

He didn't have to care for them long.

They nursed one another until they were all stricken, and then Darragh moved among them like a doctor in a fever ward, forbidding Aisling to enter the house. Each night, when he came back to their room for a few hours of sleep, he scrubbed his body and clothes with boiled water, shivering naked in the autumn air. Even freshly cleaned, he smelled of the fever when he crawled in beside her.

Aisling spent her days roaming the shore, collecting the seaweed that had ceased to have a taste to her. When she passed by the house she could hear, through the small, deep window, the moans and phlegmy hacking of a house full of women she had never really known. She often prayed for forgiveness for her cruel satisfaction over the suffering of the people who had never shown her love. Though she'd been told that God turned a deaf ear to bastards, she believed in her own version of the Lord, who looked as hungry as she, and had the kindness of Darragh.

She never saw the mean faces of her sisters again. They dropped off one by one like insects in a jar, and were taken from the house in those deceptive coffins, loaded onto carts already heavy with bodies. Though Aisling watched them driven away with her face posed in grief, she felt nothing.

On a frigid day in February, when she found the beach stripped clean of every piece of edible refuse, Darragh told her he needed to leave for a while. He was walking to Clifden, where he hoped to find relief projects that were still dispensing cornmeal. The trip there and back would take him a day, a night, and most of the next morning.

"I've left Mammy enough water, and moved her near the hearth so she can feed the fire on her own. I'll see to her when I get back. There's nothing else you can do for her, Aisling, so promise me you won't go in there."

"I promise."

Darragh left at dawn. She avoided passing the house for the first few hours, stayed below ground with the straw bedding on top of her for warmth. By midday, the woman's screams were audible even from the underground room. She managed to ignore the pleas for Darragh, but when the voice started calling *Aisling*, a name she couldn't remember any of them ever using before, she could no longer stay away.

Inside the house it was so dark, it took her a moment of blinking before she could see. The stench was so thick she was swimming in it. When the room bloomed in front of her it was bare. The few trinkets had been sold off long ago—the table and chairs, the single lace curtain, the mismatched bits of china from the aunt in Dublin who had worked as a chambermaid. All that was left were dewy stone walls and the cold earthen floor, a bed of straw and sooty blankets lying close to the hearth.

The woman beneath the bedclothes was the size of a nine-year-old child; but her face was twice what it used to be, bloated and foul. Aisling realized with a quick fear that this was what death was—after spending all your life trying to grow up, you ended it by shrinking backward to the helplessness of an ill and swollen child.

"I've no water left," the face said, and Aisling saw that she'd tipped the bucket beside her, and the puddle had long ago been swallowed by the floor.

"I'll fetch some," Aisling whispered, and she grabbed the bucket quickly, afraid the woman's hands might dart from beneath the blanket to maul her ankles. When she returned from the well, she had to tip the dented tin mug against lips that resembled two worms left to bake in the sun.

"Where's your father?" the woman said when she'd gulped her fill.

"Dead, miss," Aisling whispered. The woman ordered her to speak up, so Aisling repeated herself.

"And the boy?"

"Gone to town to look for food."

"Men are fools," the woman said, dropping her head back on the straw. Aisling was tempted to ask, Who was the bigger fool? The one for dying or the other for keeping on?

"Will you be wanting anything else?" she said instead. The woman's face clenched with what was either a threat of tears or a strong pain.

"I will," she said. "A priest. And be quick, I'm dying."

Aisling found the priest at the village church, moving swiftly in his robes among bodies laid head to head along the stone floor. She had never been inside the church before, never seen this man except from afar. She crept up behind him, half expecting her breath to leave burns on the skin of his neck. Bastard, her mind was saying, the syllables bouncing along with the panic of her heart.

"Father?" she said quietly, and he turned, his black skirts billowing across the face of a man too weak to move his head away.

"Yes?" he said. He looked unwell himself, as hungry and tired and flushed as those moaning with fever on the floor.

"It's my . . . mother. She's dying and asking for a priest."

"They're all dying," he said, sweeping his arm. "If I leave, twenty will be gone before I get back. Can you not bring her here?"

"I'm on my own," she said.

"What's your name?" the priest said, crouching to check the breath of a still woman beneath them.

"Quinn, Father." He froze. She should have lied, for now he knew exactly who and what she was. He rose quickly and reached into his cassock, she felt sure for some weapon with which to strike her out of this holy place. He removed a small clay vial instead.

"Are you familiar with the last rites?" he said, handing her the tiny container. She shook her head. A nun gestured to him from the corner, and the priest took Aisling's arm and led her through the maze of bodies.

"Mind what I do now," he said, leaning over the figure of a boy. Aisling looked at the face. It was a friend of Darragh's, whose name she could not remember, a boy who'd been there the night they shaved the mound to see who would die first. He responded to the priest's gentle questions without opening his eyes. The priest blessed him, rubbing the oil in the shape of a cross on his eyelids. Aisling memorized the words, chanting them in her mind the way Darragh had taught her to remember poems.

"God will go with you, child," the priest said, laying his hand, shiny with the oil of death, on her hair. And for the briefest moment, something she had only felt a few times—mostly in the presence of Darragh—came over her stronger than ever. The sense that she was safe, that the world was exactly as it should be, that her circumstances, finally, were more than fair. She had believed God was with her, and now this priest had made it true. She was too weak to run home, but she moved quickly, clutching the vial like a jewel in her hand.

The woman's breath was now labored and ugly.

"Where is the priest?" She wheezed.

"He couldn't come. I'm to do it," Aisling said. The woman looked confused.

"You were a fierce one when you were inside me," she said. "Kicked like the devil himself. I'd no idea what you wanted. I hadn't a moment's peace."

Aisling tipped the vial, smearing musky oil onto her thumb and forefinger.

"Are you sorry for your sins?" she said in a low voice.

"I am," the woman said, her inflection like a question, as if she were not sure she was answering correctly.

"In the name of the Father, the Son, and the Holy Spirit," Aisling chanted. "Through this holy oil and through His most sweet mercy, may the Lord forgive whatever sins thou hast committed by sight." And one by one, repeating the blessing as the priest had, Aisling anointed the eyes that had rarely looked at her, the ears that were deaf to her, the nostrils so often flared in disgust, the mouth of harsh words, the palms that stung, and the feet, dirty and layered with tough skin like her own.

Her mother's eyes grew darker, darting from Aisling's eyes to her hands, and then to the doorway, as if she were still hoping to be saved.

Aisling is not aware of her power to bring Gabe his father until she does it. When he first appeared, she knew he had been lingering awhile. He is a tall, fragile-looking man, with large, almost feminine eyes and a smile that seems bigger than the whole of him. Finding him now is as simple as turning a knob; she knows when he is there and that it takes a touch from her to let him through.

Once she let Brian out there were others. They appear behind their loved ones, shadowed like one of Oisin's prints, and Aisling must find opportunities to touch strangers—the brush of fingertips while making a purchase, the press of arms in a tight corner. When she manages contact, the ghost disappears, dissolving into the person's skin, and it is like watching ecstasy race over every inch of them with tiny feet.

Though she has tried calling him for what seems like forever, Darragh remains hidden. She can't use this gift for herself. Or Oisin. Their ghosts are still hiding.

Oisin and Aisling continue to push and pull away; she feels one of two things in his presence: overwhelmed or rejected. There are days when Oisin comes to collect her and Deirdre invites him for dinner, and for an hour they are the parody of a family. She likes this, but what she enjoys even more is walking home alone in the twilight with Oisin, who often holds her hand and asks about her day. Deirdre has remarked that he is smiling more. Maybe even Oisin has moments where he thinks all is right with the world.

Then there are the days where one or both of them is taken by a mood. When Oisin trips over something of hers and curses the loss of his privacy. When she gets so enraged that he is not Darragh she won't speak to him for hours. And when the changes in her body, which she used to delight in, make both of them uncomfortable.

She smells different now; riper, fermented like one of Gabe's molds under glass. Her sisters smelled like this, and she is now showering twice a day, using up whole bottles of baby shampoo to mask her reek. Just when she gets used to the odor, she notices coarse hairs springing from between her legs that seem to multiply into a patch of fur almost overnight. Her chest starts to ache and swell so consistently that she asks Gabe if she might have an infection. He blushes when she lifts her blouse. The afternoon she finds dark blood in her knickers she cries through Deirdre's entire explanation of sanitary napkins, heating pads, and ibuprofen.

"Part of growing up," Deirdre says lightly. "Isn't that what you wanted?"

"I don't see how *blood* is necessary," Aisling says, and Deirdre has to apologize for laughing.

The worst moments are when Oisin stares, not with the wonder he used to, but with an expression she thinks is disgust. When he speaks to her, his eyes tend to wander down, and what he finds makes

him blink and forget what he was saying. She has started wearing clothing that is way too big, ordering from the catalogues that litter every
surface of Gabe's house, and she hunches so obviously, Deirdre gives
her a lecture on posture. What Aisling finds beautiful on grown
women seems deformed on herself. One of her breasts is growing
faster than the other; she is sure her lopsidedness is visible to everyone.

When Oisin is in his studio pretending to work, she tries on his
clothes. Her favorites are his sweatshirts; she likes the way the cotton
bunches just before the cuffs—she can imagine his long pale wrists
filling the extra inches. The edges of his sleeves are worn from nervous chewing, the seams frayed into finger-size holes. When she puts
the cuffs to her face, she can smell his mouth—cigarettes, sleepy
breath, and underneath, a surprising freshness. The neck collars have
rings of sweat and dirt on the inside, which, if she touches with her
tongue, taste of salt, garlic, of Oisin after a long walk in the woods.
She prefers the smell of him to the new odor of herself. It brings a
lovely feeling, a warm, wet vibration, and a new perspective on the
place she thought was only a nuisance of hair and odor between her
legs. When he smiles at her now, she is more than grateful. She is
thrilled in every pore of her skin.

In April, the occasional day is warm enough to spend out doors.
One afternoon, Oisin bakes round loaves of gingery bread, buys lobsters at the quay, and brings Aisling to the beach. He builds a fire between the jutting boulders and boils the lobsters until they burn red,
shows her how to break them open on the rocks and suck out the
meat with messy pleasure. They throw the shells to jealous gulls. As
the twilight cools, they toast marshmallows and layer them into sweet
sandwiches with chocolate and crackers. It is just as Oisin reaches out,
smiling and wiping a sticky drop from her chin, that Aisling sees the
girl behind him.

She is the girl of light hair and bony shadows, straight from his prints, lurking like one who intends harm. Aisling closes her eyes, moves back so Oisin cannot touch her again. You can't have him, she thinks. Not yet. She is surprised when the girl retreats—Aisling hadn't thought she would be stronger than a ghost.

This is new, this particular sort of jealousy. Aisling knows what she wants and, for the first time, feels she has it in her to be vicious enough to get it.

13.

According to the Aunts, puberty hit Nieve when the twins were twelve. They didn't say puberty, a word they found coarsely American, but "a woman's time," which Nieve then translated for Oisin. Whatever they called it, Nieve seemed to be leaving Oisin behind. As if he was stuck in childhood time and she had gone on into the future alone.

When they were in Ireland, surrounded by their aunts and their exclusively female babies, a new one appearing each year, Oisin often worried that Nieve would have preferred a sister. The women in his family seemed to exist on a different level from the men; as though their relationship to each other was deeper than anything Oisin or his father and Malachy could have. The Aunts even had different laughs: one for men, which was flirtatious but somehow thin, and the laugh they saved for each other, which Oisin only heard when he was eavesdropping, and which sounded almost as if they were releasing parts of their souls into the air in between the convulsions of joy. It re-

minded Oisin, this laughter, of the light he saw within ghosts, something he was never able to see in living people.

Nieve always looked hungry around these women, as if she were
absorbing the essence of being female. Their mother, Oisin suspected,
was not the same sort of woman as the MacDaras. She preferred the
company of men, and brightened within it. When she spoke to her
sisters-in-law, Sara's face was closed, her voice clipped, polite, with a
warning underneath. I don't want to be part of this, she seemed to say
with every gesture and forced smile. In private, she referred to them
as "the Hens." So the Aunts left her alone and concentrated on Nieve.

Oisin was never allowed close enough to discover what it was the
Aunts were teaching his sister. He knew it involved physical advice,
because Nieve was changing. Her posture had straightened to reveal
the hint of breasts, like tiny fruits poking at the cotton front of her
blouse. Her face had brightened from regular scrubbing, and in their
loft bed at night, she bombarded him with smells: creams, oils, as-
tringents all battled each other and left Oisin with welling, itchy eyes
and a longing for the old, familiar smell of his sister.

They were telling her secrets as well. Secrets Nieve would remember when playing at the old fort with Oisin, with a knowing
smile that irritated him. Over endless pots of tea, with the haze
from their cigarettes looming into a large cloud, babies hanging off
them like uncontrollable limbs, the women would whoop, then
whisper and scold, Nieve in the middle of it all, her eyes bulging as
she tried to take it in. Oisin would watch this through the small,
deep window. Their faces were huge, fluid, every expression exaggerated as if they were on the stage. Their eyes bulged, lips contorted, they managed to look horrified, sly, coquettish, and fierce all
within one sentence. Their laughter could rise to a collective scream,
and they worked themselves into a frenzy, tending toward food

fights and chasing one another with dish towels. Their babies found them endlessly entertaining.

On his way past them to the bathroom, when the women hushed their tones and stirred tea loudly for camouflage, Oisin would hear stray words. *Him. Wait. Kiss. Love.* Without the context of a sentence, the words seemed to have heavy significance. Was Nieve learning secrets about love, about sex? And if it was men they spoke of, why weren't the men allowed to hear it? Oisin would pass by a table of dark curls and flashing eyes, hoping to be included, but he was merely given a scone and a nuzzle and sent on his way again, wondering how he was supposed to know anything about women when he was surrounded by women who told him nothing.

He could barely distinguish the Aunts when they were huddled like this. They all treated him the same way—much like they treated their brothers and husbands—with kind attentiveness, but removed, as though the men were a part of their daily routine which they'd long ago ceased to concentrate on. They seemed to prefer talking *about* men to talking *with* them. Oisin had always felt—occasionally with a rage that he was afraid to express—that these women did not take him seriously.

What Oisin knew about love he learned from the ghosts who woke him nightly. He spent the wee hours comforting weeping dead women, who told him, between phlegmy sobs, of accidents that had resulted in unrequited love. It seemed to Oisin that love was often doomed to misunderstanding, especially in Ireland, where people rarely spoke of what they felt until it was too late.

Oisin was sure that what Nieve was learning of love from his aunts was of a more useful nature than the muddled lessons that came from his ghosts. What Oisin wanted to know was how to kiss a girl without her seeing at close range the red, painful pimples that now clustered around his nose. Nieve, he felt sure, was learning the basics, the anatomy, the mystery of what it was rumored you were supposed to do with your tongue. All Oisin was learning was what it was like to be past your prime and brokenhearted.

At home in Boston, Nieve was no longer her lively, bossy self. She was brooding, distracted; she hardly looked at him anymore but seemed to be fixed on something he could not see. "I'm just thinking," she said when he asked, but the tone suggested that her thoughts were beyond him. She spent hours on the telephone, making him suspect she had a boyfriend, but every time he eavesdropped he heard her addressing a different name. While only a year ago they had bathed together to save hot water, now Nieve was allowed on her own in the one bathroom, and his mother insisted they leave her undisturbed, even if it meant Oisin and his father had to pee on the bushes in the backyard. As if Nieve's ablutions were now so complicated and precious that she needed more time and privacy than Oisin, who was reduced to urinating in public. (Once Oisin was told by another kid at school that girls' time in the bathroom involved *bleeding*, he stopped complaining.)

Oddest of all was the way Nieve's new status as a young woman seemed to have sparked an allegiance in his mother. Sara was drinking less, and suddenly the two were like a television version of mother and daughter, sharing clothing and doing each other's hair, Nieve eating the attention up as though she'd been starved. As though she'd forgotten her mother was the enemy.

Oisin felt closer to crying than he had in years when Nieve announced at dinner that she wanted her own room. He assumed their mother would wave the request away, the way she had always dismissed Nieve. But instead, she took Nieve so seriously, Oisin thought she might suggest moving house to satisfy her. There were only two bedrooms in their single-floor home; guests slept on the sofa bed. His mother and Nieve stayed up late that night drawing plans on graph paper. They considered a plywood partition in the children's room, but they would need their father to erect it, and he was away at sea. They ended up transforming the breakfast nook, a glassed-in portion of the kitchen, into a bedroom. It was the size of a large closet, and so cold that in the winter, oatmeal congealed before the first bite. Nieve hung a beige curtain from the ceiling to enclose the two port-holes that looked into the room, and reattached the door that had been removed years ago to open up the space. Oisin thought the room was so pathetic he was sure Nieve would change her mind, but when they'd finished, his mother told him that he would be the one moving into it.

"Try to understand, Oisin," his mother cooed, while in the back-ground he could already hear the rustle of hangers: Nieve transferring his clothes. "Girls need more space than boys do. You won't be cold, we've caulked the windows. You spend half your nights in the kitchen anyway."

So Oisin, who felt that arguing with the determined Nieve would be a waste of his energy, moved gloomily into what he came to think of as his cave, which barely had space for his bed and dresser. At first it was so cold he could see his breath, so his mother covered the wall of windows with thick plastic, heated with a hair dryer until it tight-ened to a bounce. The barrier, blotchy with clouds of condensation, warped the view of the backyard trees into large, threatening shapes. Though his mother promised to reorganize, the shelves in the corner of Oisin's room held dusty cans of peas and pear halves in syrup for the rest of the time he lived there. Many mornings his father would crawl past him to fetch the cereal, glancing at Oisin as though he were disappointed in, but empathetic toward, the subservient male he'd become.

Nieve's new room went through various personality changes. At first, it was decorated with shocking pink, yellow, and orange daisies. Her curtains matched her duvet cover, which coordinated with her sheets, which echoed an explosion of miniature pillows. The room's innocent appearance contrasted sharply with the odor: the musky, mature scent of Rún perfume, given to Nieve by the Aunts, which she applied in liberal splashes made possible by removing the aerosol tip.

Within a year the curtains (never finished, the hems still pinned because Nieve, who had made them herself, had grown impatient) were ripped down and replaced with new, more fashionable blinds, which blinked open and closed at the turn of a thin stick. They were such a deep red that when the sun shone behind them, her room looked like a smoldering coal. The floral duvet was abandoned for a collection of mangy Mexican blankets. By the time she was thirteen, all that was left of her original sanctuary was the carpet, meant to represent grass, so dirty it looked more like army camouflage. Formerly strewn with stuffed toys and china animals, the shelves were replaced with thin books of music, held upright by heavy glass ashtrays, which she'd purchased originally in a collection of ten from the five-and-dime, and later, rather than empty them, she had replaced them with ten more. There was still the smell, so faint it was more like a memory, of the perfume, but now it was overwhelmed by cigarette smoke and the hypnotizing spice of the candles Nieve burned constantly. These volcanoes of wax were the only light, as she never touched the switch of her lamp. She stayed in her room all the time, scraping sorrowful tunes out of the fiddle Malachy had given her, or listening in half-darkness to later Beatles albums, which from outside her door sounded like an ancient exodus—drumbeats, bangles, and a moaning sound from an instrument Oisin could not identify.

The transformation of the room that had held their childhood seemed to coincide with their growing apart, and with Nieve's journey on a path he could never find the entrance to. In his memory it seemed they jumped from eleven to fifteen in a weekend. But at the time, it all happened so slowly that it was easy for him to believe that puberty and estrangement were temporary conditions.

Once the twins started the eighth grade, they were no longer inseparable. Nieve was one of the girls now—he never saw her alone, but only as part of a teeming mass of ironed hair, eye shadow, and the damp-smelling plaid of Catholic school uniforms. Oisin, who had once barely noticed the female half of his school, was now suffocating in a feminine haze. These girls towered above him; his vision lined up directly with the breasts straining their navy sweaters. Their uniforms, which were meant to be depersonalizing and virginal, were a part of his erotic dreams for years. For some reason, the fact that all the girls wore the same clothes made it easier to picture them naked. He took clues from their knees—pale and goose-pimpled above their navy socks, cushioned, long, shapely, or scarred—and undressed them upward in his mind.

Nieve was the prettiest girl in the eighth grade, which made Oisin nervous. He didn't want perverts like him drooling over her knees. Luckily Nieve, like her aunts, seemed more interested in talking about boys than to them.

Girls, Oisin soon discovered, were not to be trusted. It wasn't just the weakening physical effect they had, but the contradictory behavior that worried Oisin. There were days where girls smiled at him, passed him quizzes in which he was asked if and how much he liked girls a, b, c, and d. Nieve's closest friends, who, to his dismay, had the most promising knees, sometimes called his name out together, like they were singing it, in the cafeteria. He used his lunch tray to hide the effect of their voices.

More often, though, Oisin was snubbed, giggled at in gym shorts, bumped aside in the hall by female arms that felt fiercer than they looked. He felt that he was considered a joke among these girls. He was never asked to walk them home, never invited to the parties that more popular boys bragged about in the bathroom. Popular boys were tall enough to kiss without embarrassing themselves, had hair that stayed in its part, ears that lay flat against their skulls, poreless, ruddy skin. Oisin began to suspect that beauty had a more powerful effect on people than any other characteristic. Beauty was accepted, often worshipped, instantly. Anything less had to prove itself.

Worst of all was that his sister, whose mind had once been as familiar as his own, was one of these beautiful people. Though she still spoke to him at home, in school he sometimes felt that he was not attractive enough to be worthy of her time.

Weekends were lonely. Nieve spent every Friday and Saturday night at a girlfriend's house. She would pack a tiny round suitcase with her best pajamas, her toothbrush, and the new underwear Oisin had glimpsed in the laundry room—no longer flowers on cotton, but slippery, suggestive—and bring it with her to school on Fridays. Oisin wouldn't see her until Sunday at dinner, where she always wore a sleepy, satisfied look, and nodded at his questions as though she were only pretending to listen.

On the nights when she was away, Oisin would slip into his old bedroom, lie on top of Nieve's blankets, and stare at the ceiling, inhaling the smells of the room which held no memory of his twelve years there. He would lie this way for hours, wondering why his sister was so enthralled with people he found so two-faced and irritating, people, he felt, who weren't worthy of her, and, worst of all, people other than him, her twin, her best friend for all of her life.

One Saturday, Oisin was doing his homework when he heard the front door slam and a wail so intense and inhuman, he thought it must be another banshee. When he ran into the kitchen, he found his sister on the floor, holding on to his mother's lap and crying, her words unintelligible, like sucking noises within the flood of phlegm. Oisin, who was ushered out of the room by his mother, tried to get the story from Nieve later. Her friends had turned against her, but the reason was unclear. What could they have possibly done that would make his sister, who rarely cried, howl like that? Nieve had only wailed louder at his questions and sent him away. Oisin, in a spurt of fear, wondered where the sister who was braver and smarter than he was had gone. They are nothing, he wanted to say. You're the best one, Nieve. But he kept that to himself, and secretly hoped that crying over nothing was just part of becoming a woman.

By Monday it was all over. The girls sniffled and passed heart-strewn notes in class. Oisin saw them at recess, four identically dressed, lovely girls, touching Nieve and smiling as though she were back from the dead. The look in their eyes made Oisin remember himself as a small boy, how he had once gone through each day with his body almost constantly touching Nieve's, as though by contact alone, he could become her.

When Oisin was older, he would see this over and over again, this intensity—betrayal followed by passionate reconciliation—and know that it was nothing like the way men were friends. He came to think that this kind of intimacy was what men secretly wanted, and, eventually, there was nothing that would make him feel so alone as the sight of two women who loved each other.

Oisin slipped into Nieve's world briefly by invitation of Maggie Doyle. He had never liked Maggie—she had a voice so loud it was almost violent—but he was grateful enough to imagine her the girl of his dreams when she invited him to her party. Oddly, she had a crush on him, and even Nieve seemed excited at Oisin carving a way for himself in the popular crowd. She took him shopping for clothes, helped him tame his cowlicks with hairspray, slipped him a tube of benzoyl peroxide.

The party was an awkward disappointment. Boys and girls huddled on either side of Maggie's solemn, snack-strewn living room, waiting for their turn to pair off and descend the dark stairs for fifteen minutes of tense pleasure in the basement. Oisin had heard these sessions recounted in the boys' bathroom. It was a test of manhood, how far one could get in such a limited time frame.

When it was Oisin's turn, he was sent down first to wait for Maggie. The basement was cold, the floors covered in a cement-hued carpet, the only furniture a couch fashioned from a raised platform with floral plastic cushions that stuck to the back of his jeans. Oisin sat down and willed his knees to stop shaking, as the motion evoked an obscene squeaking from the couch. When girl's shoes began to descend the stairs, he was sure that the instant he heard Maggie's drill sergeant voice he would vomit.

It was not Maggie but Nieve. For a moment he thought she would say "This is stupid, let's go home," but she settled beside him with a businesslike manner.

"Maggie's upset because you haven't spoken to her all night," Nieve said.

As the boys had been on one side of the room while the girls huddled at the other, Oisin wondered how he was supposed to have accomplished this, but he said nothing. He was secretly relieved. He was beginning to feel, on this sticky plastic seat, like he was awaiting a shot in the doctor's office.

"Okay," Oisin said, standing up. Nieve pulled him back down.

"But Sharon Feeney said she thought you were sort of cute, so she's coming down instead." Oisin imagined them upstairs, trading him back and forth like an unpopular baseball card.

Nieve, her job finished, got up to leave. Oisin grabbed her wrist. He was suddenly afraid, as if Nieve had announced that a headless ghost was due for a visit.

"Tell me what to do," he said. Nieve smiled and seemed to really look at him for the first time in weeks.

"Kiss her," she said. Oisin held tight to her wrist.

"How?" he said. Nieve sat back down beside him, smoothed her hair, and with a graceful movement he barely registered, leaned in and pressed her mouth to his. It was so brief, there was no time to be surprised.

"Just like that," Nieve said, and then she left him there, her thick soles clumping up the steps over his head to the main floor.

Oisin had his fifteen minutes. Fifteen wet and slightly sour minutes that left his jaw cramped and Sharon looking mauled and disappointed. He emerged from the basement relieved at having gotten it over with, and with no desire to descend again.

Years later, when Oisin was invited to reminisce about the occasion of his first kiss, he told the story with humor, unable to remember the girl's name, but recounting his horror at the size of her tongue.

But even now, in those weightless, still frightening seconds before he first kisses a woman, what comes to Oisin's mind is the warm, dry softness of his sister's mouth, and black eyes that looked at him, in a way that was sadly familiar, though far too brief, as if he were the only boy on earth.

PART THREE

Summer

We are born with the dead:

See, they return, and bring us with them.

T. S. ELIOT

The Four Quartets

14.

Aisling is bringing the dead back to the islanders. Odd experiences are being whispered about in the local shop. Mira has been returning home to find her kitchen mysteriously rearranged in the decorative preferences of her late mother. Katherine Darcy, after giving birth to a stillborn boy last autumn, has watched her milk return, and in the mornings feels a small mouth drinking steadily at her breast. Doreen Hogan, who was widowed during her first pregnancy, thought that her eight-year-old daughter was being stalked by a pervert, when the girl mentioned casually that a strange man often walked with her along the beach. After an interrogation, she described the man as her dead father. Doreen now hides behind sea grass and watches the familiar figure of her husband, so tall he needs to hunch over to listen to his daughter as they stroll at the tide line. Deirdre's uncle John admitted to her with a blush that his wife, who died of lung cancer ten years ago, has lately appeared lying beside him at night, her hair done up in the same old cushioned curlers. "She still smokes in bed," said John, his voice pleasantly irritated. And Deirdre, when she checks on Gabe in his sleep, sometimes sees a faint image of her mother, napping upright in an armchair parked by his pillow.

Deirdre watches what happens when islanders shake Aisling's hand, or stop to talk to her on the road. She sees a change in their face, a softening, as though some pressure is lifting off their features. And she knows that they are smelling, feeling, or hearing someone they believed was gone forever.

"Are they really here?" she heard Gabe ask Aisling. "Or are you just re-creating them?"

Aisling shrugged at first, with the look of annoyed boredom that hurts Gabe more than anything these days. But after he pressed her, her eyes clouded and she said only: "I don't know."

She is giving the dead back to the living, passing out pieces and images around like small gifts, and even she is not quite sure where they're coming from. At first, Oisin is unaware of this and, when Deirdre tells him, seems betrayed by it. She wonders who it is that Oisin—content with his own company for so long—wants back.

Deirdre is able to ask Aisling for Brian now, though she tries not to ask too often. She needs only to extend her hand, and her fingers on the girl's skin bring Brian so instantly and violently alive, she must choose between bearing the pain of it or giving up the pleasure. Though she has spent years mourning the end of their life together, now she knows how much has slipped away; she has forgotten what it felt like to have him next to her, to have him inside her, in subtle, everyday ways.

It wasn't until Brian died that Deirdre began to wonder who she was. His absence left a bigger hole than it should have. Not that she felt a part of her had died, or even that she could not live without him—they were not those type of fairy-tale lovers. It was just that she realized, once he was gone, that Brian was the last in a long line of molds she had used to cast herself. In the void, with no one to compare herself to, her personality seemed blurry. She imagined her soul pieced together loosely with images and impressions of others; if shaken hard enough they fell away like scales and nothing was left at the center.

She had always been more of a watcher than a participator. When she was a child, her mother often sent her from the room because she made guests nervous with her critical gaze. She was not known to be talkative, but when she did speak, what she said was never random or unfocused—her rare sentences appeared to have been marinating in her mind for days. The marinating theory came from Brian, his observation after they met in college; most people only thought her shy. The moment he said it she was positive she would fall for him. She liked the way it made her sound.

She had a tendency to fall for eccentric, noticeable men. Men who were the center of attention. She often felt cursed with plainness, so she fed off the spark of others. She would shadow these men and end up resenting how they made her invisible. These men liked her because she didn't compete with them, and since she was so reticent with others, they thought they were the only ones who knew her soul. They often felt stripped bare by their own extroversion; Deirdre was something they could keep to themselves, their special secret.

By the time she met Brian, Deirdre had abandoned all hope of becoming the exciting, gregarious woman she dreamed of being. She was too far behind to change her personality by then. She was best at playing sidekick to the personality of someone else. And Brian had the best personality.

He was handsome but not quite gorgeous enough to intimidate. People thought he was a genius, but Deirdre knew it wasn't his

thoughts that were so original but the way he presented them. He was
the most articulate man she had ever met, able to communicate with
and impress everyone. He would have been a successful politician, but
he chose to be a teacher because he was idealistic about making a difference one-on-one. He made people laugh. And, when they were
alone, away from all the eyes that focused on him, Deirdre was the one
who made him laugh. This made her prouder than she liked to admit.

The first time they made love, in a darkness- and intimacy-fueled
confession, Deirdre told Brian that she often felt invisible. When she
woke the next morning, he had already left for his early class, and
there was a poem written in red ink on her pillowcase.

To me
you are
not
invisible.
You are
like air
and
strokes:
Unseen and sweetly felt.

She felt immediately in love with this image of her, and, for a
while, forgot to be disappointed by the word *unseen.*

After Brian died, Deirdre began collecting other people's impressions of her. She would flip through them like a file of unrelated doc-
uments, trying to find the one that sounded close to the truth. The
brave widow. A mother who laughs easily. Someone who forgets to return phone calls. Who gives the impression of listening in on private
conversations. Smart enough to make most men nervous. A natural

dancer and a ferocious reader. An insomniac. A person strange dogs instantly adore and respect. A magnificent kisser.

She had trouble separating what was her own and what she had borrowed from others. Often she found herself behaving in a way that she recognized as a character from a novel. She tried to speak about this to her friends, but they found her fears ridiculous. They said they knew who she was. But when she drilled them for definitions, the ones they came up with always had something missing or inaccurate.

She fell into a serious depression, where fear seemed to swallow up even the most benign actions. She couldn't drive, couldn't do her shopping on the mainland; she took the entire term off from work, feigning illness. She stopped reading because every word seemed like a criticism aimed at her. She stayed alone in the house whenever she could because the faces of other people reminded her that she did not know who she was. Gabe, who had inherited his father's ease with the world, took to answering the phone and ordering groceries from the shop.

Oddly, it was the one night with Oisin—after they met on a walk in the woods and silently agreed to go back to his place—that saved her. Not that he gave her advice or presented her with a new image of herself. She had thought it would be the same as with other men—that his attraction would define her in some way. But all Oisin did was kiss her, touch her, and enter her—quietly, reverently, but with a sense of distance that for some reason allowed her intense pleasure. With Brian she had been so self-conscious during sex, had felt such a responsibility to appear to be carried away that she never actually let go. She had developed a scale of purposeful noises over the years and eventually, like a lie told over and over, she forgot they weren't genuine.

With Oisin there was only the sound of their breathing. Oisin led her hand down to her own surprising wetness, and held on to her fingers loosely to learn how she touched herself. Then he imitated it perfectly, as if he'd known her body for years. She was not as impressed by his abilities as she was by her own abandon. The whole experience left her feeling unencumbered and free and, oddly, herself. It was the first time she had ever watched a man's face during his orgasm and not felt lonely.

She was under no delusions about Oisin's reputation. After that night she did not wait for him to call, and when he didn't, she wasn't disappointed. If they met by accident he was warmer than before but never lingered. For once it wasn't about what he wanted or what she expected, it wasn't even about how they were together. What that night became for her was the moment she stepped away from all her definitions and into herself. Suddenly it no longer mattered who she was, only *that* she was. She stopped editing her thoughts and analyzing her actions. When she looked in the mirror, her brown eyes were tired or angry, often amused, but no longer plain. Beneath the fears and posing, she had been there all along.

In June, after school lets out for the summer, Deirdre's three nieces arrive from Boston for their annual visit. Colette, Mags, and Jemma, seventeen, fifteen, and thirteen, are perfect examples of the well-adjusted teenage girl. They are so happy and confident, they sometimes make Deirdre feel more dysfunctional than usual. But they are the daughters of Brian's brother and have so much of Brian in them that Deirdre asks them back every summer. This year, she introduces Aisling to them as a normal though lonely teenager, in the hopes that they will all become friends. Within a matter of days, Aisling is addicted to being one of the girls.

Aisling adopts and discards mannerisms of all three nieces. The day that a woman praised Colette for her posture, Aisling began standing up straight, emphasizing her height and her breasts. She is liable to be positively polite (Colette) and obnoxiously forward (Mags) within the same fifteen minutes. For a while, after she discovered Jemma's sensitivity, Aisling burst into tears at the slightest provocation.

Deirdre knows that part of growing up comes from example, but she is also familiar with the danger of losing yourself in the influence of others. She doesn't think Oisin recognizes or even understands this. Boys don't go through quite the same thing. What *they* need to prove she has never been sure, but she knows that girls are afraid of sliding into oblivion; they think that not being noticed is the worst thing that can happen to them. She has been watching fifteen-year-olds for years, trying to teach them to write an essay while their minds float three feet away from their bodies. She can tell Aisling's age by the way she goes from solemn to silly in the space of seconds. There is something transparent about teenagers, as if their souls are sliced wide open; they have a mix of arrogance and vulnerability that makes adults alternately furious and protective. Why is everything such a *drama?* mothers often ask Deirdre. They have either forgotten or blocked out those years where every moment seemed to be drowning in importance.

Set free to run around on the island, Aisling doesn't quite know what to do with herself. She studies Deirdre's nieces for clues about when to smile, laugh, answer, snub, react, or feign ignorance. Gone is the ease with which she interacted with Gabe; Aisling is a teenager now, with that look in her eyes that insists nothing is easy. Gabe misses her, and Deirdre tried to reassure him at first, but she only made it worse. He is smart enough to realize when he's been left behind.

When Deirdre goes to the shop now, she often sees Aisling hanging on every look of Danny McGorey. As though everything he does is either a rejection or confirmation of her. Deirdre wants to take her aside and tell her everything it took her thirty-four years to learn—that it doesn't matter how other people see you as much as how you see yourself; that someday she will have trouble remembering Danny's name. But she knows that direct advice gets you nowhere. You have to slide your wisdom in by example when they're not looking, the way you once inched your fingers under the pillow to replace tiny teeth with quarters.

The change in Oisin is so subtle, Deirdre wonders if anyone has noticed besides herself and Gabe. He acts the same around the islanders—barely acknowledging them, as if he's still lost in his own world. But Deirdre can see the difference in his eyes. There is no longer that glassy film over his pupils; his eyes are sharp and curious. He watches people now, like Aisling, as though he is collecting impressions, which he then lays out and studies later on. He has been gone from the world of the living for so long, he needs to learn all over again how to be a part of it.

He practices on Deirdre. When he meets her in the woods, he asks polite questions about Gabe or her nieces or what she is reading; he comments on the weather. She tries not to laugh at the painful look that comes over his face during these forced interactions. When Aisling is around, he is more relaxed. He smiles now, so often that the wrinkles by his eyes have curved from furrows of anxiety into something resembling laugh lines.

Her nieces are mad about him. They transform into fools if he comes unexpectedly to the house, flipping their hair around in a way

Deirdre worries will damage their necks. Oisin can't help but flirt with them—it's his only natural social skill. His attraction to Aisling is what worries Deirdre—the tension between them is palpable, like lush material stretched to the point of ripping. Oisin is careful with her, he maintains a physical distance while trying not to push her away, and the effort seems to exhaust him; Deirdre suspects that he has rarely had to deny his lust before. She remembers her own infatuations with older male friends of her parents', then her chemistry teacher in high school, and finds a part of her hoping along with Aisling that Oisin will lose his composure and carry her off into the grown-up world of lovers. Her adult conscience chides her for this, making silent speeches about the responsibility the old must take for the impetuous young. Oisin is supposed to be the one with the future in mind while Aisling loses herself in the present. But they are such an odd twosome, a girl growing up too fast and a man who stopped maturing too early, she wonders if the normal rules apply.

One night, while waiting for the girls to get home, over their second glass of wine, Oisin tries to kiss Deirdre. Startled and apologetic murmuring follows: *don't, sorry, never mind,* and Deirdre leaves him on the couch, alarmed at how much her mouth wants this to happen. She remembers their first kiss—how surprised she was at the freshness of his breath; she had expected him to taste as ruined as he sometimes looks.

When she returns with coffee, Oisin has his head in his hands. She resists the urge to comfort him, to kiss him after all and swallow the awkwardness.

"I'm sorry," Oisin says, fumbling with his cup and saucer. "I don't know why I did that."

Deirdre knows why. It is the same reason his touch is so polished—sex is the only way he knows how to reach people.

"I'm not sure who I am anymore," says Oisin, forcing a sarcastic laugh to hide his wobbly voice. "How am I supposed to help her know who *she* is?"

"Do you love her, Oisin?" Deirdre says, and as his eyes flick away, she adds silently: *Do you love anyone?*

It seems Oisin can't or won't answer, so Deirdre continues. "That's all she really needs." She can hear the girls laughing their way up the path. "In case you haven't noticed, she's figuring out the rest by herself."

Then the girls come slamming in, and, amid the shedding of shoes and giggled greetings, Deirdre catches Aisling and Oisin looking at each other; one glance seems to hold within it every fear and desire Deirdre has ever felt in her life; as if both of them are simultaneously children, teenagers, and remorsefully middle-aged.

15.

Oisin MacDara's first sexual experience was not a human one. When he was in art college, and, while talking to his friends, the topic of losing one's virginity came up, Oisin's answer was simple: fifteen years old, South Boston, my sister's bedroom. That was actually the second time, but it was an easier answer than the truth, which he never spoke of. He was fourteen, it was summer in Ireland, and it happened in a graveyard.

The seduction started in his dreams. During these dreams it was as if his mind was awake, watching as his body slept beside the curled form of Nieve. There would be a breeze, then a slight shift at the bottom of the duvet, a swelling that moved upward, but seemed to have no shape, until it reached his neck and turned into a body. It was not a body he could see, it hovered above him light as air, then moved down against him, not all at once, but in pieces; a light flutter of fingers at his neck, a soft stomach pressing warmth into his groin. His wrists would be anchored so he couldn't reach out, and a mouth would move like a smile across his chest, occasionally releasing the shocking wetness of tongue. He would arch his hips as the body moved down, and when he felt his penis slide into a cupping of flesh, he knew without seeing that he was being cradled by breasts. They were so unlike any part of his body, fluid and firm at the same time, like, he imagined, the consistency of clouds, smooth skin punctuated by rough nipples that tickled the hollows of his hips. He would come violently within the manipulation of these breasts, and the eruption would seem endless, repetitive, nothing like what he dragged from himself with his hand, which, in comparison, was a bare hiccup of pleasure. Oisin would wake up fully clothed and sticky with semen, ashamed at the sight of his sister sleeping innocently beside him. He took to rising early in the mornings, to rinse his pajama bottoms out in the bathroom sink. Afraid to hang them on the clothesline, Oisin would fold his pajamas and bury them under his pillow. By nighttime they would still be damp, the cold cling of the material an uncomfortable but exciting hint of future dreams.

He was convinced it was all in his imagination until one night, sleepless with anticipation, there was a voice, a voice with the musical faraway tone he knew belonged to a ghost.

"Not here, Oisin," the voice said, and he was led away by a small, feminine hand, a hand he could not see but whose delicate bones he could feel pressing against his fingers.

It brought him to the graveyard. With bare, cold feet pricked by nettles, he passed quietly by the stone that listed the years of his grandfather's life and the tiny inset that bore the names of lost Mac-Dara babies. By the lone oak tree in the corner of the stone-walled yard, the invisible body urged him backward, until he was leaning with the bark biting into his spine, while kinder teeth nibbled and pulled at his ears.

"Why can't I see you?" he whispered as ghostly hands, lips, eye-lashes, and breasts coaxed him down, until he was lying across a plait of roots, looking up at branches thick with fingered leaves, his body releasing tiny explosions with every unpredicted touch.

But, night after night, he would not see her, not until after hours of a mouth sucking him to the brink and then releasing at the last minute; not until the ache in his groin spread across his whole body with a desperation he fought not to let go of; not until the smell of clean earth, which came from the long hair that traced his body, left its taste on his own skin; not until tight flesh lowered slowly over him, releasing and gripping, drawing his penis into a quality of warmth and wetness that he had not known existed; not until he'd been ridden and stroked and pulled and swallowed and he felt her entire body clench so hard it dragged all his muscles toward it; it wasn't until the moment before her release that he ever saw her. Blue-white, the stars showing through her shoulders, hair like a red thorn bush with branches clinging to her breasts, eyes that locked on his and echoed the pulsing within her with small silvery circles that rippled out from her pupils and disappeared in the air. He would try, each time he came, to keep his eyes on her, but like the reflex when he sneezed, his lids would clench at the moment of or-gasm, and when he opened them again, she would be gone, the air cool and empty on his damp body. He would stumble back to the house alone, and sneak by his parents on the mattress in the front room, climb up the creaking ladder and slither in beside Nieve. It was only afterward that he had time to be afraid, and, exhausted and trembling, with his legs curled against his chest, he wondered if lust would always be strong enough to camouflage any doubt or fear. Often, his early dawn dreams would replay the encounter, and rather than a fiery-headed ghost, it would be Nieve's face he saw

moving above him in ecstasy. He spent his days blushing and avoiding his sister's eyes.

Oisin's affair with the ghost lasted for three weeks of July, until,
weary with lost sleep, reading a book his grandmother had given him
on Irish ghosts, he came across a chapter titled "*Leannan Sí*—Otherworld Lover." It recorded stories of angelic, white-clothed women
who led men to graveyards, seduced them, and left them cold and
dead between the stones. This terrified the superstitious Oisin. He
started to worry about that moment of ejaculation when he felt almost as if he was dying, as if everything within him was being pushed
out the small opening of his penis. That night he refused to follow
her to the graveyard. She never came back to the house for him, but
for the rest of the summer, he often felt her presence in the form of
an ache that was not his own, that he imagined to be the longings of
her invisible body, as she waited for him in the shadows of slate head-
stones. He drew her a hundred times, disappointed in the portraits,
which looked merely like beautiful girls.

He never felt her touch again, but she stayed with him, overshad-
owing every development of his intimate life with women. Though he
continued to reach new levels of passion, there was a quality to that
first encounter, bound up in the weightlessness that transformed to
pressure then lifted again, which he could never capture with flesh-
and-blood women.

When Oisin was nineteen, he was seduced by his thirty-two-year-
old sculpture professor. In an absent, drunken moment, naked in
front of her wood fire, when she coyly asked him where he had
learned to move like that, Oisin answered: In a graveyard. His professor found this so fascinating and sexy, he dropped the class soon afterward, fearful that she would suggest a rendezvous in the nearby
Jesuit cemetery.

Oisin has been known to close his eyes so consistently while making love, not needing to open them for navigation, which he performs by touch alone, that many women, usually just before they break it off with him, have the uneasy feeling that he has an aversion to looking at them, that perhaps, behind the blue-veined patterns of his eyelids, he is imagining that he is inside of someone else.

In August, Rose, Malachy's wife, died delivering her sixth stillborn child. Oisin, hovering within a libidinous daze, an aftereffect of his graveyard trysts, had barely noticed that Rose was pregnant again. She'd been pregnant almost every other summer they were in Ireland, and swollen was her normal form. After the loss of each baby, only Oisin could hear the ghostly cries that followed. Every time, Rose seemed to shrink a bit more, her shoulders receding into her torso, her eyes sagging with the permanent purple bruises of sorrow.

Oisin once overheard a conversation between his father and Malachy; they were preparing to open the bar, and Oisin was sweeping up the previous night's cigarette butts and chip bags. "I've tried to stay away from her, Declan," Malachy whispered mournfully. "The doctor says another baby could kill her. But she's so stubborn, and I forget myself when she kisses me." Oisin had an embarrassing vision of Rose (who looked so much like the Virgin Mary that, when he was small, he'd assumed she possessed the same virtues), pressing her stomach against his uncle Malachy's hips, kissing him with the same feral, tongue-pulling determination that Oisin's invisible lover had used. Was Malachy's passion that strong, he wondered, that it could even supersede the fear of death? Apparently so, for Rose had been pregnant again, bedridden for the last six weeks under doctor's orders.

The night Rose died and came to get him, Oisin was so bleary

with sleep, he thought at first she was only there to tuck him in. Rose
had always liked to participate in the everyday rituals of her nieces
and nephew; she was often giving baths, pulling on pajamas, or feeding ten cousins at her cramped kitchen table. Like Malachy, she had
a special attachment to Oisin and Nieve (her first stillborn child was
delivered the same year as the twins), and it was not unusual for
Oisin to find himself crushed in one of her spontaneous embraces,
or open his eyes in the night to see Rose watching him sleep. While
Malachy gave Nieve fiddle lessons and encouraged Oisin's drawing,
Rose often had the twins for a sleepover in her extra bedroom, which,
prepared obsessively over the years for expected children, was filled
with toys and silent musical mobiles. There were bunk beds against
the wall, across from an antique oak crib and a changing table
painted in a Noah's Ark theme of twin baby animals. Oisin hated to
sleep there; he was kept awake all night by ghostly gurgles and mews,
as if all the babies had sneaked back to admire the presents they
never received. His grandmother insisted that it meant a lot to Rose,
so Oisin never got through a summer without a night in that ghoul-
ish nursery.

　　Oisin barely stirred when Rose climbed up to the loft. She sat
down on the bed, smoothing the duvet into valleys on either side of
Oisin's hips. He let out a grateful murmur, then set his mind to go
back to sleep. But, even with his eyes closed, he could sense it. The energy that manipulated his body until he felt like he was breathing to
someone else's rhythm. It was not something he had ever felt with a
living person. Only the dead made him feel so vividly and vulnerably
alive.

　　He opened his eyes. Rose's face smiled above him; the stain of
grief beneath her eyes had vanished and was replaced by the particular glow that Oisin had first seen on his grandfather. As though every

molecule of her form was dancing, making her appear blurred but, somehow, more substantial than she had been alive. This was the quality Oisin had tried, unsuccessfully, to convey in his drawing: the opposite of life, as different as night was to day, but so unlike anything in the physical world that he had no idea how to capture it.

It was a while before he noticed the babies. What he had thought was Rose's permanently swollen stomach was actually a cross of heavy cloth, tied up behind her shoulders and waist, cocooning a number of miniature bodies. Oisin counted six tiny heads within the slings, bald or with dark, flimsy hair; their faces were the mottled, squashed, and exhausted features of newborns. Oisin noted, with a mixture of dread and relief, that Rose had not missed any second of their lives. One baby, the smallest, his head barely the width of Oisin's palm, was sucking with rhythmic, contented noises at Rose's exposed breast. For reasons he did not want to think about, this vision gave Oisin an erection. He sat up and rearranged the bedclothes. Through the round loft window, he saw the glow of artificial light coming from Malachy's house and heard the muffled sounds of a gathering—the broken, wavelike moan of Malachy in grief. Oisin was suddenly aware of the stillness of the ground floor below him; everyone had slipped out to Malachy's house. Even Nieve was gone, her side of the duvet left folded back in her haste.

"Malachy's crying," Oisin said. Rose nodded solemnly, but with the hint of a smile.

"He's always loved me," she said. Oisin held back his instinctive response. Everyone knew that Malachy worshipped Rose; why did she say it as if it were in doubt?

"Would you like me to walk with you, Auntie?" Oisin said. Often this was what the benign ghosts wanted from him: human company for a mile or so on the potholed roads, until they felt ready to go ahead alone. Oisin had spent many nights marching through moonless dark, his feet thudding in unison with ghostly limbs.

"That would be lovely, Oisin," his aunt said, her voice as seductively musical as the ghost who had kissed every inch of his skin. "I want to tell you about your mother," Rose said.

What Rose could possibly have to say about Sara, Oisin didn't know; the two women had barely spoken to each other in all the summers they'd spent as neighbors. But Oisin was quite used to odd requests from nightly visitors; he had played soccer on a dark football pitch, wound yarn for furious knitters, sung rebel songs until his voice cracked, slipped money into shop owners' tills to pay for the dead's debts. He considered himself fairly generous and amiable toward the otherworld's requests. So he rose from bed, put on Wellingtons, a sweatshirt, and a wax jacket over his pajamas, and walked out under the stars with Rose and her mewling babies, unaware that he was about to be told the most important secret of his mother's life.

Y our mother married for love," Rose began. "That is, in order to be near the man she loved, she married his twin."

Oisin stopped walking then, understanding settling over him like fear. Rose took his hand.

"It's all right, Oisin," she said. "See for yourself."

His mother's story came to him through Rose's light hand. He no longer listened but watched, as if he was dreaming of his mother, able to observe her and see through her eyes at the same time. Before he forgot himself altogether, he wondered whether Rose had the whole world in there, that perhaps, like the intricate paths lining her palm, he might be able to follow any life, depending on where he touched.

S ara met the MacDara brothers in Boston, during her first year of college. In 1955—and in the family in which Sara was raised—college was more an opportunity for husband shopping than education. Sara despised most of the men who tried to court her; they were all younger versions of her father. Unlike most of her classmates, Sara had never been a Daddy's girl. William Linnet was a cold, absent father who left Sara's early upbringing to his wife, and later, after he had Mrs. Linnet institutionalized, to a series of nannies. Though he was by no means a warm man to begin with, it wasn't until he discovered his wife's illness, and the deception surrounding it, that he became cruel. For his wife, Veronica, had come from a family tree of mental instability, a lineage where no wife, mother, or daughter had made it to thirty without a breakdown. For generations, every woman in Veronica's family had invented the same lies about her gene pool, in the hopes that she would turn out differently from the rest. When William signed his wife over to the Floating Hospital for the Insane (Sara grew up imagining her mother in a levitating hospital ward), he found Veronica's supposedly dead mother on the name board of the paranoid schizophrenics floor. The hospital had housed one or more of Veronica's relatives for more than a century.

What little tenderness William felt for his daughter, Sara, ended with her mother's departure. He had invested in the illusion of a normal family and had ended up with a wife who tried to poison him, and, when she failed, smeared herself with her own excrement. He watched fearfully from the sidelines as Sara grew up, waiting for the onset of depression, manic energy, or schizophrenia. He married again and his new wife, Marjory (not the sharpest knife in the drawer, the help was apt to say, but sane nonetheless), gave him two sons; both boys had their own nannies and were kept almost completely away from their stepsister, who was sequestered on the fourth floor. Sara learned to get attention from her father by pretending to plan her suicide. She collected razor blades, hung nooses from the attic beams, set fire to her room. He harbored a shameful hope that one day she would succeed in killing herself.

William sent Sara to university in Boston to get rid of her, hoping she would find another man to take on the responsibility of her heritage. Sara, anxious to be out in the world after ten years of paranoid supervision, was perfectly willing to do just that—but the man she was looking for, some medium between her emotionless father and her psychotic mother, was not easy to find in the halls of an Ivy League Yankee school.

So she went elsewhere. Her roommate, Molly, was a scholarship student from South Boston. On the weekends, she took Sara to her local pubs, where men in flannel work shirts drank dark beer, tapping their boots to the traditional Irish bands. These men were rough, uncultured, raucous, and attentive. In Sara's eyes, they were more alive than the few men she'd been allowed to see socially at home, who wore summer suits and sipped mint-laced cocktails.

She knew Malachy was the one from the first moment she saw him. Playing the fiddle, his fingers moving so fast they blurred, the brown curls on his forehead damp and dancing, his indigo blue eyes striking even from a distance; he looked like a man who could teach her about ecstasy. Full lips, an uninhibited laugh, dimples carved in careless stubble. He caught Sara's eye, and with a smooth marriage of wink, smile, and nod, he acknowledged her. In that gesture, she saw her life like a map laid out in front of her: permanent roads of happiness, rivers of love, a mountain range of passion.

Two hours later, when she found out he had a wife at home in Ireland, it was already too late. She had heard his voice, felt his strong hand at her waist, been twirled around the smoky room, her heart beating to the rhythm of his stomping feet. This was what she wanted, this feeling she had in the presence of Malachy, as if she were floating, falling, rising, all at once. It was too powerful to forget, too real to dismiss and look for another, more available man. (Sara, who—like the women before her—was convinced she was nothing like her mother, had actually inherited a tendency toward the fatalistic, which at its best was irrational, at its worst, psychotic. If Sara wanted something, she would get it or die; there were no other options.)

When she went home that night, Malachy permanently splintered under her skin, Sara made a plan. A wife, she thought, is not enough to stand in the way of true passion. Sara knew how to make herself look, smell, feel, and sound irresistible. And for fourteen years, that is exactly what she did.

Three months after she met him, Malachy, who had only come to Boston to make money, was due to go home. Sara had dug herself a place in his life; his friends accepted her, the musicians flirted with her, and his twin brother had become the official escort for her nights out. Declan MacDara was a muted version of his brother: Malachy gone limp. Lank hair, dull eyes, a shy, mumbling voice that was drowned out by his brother's animation. Though they looked like two versions of the same person, it was impossible to confuse them. The energy that emanated from Malachy was absent in Declan; beside his brother, Declan was a burned-out lightbulb. He hovered at Sara's elbow, silent and unobtrusive. She barely knew he was there.

Though Malachy had been nothing but a gentleman all the time she'd known him, Sara believed he felt the same as she did. Everything he said to her was soaked in hidden meaning. So, the week before Malachy left for Ireland, when he stared at her with those dusk-colored eyes and said simply, "You know Declan fancies you," Sara took it as a coded message. He was too traditional, too old-fashioned to leave his wife; but he was showing her the only way they could be together.

"Yes," Sara murmured, her heart's hammer drowning her voice.

"He'll want to ask your father for your hand," Malachy said. He who was so confident was blushing with this admission.

"My father will say no," Sara said. Malachy blanched. "He'll have to ask me instead," she added.

Malachy grinned, cocked his head, and looked at her with such amused admiration, she felt sure, for the hundredth time, that he was about to kiss her. Instead, he lifted his glass.

"To family," he said, then swallowed half the pint at once, like the thirstiest man in the world.

In the years to come, Sara would cherish that moment, reframing it in her mind as Malachy's inventive, passionate proposal.

S ara married Declan as quickly as the Catholic church would allow. She sent a telegram to her father, and received back a formal letter of disapproval. She'd expected as much. Though he claimed a distaste for her choice—immigrant, Catholic, working class—she knew her father had been planning to write her off for years. Sara felt so relieved at driving her father out of her life that she didn't even care about losing access to his money. What was money when she had the more permanent security of love?

The ceremony took place in Clifden, the small Connemara town where the MacDaras lived. On her wedding night, Sara, choked with gin and the shock of meeting Malachy's wife, woke briefly from her fantasy world at the moment Declan forced himself inside her. She screamed with the pain, Declan covered her mouth with a damp, bitter-tasting hand, and for a few minutes she thrashed, bit, and kicked as he battered into her. When it was over, Declan stumbled to the corner of the room and vomited repeatedly in the tiny sink. By the time he came back to bed, Sara was crying.

"Never do that to me again," she whispered, and Declan, who found women mysterious and Sara unfathomable, grunted in agreement.

Sara wanted to stay in Ireland, but Declan could make more money as a fisherman based in Boston. Declan, who believed that men should make unconsulted decisions, a rebellious response to the tough women he grew up with, closed his ears to Sara's pleas. They settled in South Boston, and Declan went to sea seven months of every year. That first violent night left Sara pregnant with the twins. Their life fell into a routine that had its foundation in their separation: winters in Boston where Declan was rarely home; summers in Ireland where Sara barely looked at him.

Sex only united them a handful of times in the next decade. Sara attributed what she thought of as her few infidelities to Malachy to a red wine allergy. Too much Merlot made her libido, normally buried in a fantasy world, flare into physical existence. Her senses blurred Declan's face into his twin's. With her eyes closed tight in concentration, she could kiss her husband and taste Malachy's mouth. She would snap out of it the instant Declan penetrated her and begin to fight him as on the first night, and they wouldn't finish what she had started. Eventually, Declan avoided these rare invitations; they left him with the revolting impression that he was raping his own wife.

Sara's happiness grew to depend on the most benign gestures from Malachy; Christmas cards, presents for the twins, the smile against her ear as they danced at family weddings. She kept obsessive track of them in the coded notebook of her mind, a hierarchy of the evidence of their love. If Malachy entered a room without looking at her before anyone else, she would be bedridden with a clenched chest and rapid heart, barely able to breathe at the thought that he no longer wanted her. Eventually, her pulse would send her searching for him, drinking at the bar until she could barely see, waiting through seven hours of jigs and reels for one wink over Malachy's fiddle. And she would be instantly cured, she would stumble home feeling as though she was flying, repeating their history in her mind, knowing again that nothing else mattered: she was wanted.

Her determination never faltered. She never seduced him, never even stole a kiss. She didn't want an affair with Malachy, she wanted it all. She was waiting for the miracle that would unchain him, waiting for his freedom which would bring his unspoken promise to fruition.

Sara had been waiting, Oisin thought, as Rose let go of his hand, for Malachy's wife to die.

Oisin was exhausted, sweat-soaked and chilled as if from a fever. It was one thing to be visited by ghosts, quite another to be infused with another person's life. Knowing such things about his par-

ents was like seeing them naked. Oisin had a vivid image of inter-
rupting them in bed, their faces clenched and hideous in loveless sex.

"Watch over your family, Oisin," Aunt Rose said, babies mewling
at her chest. "It's not only your mother who suffers when she does not
get what she wants."

Oisin thought she was referring to his father, bitter and robbed of
love, or Malachy, who might be weakened by his grief. It didn't occur
to him, not then, that Nieve, who had always seemed so removed from
his mother, was the one who would inherit her pain. It was like a punishment stamped on her genes, right alongside the chromosomes that
made her beautiful and a woman.

16.

"T his place reeks of heartbreak," Deirdre says.

Gabe and Oisin are sitting on Oisin's sofa, their faces as sunken as the beige cushions beneath them.

"Your son has been stood up," Oisin says, avoiding Gabe's betrayed glare. Deirdre hides a smile as she gives Gabe a bolstering hug.

"They're not even special," Gabe says. Oisin has felt the same whine deep in his throat for days, and he envies Gabe for being able to voice it. "They're *average*, they could have come off an assembly line of teenage girls."

"Jealousy doesn't suit you, Gabriel," Deirdre says.

"I'm not jealous," Gabe mumbles, head down, letting his mother caress his hair.

Gabe is not the only one who resents these girls. For Oisin, Deirdre's nieces conjure memories of every girl he was afraid of in high school. They are young and beautiful and, worse, seem to know it, and he feels fourteen again under their collective, flirtatiously disapproving gaze.

They swarm through his house during the day for refueling—snacks, the swapping of tank tops, the furious brushing of their hair. All of this amid giggles and conversation so low and slang-ridden it seems like a foreign language. They leave behind a fog of same-sex cologne, a ransacked bathroom, and a quality of loneliness Oisin hasn't felt since he was a teenager.

The oldest is Colette at seventeen, a severe girl composed of angles and planes. A shank of blond hair, collarbones reaching out further than her miniature breasts. Even her mouth forms a straight line—no smiles or frowns, but a steady, detached expression.

The middle sister, Mags, is the tomboy, but nothing like the tomboys Oisin remembers. Mags has the sculpted short hair of a model, parted in zigzags, kept off her unlined forehead by plastic, bug-shaped barrettes. Her sneakers must cost $150, and he's seen at least four different pairs; she's a bouncing advertisement for the top name brands. Cutoff denim shorts and men's white T-shirts seem sexier on her than an evening dress. She has coltish, muscular legs, and Oisin has to stop himself from following them with his eyes.

But it's the baby, Jemma, who gives him the most trouble. Barely thirteen years old and the most voluptuous creature he's seen in a while. A girl brimming with the seductiveness of a woman, but not quite sure what to do with it. She has almost dripping moist lips, soft brown curls that bounce teasingly across her cheeks, and a habit of touching her own body—her calf, her neck, the curve beneath her breasts, with such thoughtless pleasure that Oisin almost doubles over with guilty lust every time she enters the house.

He is afraid he is becoming a cliché—the perverted middle-aged man—sexually desperate, past his prime, leering after his daughter's teenage friends. He feels an inflated sense of accomplishment when he makes one of them laugh, he has actually winked at each of them at least once before he could censor himself. Not that he's never eyed teenage girls before—most men do—but it seems different now. He's supposed to be a guardian and he's acting like a horny older brother.

He is brooding in the twilight again, now that, after eight months of never having privacy, he is left alone at the end of each day. He has given Aisling the same curfew as Deirdre's nieces, though he'd prefer her home before dark. (He remembers fifteen; there was a sense of invincibility that heightened once the sun went down.) Solitude, which he once cherished, is dangerous now. Because after an hour of worrying over his attraction to teenage girls, his real fear wiggles out into the blue night air: These girls only camouflage the desire he can't justify. Because the one he really wants was a little girl crawling into his bed with nightmares only months ago.

Aisling's awkward phase has been painful for him. Her disgust at the changes in her body was obvious, and, he knew from experience, so impossible to comfort that he tiptoed around her and made it worse. She hid within voluminous sweatshirts, hobbled around like a hunchback, washed and perfumed herself so vigorously that he developed allergic, rapid-fire sneezing. He found familiar traces of squeezed zits on the bathroom mirror. His empathy over her acne was so overwhelming he almost mentioned it, but opted instead to ignore it, when he remembered his own long-ago hope that his blemishes weren't as noticeable to others. He tried not to look pointedly at her face; he wound up lowering his eyes to a body which, though hidden by extra clothes, hardly seemed an appropriate place to stare. His demeanor went quickly from tentative to stammering, and she would walk away from him looking mortified. He was grateful for Gabe, who at ten was still young enough not to care if Aisling was girl, boy, or reptile, as long as she remained fun to be with. One day he found the two of them studying the innards of a zit under Gabe's microscope, and he thought *There's one approach I never considered.*

All this happened last month, when she was still trapped in puberty. The pimples are gone now, her skin shows no evidence of its recent battle. She has grown into her new body and flatters it with stringy tank tops, Miracle bras, and short shorts. She is almost as tall as Oisin, taller if she wears platform sandals, and she waxes her long legs until they look as soft as the rest of her. Colette has pierced Aisling's ears with tiny silver hoops, and every few days Aisling applies a new temporary tattoo to the luscious place just below her belly button. Her adult teeth are straight and gleaming, her upper lip forms a perfect heart curve. Her eyes are still the most striking of her features—huge and gold, highlighted now by sparkling powder, but with so much more depth to them, as if she holds traces of everything she's experienced in the past months, that Oisin feels lost if he focuses on them for too long. She is remarkably more beautiful than the other three, but he can tell she's not aware of it, because she looks at them with envy. With the face of an angel and a body without a flaw, Aisling is followed by the eyes of the islanders now, most of whom watch her with something close to reverence. Still, Oisin has almost flattened a number of male tourists who leered at her sunbathing on the dock by the ferry. He made her exchange her bikini for a racing suit.

He misses her, so much that he is plagued by physical cramps of longing. She is no longer his pretty little shadow. Now she comes creeping in an hour after her curfew, smelling of bonfires and cheap beer, her lips swollen and used, twitching with secret smiles. She's kissing, and who knows what else, and he is torn between the instinct to ground her and a desire to show her personally what a real kiss should feel like. In his dreams, each day is edited and replayed with a series of seductions. He christens each morning with a cold shower.

He hasn't needed self-discipline with regard to sex since he was a boy, believes he is wavering but relatively under control, trusts that eventually he will outgrow this embarrassing lustful stage. He thinks Aisling is safe, until she begins to flirt with him.

In the beginning, he blames it on his imagination. When she brushes against his hip in the kitchen, he scalds himself on purpose to deflate his arousal. He often feels as though he's being watched, and when he turns to her, she looks down, and what he thinks is a blush blazes across her forehead. She has abandoned her girlish pajama sets and parades around in a T-shirt too short to cover her bikini underpants. (It takes great self-discipline not to watch her bottom move beneath the silk on her way to the bathroom, but most of the time he manages.) When she talks to him, she leans against the support beam in the living room, her arms tucked behind her, only her shoulders touching the wood, the rest of her body arching forward, fidgeting just enough to lend a bounce to her breasts. One day she offers to cut his hair; he tries to refuse, but gives in to the rejected look that comes over her pretty face. There's no need to punish her for his weaknesses, he thinks.

But from the moment she starts dribbling water over his head, he knows he's being seduced. She's new at this, and fumbling, but effective. She runs trembling fingers across his neck, presses her breasts into his back. While trimming over his ears, she glances at his eyes, and he can see the intentions battling with fear in her face.

"Leave my ears," he croaks, and when she laughs, he thinks: Uh-oh. This is not her normal laugh. It's the laugh they reserve for boys, the one that says she's not really amused, but she knows even her laughter will be attractive. When she breathes against his earlobe, he stops the haircut with the excuse of artistic inspiration, running to his studio with the towel still draped around his shoulders. Later, when she is out with the girls, he has to trim the rest himself in the mirror, scolding his reflection. And though he senses something unnatural, practiced, in the way she is with him now, he is already longing for that purposeful touch of hers again.

O isin visits the island shop three or four times a day, because he has a chance of glimpsing Aisling amid the throng of children who pad in and out, fortifying themselves with ice pops and Coke. More than once he sees her straddling the front tire of Danny Mc-Gorey's bicycle. He doesn't like this Danny; he's rough-mouthed, gorgeous, and has that look of bad-boy mischievous humor that Oisin didn't perfect until college. He is disappointed to think such cheap tactics would work on Aisling, but they probably do. He recalls it was always the smartest girls who lost their minds the fastest.

He remembers a lot about being a boy that disturbs him now. That single-minded devotion to getting inside a girl. Lately he has been picturing, with shame, Peggy, a sixteen-year-old virgin he seduced when he was a senior in high school. He used to coax her into his bedroom (by this time he lived alone with his father, who was rarely there, and when he was, rarely sober) and pretend that kissing was all he intended. Peggy loved to kiss, was not ready for anything else, but in the weight-less, breathy heat of his room he managed to convince her that irresistible forces were leading them along. He pretended that the shedding of clothes and the step-by-step manipulation of every inch of her was something he had not plotted, an accident he had not been thinking impatiently about during all that exploratory mouth work. Though he never said it, he knew he was leading her to believe that he cared about her. Somewhere in the world Peggy is approaching middle age, and in her memory, Oisin lives on as the first to break her heart.

He sees the same brainless determination in the twitchy eyes of Danny McGorey. He wonders how far the boy has managed to persuade Aisling to go. Of course, there is the other option, that Aisling is the eager one, that she initiates and welcomes sex in the same way she delighted in her teeth falling out: as a sign of life. This idea disturbs him even more. Her passion for experience would be wasted, he tells himself, on a horny young boy. Or perhaps he's only jealous that he is no longer a boy himself, that he no longer has that energy, which plunges without thought of consequence, that he has lost youth, which arouses like nothing else can.

On the night Aisling comes home drunk, the look on her face as she comes through the door, and the careful, exaggerated way she moves her arms and legs, brings before him a vivid image of his mother trying to set the dinner table, so loaded she can barely stand.

"Has your boyfriend been raiding the old man's scotch supply again?" Oisin sneers in response to Aisling's sloppy smile of a greeting. She looks confused, starts to answer twice, but can't manage the logistics of the number of lies she's trying to organize.

"Ah, fuck it," she says finally, thumping into the seat across from him. Lately a new voice has been erupting out of her: the low-toned, cynical voice distinctive to the young who are beginning to imagine themselves world-weary and old.

"Is it losers in general you're interested in, or are you attracted to Davey in particular?" Oisin is appalled at the parental clichés forming a queue on his tongue.

"*Danny*," Aisling corrects him. "And you wouldn't understand." She's having trouble speaking clearly, and looks regretful and trapped in her armchair.

"Of course not," Oisin barks. "I'm an old man. The depth of your feeling is unfathomable to me."

"Okay, I'm going to bed," Aisling says, hoisting herself into a wobbly stand.

"Just tell me one thing," Oisin says. She rolls her eyes. "Is he nice to you?"

"Sure," Aisling says, but she looks confused.

"As nice as Gabe was?"

"Gabe is a child." She snorts.

"So were you, a month ago," Oisin says. "Gabe gave you something. What does this Donnie give you?"

"*Danny*," she says, with less conviction this time. She's trying so hard to think, he can imagine her brain dehydrating from the alcohol.

"He thinks I'm sexy," she says finally. Oisin laughs cruelly.

"That's original," he says. "Your expectations are astoundingly high. Every man that passes by looks at you; you don't need a moron to tell you that."

Aisling has backed up against the support beam, assuming her seductive position instinctively, though her head is hanging like she's gone suddenly shy. She mumbles something he doesn't catch.

"What?" he says. She looks up at him, gold eyes blazing, the blame of the world in her face.

"You don't think so," she says.

"Don't be ridiculous," he says. He should know better than to dodge that question, but he's approaching dangerous territory.

"You never look at me the way you look at them," she says.

"What in hell are you talking about?"

"I'm not blind," Aisling says. She's close to crying now. "I see the way you look at Colette and Mags and Jemma, even Deirdre. It's the way Danny looks at me, and I don't care what you say, it *means* something. It does."

"It doesn't mean as much as you think," Oisin says. He sees immediately that she's taken this the wrong way. She's crying now, swiping angrily at the tears dropping from her nose.

"I know it means you don't want me," she says quietly.

"Want you?" he says angrily, though what he's feeling isn't anger. "That's all you need to know, is it? Whether you have the same effect on me as you do on that boy?"

Later, he'll tell himself that he did it without thinking, but that won't be the truth. He is thinking, and hoping, and pretending that he is still the sort of man he was a year ago, one from whom such behavior is expected and excused. A man with nothing to lose.

He walks quickly to her and leans into her waiting body, pressing her against the wooden beam with all the urgency he's ever felt in his life.

"How's that?" he says, pressing harder, letting himself shudder. He puts his hands to her face, lifts it, expecting to see the fear that will stop him. But her eyes are glowing; she looks delighted. He presses his forehead against hers, lining up the slopes of their noses.

She saves him with a question.

"Are you going to kiss me?" she says.

Oisin is gone. Ripping away from her, out the door, the summer air mocking the pleasure which he has no right to be feeling. She is still so innocent. He sees her wrapping kisses in blue tissue paper, storing them along with all she has collected so far.

When he returns at dawn, he finds Aisling hunched and vomiting in the bathroom, the toilet sprayed with the blue Kool-Aid concoction she must have been guzzling earlier. He gathers her hair at the back of her neck, rubs circles into her back until the retching stops and she feels safe enough to let go of the bowl.

"I'm doing this all wrong," she says breathlessly.

"No, you've got it right," Oisin says. "Drink too much, get sick, vow never to drink too much again. You've passed with flying colors."

"That's not what I meant," she says, but she's laughing.

He gives her a peppermint and a glass of water, guides her to bed and tucks her in, and for a few moments the awkwardness of the last months is gone, their jealousy and longing are folded away, and they know in their silence who they are to each other again.

17.

The summer he was fifteen, a year after Aunt Rose died, Oisin waited for his mother to betray them. Malachy, though hunched in shadow, was finally free. And Oisin, more than anyone, had faith in the persuasive gifts of his beautiful mother.

One night while this fear kept him from sleeping, he whispered his mother's secret to Nieve.

"We all know Mama's got a thing for Malachy," she said. We apparently referred to the women.

"Did you know Mama's family was crazy?" Oisin whispered. He felt stupid; he'd been guarding a secret that he'd been the last to hear.

"I'm not surprised," Nieve said, and she slept, leaving Oisin awake and worried. He wondered if it was because Nieve was a girl that she learned everything first. The Aunts let her into the center while he was left nosing around the edges. He might have had second sight, but he was kept blind to the living.

The women took on the job of keeping Sara away from Malachy.

Aunt Emer moved into his spare room, his mother fed him as though he had regressed to a toddler, hovering and cooing encouragement to his slack appetite. Nieve sequestered him for fiddle lessons when he wasn't in the fields. And, at night, the Aunts started drinking at the pub, something they'd previously only done at Christmas.

Before that summer MacDara's had been frequented mostly by local men. Sara went in sometimes, and there were female tourists who sat together in the snug at the corner of the bar—the only ones drinking spirits in a room full of black pints. Once Oisin's Aunts descended on the place, however, the women of the village began stopping by as well. They brought their babies, leaving them in prams to be lulled by laughter, music, and smoke thick as fog. Oisin, who had watched this room from behind the tall bar since he was five, was awed at the transformation. The pub had once smelled purely of Guinness, hay, manure, salted fish, and pipe tobacco. The men had gathered at high stools around the three-sided bar, wool caps and jackets left on, joking in a language all their own, half Irish, half English.

With the entrance of women, the pub changed drastically. Blending with the masculine odors were sharp perfumes, soft powders, the sour complexity of baby formula. The younger men came alive, started showing up for their drinks in starched shirts. Declan cleared an area for dancing, stocked the shelves with a variety of gins, vodkas, and rums, multicolored fizzy drinks, and child-size chocolate bars. Oisin was put to work pulling pints and left in charge of the complicated arrangement of spirit bottles—an upside-down revolving circle with measuring dispensers. He learned to keep the orders of fifteen people in his head while preparing as many drinks. (Occasionally he found himself with an extra Guinness, which he had absentmindedly poured for a ghost who had dropped by to watch the festivities.)

Nieve worked as a waitress, balancing loaded trays above her head, weaving her way through the compliments of the men she served.

The women brought a new energy to the air, stronger laughter, possibility sparkling in the eyes of the young. Every night was like a church dance, men crowding at the bar eagerly ordering gin lemonades, couples weaving home over the dawn-lit roads. Oisin would feel sorry when he glanced at the corner of the bar where the old men now huddled together looking lost and not just a bit betrayed. They ordered their pints by nodding almost imperceptibly at Oisin, paid out the price exactly in coins piled in neat stacks. Once they had flirted with Sara and the occasional female tourist. But this was too many women for them. They stuck together, drinking faster as though afraid the lines would run dry, mumbling and frowning, forcing a smile over their horrified expressions when their wives or daughters called to them from across the buoyant room.

The transformation had its intended effect. Sara could hardly catch sight of Malachy, let alone sit beside him as he played the way she used to. He was blocked on all sides by sisters, hovered over by young local women who had loved him secretly since they were eleven. Malachy played with a smile, but his eyes no longer had the music in them. Only late at night, when he slowed down with an air or two, did he come alive, pulling his grief for Rose off the crying strings.

The Aunts developed a sixth sense with regards to Sara. If she slipped out for a walk, one of them would set out with a snack to bring to Malachy in the fields. At dinner they surrounded him with their children and were constantly asking Sara to fetch something for the table. At the pub they were like a small army, uniformed in shiny curls and indigo eyes, their weapons disguised behind their smiles. Oisin almost felt sorry for his mother, who seemed no match for his ferociously protective aunts.

Sara was drinking again, so heavily that Oisin or Nieve were often let off early with the job of guiding her home. With Oisin, she would cry from the moment they left the pub until he put her into bed, loud, wracking sobs which she could not speak through, her few indecipherable words like tiny yelps of pain. When he got her to the cottage he would have to help her take her clothes off. He pulled at the garments quickly, blindly, taking care not to contact any bare skin. Once in bed, his mother would jerk him down on top of her, hug him in a fierce, erotic embrace, her hips arching up against his stiff, terrified body. He learned to jump away at the first opportunity, kiss her forehead quickly, and untangle himself from her arms under the guise of tucking her beneath the duvet.

"You'll always take care of me, Oisin," his mother would slur through her tear-soaked hair. It was not a question, so he never bothered to answer.

He often walked back to the bar to finish off the night, the cool air deflating his unfathomable erection. He no longer had any control over his body. His penis, his skin, his hair follicles and sweat glands seemed to have minds of their own, and they were ganging up on him, the way the Aunts were rallying against Sara, shoving him into a place where he was unattractive, inappropriate, and alone.

Whenever Nieve took Sara home, she returned with bruises. The brief time during which Nieve and Sara had seemed to be coconspirators had ended with Rose's death. Nieve's lip would be split, her neck scratched, her upper arms gripped in blue. If Declan asked, she shrugged him off with a story of their mother falling into a ditch.

When Oisin saw her one morning with an eye swollen shut, sprouting a purple and green bruise, he followed her outside where she was hanging the wash.

"Is she hurting you, Nee?" he said. He knew this subject fell into

the category of secrets. That it required whispering, denial, and swallowed opinions, in the same way that the topic of Sara's drinking was
skirted by the Aunts.

"Just leave it, Oisin," Nieve said, snapping the wrinkles out of a
damp sheet.

"Come on," Oisin tried, but Nieve turned her back, jabbing the
line with clothespins.

"Get your own life," she said. "Mine's none of your business."

Oisin was so embarrassed, and later so angry, that he stopped in-
quiring at her bruises. But he volunteered to take his mother home,
thinking it was safer for everyone, though he often felt afterward as if
he were sporting invisible bruises of his own.

That summer, it wasn't the Aunts who took Nieve away, though
she could still be found cocooned in their smoky lair. The new
thieves were boys. Half the men under twenty-five chose MacDara's
over the other local because of Nieve. Clearly they could accomplish
nothing under the guard of Malachy and Declan, so Nieve was lured
outside for quick declarations of love between rounds. Oisin, who
sometimes managed to eavesdrop, was confused by the unmasculine
behavior he saw. In Boston, a boy would die before admitting feelings for a girl—it was well known that the best way to attract a
woman was to pretend she didn't exist. Ireland seemed to have different rules. Local boys recited poetry to Nieve in the car park, pro-
posed marriage over the top of a pint, avowed her beauty with
tearful, sincere eyes. Oisin knew they were after the same thing, one
thing. But he could not bring himself to warn Nieve of this; he
didn't want to admit that he knew the perversity of the young male
mind. Instead he kept an eye on her out the steamy pub windows,

hoping he would not be called upon to defend his sister's honor against a fisherman twice his size.

Oisin was newly troubled by his sister that summer. She was infused with more than her share of energy; everything she did, at work or home, she did rapidly. In a place where people took their time, Nieve's rush was noticeable enough to be disturbing. She began clearing the dinner table before people finished eating, knocked Oisin out of bed so she could straighten the sheets, was known to reorganize the kitchen cabinets and wash the floors while everyone else was still asleep. She ironed everything. Sheets, napkins, tablecloths, even Oisin's underwear. The ironing board was rarely put away, the small house was always slightly steamy, Nieve began to smell of starch. When she wasn't cleaning, she practiced the fiddle until her fingers bled or wrote pages and pages in what Oisin assumed was a diary, crouched alone in the fort where they had once played together. Even her mannerisms had sped up; her eyes couldn't focus but darted past every object to see what was coming next, she smoothed her hands over her hair so often that the sheet of blond looked dull and mauled by the middle of the day. She spoke with such tense speed that even the most benign utterances seemed to suggest that something awful was about to happen.

The Aunts, who nodded knowingly and whispered the word *hormones* when she passed, tried to get Nieve to stop, sit down, relax. They said nothing when she started smoking their cigarettes, thinking that it would have the same calming effect on her they believed it had on them. What was smoking if not an excuse to sit still for ten minutes? But Nieve kept moving, simply added trails of smoke to the race. She was such an aggressive smoker, inhaling loud and fast, the ember on her Benson & Hedges stretching in an angry burn, that Oisin often thought her lungs would burst with the pressure.

She wasn't sleeping. She would come to bed after Oisin and leave it before he did. By August, she'd stopped climbing up to the loft at all. At breakfast she would be wide-eyed and jumpy, never tired. He worried that she was sneaking out to meet boys, but whenever he checked, he found her crouched somewhere with a flashlight, writing furiously in her notebook. She hid this diary under her side of their mattress. Once, when she was outside pruning the bushes with the Aunts, Oisin pulled out the red notebook and let it fall open where it was marked. It was difficult to decipher, because her handwriting had sped up with the rest of her, and words were unfinished, their second halves an impatient scrawl. He was only able to read a couple of sentences before a noise downstairs made him shove it guiltily away.

I don't need to sleep anymore. I think this means I am no longer a child.

Though it made little sense to him, Oisin was disturbed. He had assumed Nieve's strangeness to be temporary, like puberty. But what if this new, frantic, removed person was merely the permanent, adult version of his sister? How would he ever manage to keep up with her? He was sure to be left behind.

O sin hadn't had sex since his ghostly rendezvous. There had been a series of ravenous kissing sessions, and finger-damaging struggles with the bra hooks of high school girls, who only seemed interested in him for an hour, and always in darkness.

In daylight he could have been a poster child for awkward adolescence—his skin resembling a dermatologist's diagram of the various stages of acne. He grew his hair long in an attempt to hide his prominent ears and bumpy face, but the grease from his head seemed to make his skin worse. He was still plagued by infections in his eyes, clumps of his eyelashes had fallen out completely, and this combined

with his picked skin often made his face look exposed and raw like a
burn victim's. Most girls looked at him with badly camouflaged disgust. He couldn't blame them, but he resented them nonetheless, resented their lush, flawless bodies (compared to him, everyone seemed
flawless) that he would never be allowed to see unclothed. At fifteen,
all he wanted in the world was access to a naked woman.

In Ireland, every girl who had ever tormented him seemed to amal-
gamate into his cousin. Sophie was the daughter of Aunt Maeve, who
lived in Australia, and she'd been sent to Ireland on some sort of pro-
bation. Oisin wasn't told what she was reforming from, but he could
guess. Seventeen, her breasts so large it was almost impossible to see
beyond them, she seemed to deposit sex everywhere she went, like the
glistening trail left by a slug. She was constantly straddling things—
fences, the backs of chairs, fallen tree limbs—and her mouth chewed
and sucked at itself furiously, as if it were impatient for something to
devour. Oisin spent his days tortured by a constant, painful erection;
sometimes he couldn't wait until nighttime to relieve it, and would
hide in the old fort Malachy had built, masturbating furiously into
the damp ground, barely breathing as he listened for approaching
footsteps.

Sophie had a boyfriend, Enda, a local boy with clear, milky skin
and straight black hair that flashed in the sun. One night, walking in
the graveyard, hoping to encounter his old ghostly lover, Oisin came
upon Sophie and Enda half-dressed and writhing beneath a tomb-
stone. Enda's hand was hidden in the fabric of Sophie's skirt, his arm
strained and obscenely muscled in the moonlight. He was thudding
his groin against her side, following the rhythm of his wrist, making
small, painful noises into the shadows of her neck. Sophie's underwear, strewn with childish flowers, was pulled halfway down her legs
and forgotten, stretched out of shape between her knees. She looked

straight at Oisin. She made no gesture of alarm or even recognition, but kept her eyes on him as if he were the logical place to be looking. She appeared amused and slightly bored, and seemed to be about to say something to Oisin when a thrust from Enda's hand transformed her. All at once, her neck arched, her eyes closed, her mouth fell open, her thin fingers pulled at his pale back. Somehow Oisin knew that it was not a show for his benefit, but that Enda, with his desperate prodding, had finally encountered, within Sophie's secret depths, a place that mattered. He left them there, Enda grunting, proud of himself, and Sophie rhythmically whispering what Oisin thought was either instructions or encouragement. He went back to his empty loft bed and spent the rest of the night stroking himself to the remembered cadence of her whispers, imagining that he knew exactly when, where, and how much to touch her to send her reeling.

In August, the Aunts received a hasty, misspelled letter from Sophie's mother. She had fallen in love with a German tourist and was now traveling with him, she would send for Sophie when they were settled. Enclosed was a picture of Aunt Maeve, with her dark MacDara beauty, and a short, unattractive but beaming man. Apparently, similar abandonment had occurred before, and Sophie, though quiet, didn't seem too concerned. The Aunts were furious; they huddled in smoke-haloed conferences, muttering in secret, indecipherable sister-language. Occasionally, one Aunt would lose her composure and Oisin would overhear a single sentence, and be left to fill in the rest on his own.

"It started in secondary school with that Ryan Kennedy."

"We're lucky if *she* knows who the father is."

"It's not as though she's the prize among us."

Oisin was intrigued by their jealousy. He watched their eyes glaze over, looking inward with dissatisfaction, and he wondered if they had ever been tempted to run away with inappropriate men. Perhaps every woman—despite the way they all ridiculed the opposite sex— had a secret part of her soul that lay waiting for a man to sweep her away. And if this was true, if it was possible for a froggy-eyed, ungracefully balding German man to seduce Aunt Maeve into delinquent flight, why couldn't Oisin get girls to look at him with anything but vetoed consideration?

One afternoon, after an hour of masturbating under dripping ferns, Oisin stumbled out of the fort and found Sophie straddling a tree trunk, watching him with the same inappropriate boldness she had when with Enda. Oisin, weak-kneed and mortified, tried to walk past her, but she blocked his way by extending one of her long legs. He had a brief impulse to grab her bare foot and insert it into the damp fly of his jeans.

"Do you think of me when you do that?" Sophie said, and Oisin backed away from the temptation of her foot.

"No!" he said, and he could hear the exaggerated, fearful protest in his tone. Sophie frowned.

"Why not?" she said, and he was instantly sorry for his answer. Could she possibly want him to fantasize about her? He was too flustered to take it back, too embarrassed to say, yes, every time, only you, and stood stupidly wordless for so long that she grew bored with him and lowered her leg. He heard her chuckling as he ran down the path.

He missed Nieve. Once, his sister would have teased him and then told him what to do, recommended skin products, divulged the secrets of girls, translated the signals that he could not read. Or maybe not. His twin resided within the foggy world of female mysteries. Perhaps even Nieve, like the rest of them, wanted to hoard everything that was distinctly female in a place that he could glimpse but never truly reach. Like a kiss that never went any further but cruelly suggested what the rest of her body might do.

Sara must have known that the Aunts' guard on Malachy would relax sooner or later, and when it did she was ready. One Friday night both Sara and her mother-in-law stayed home with colds, and the Aunts, freed from their watch, lost track of their gin limit. By the time Sara skipped into the crowd at midnight, the Aunts were drunk. Fiona was crying to herself between two old men at the bar, who were awkwardly patting her back and supplying her with hankies and gin. Dervla was planted in the lap of a local farmer, pretending to be interested in his talk of a new tractor, sliding her thigh against his hidden erection. Emer was singing, and had half the pub mesmerized by her angelic voice.

Oisin saw Sara come in, watched her move over to Malachy and whisper in his ear. Then she left again, smiling. Nieve was nowhere in sight; she had been lured away by one of her admirers. Oisin's father was out back struggling with an empty keg. Oisin watched, frozen, as Malachy walked out the door, as if pulled by an invisible string. He could have run for his father, could have roused the attention of his inebriated aunts. But there was a part of him that wanted to see his mother succeed, just enough to satisfy the wanting that came off her like an odor, the wanting which sometimes made her confuse Oisin with the man who could satisfy it. So when his father came in with the new keg and asked where Malachy had gone to, Oisin just shrugged and busied himself washing the creamy rims off the pint glasses.

The first thing Oisin noticed when his mother returned was blood. Blood covering her white eyelet blouse, dripping like wax onto her smooth legs. Then he saw Nieve. Malachy was with them, holding Nieve's arm in the air, her wrist wrapped in a handkerchief soaked black with more blood. They were surrounded in an instant, the Aunts shocked into sobriety, Declan rushing forward with clean towels. While Declan and Fiona tended Nieve's wound by the sink, Dervla and Emer pulled Malachy aside like a child in the way during an emergency. Oisin watched Fiona unwrap his sister's wrist, saw briefly a raw, almost beautiful wound, a slice that had just missed the delicate pulsing of a thin, bluish vein. He felt the shimmer of a déjà vu, but couldn't identify its origin. Nieve was laughing.

"I slipped, that's all. I scraped my wrist on the rocks."

Malachy was shaking his head at the scolding drone of his sisters, repeating himself in the hopes of being heard: "I was only trying to talk to her."

Fiona pulled a clean towel tight around Nieve's arm, holding it in the air while Declan went to ring the doctor. The bar had gone quiet, the customers filed out mumbling their thanks, men hurriedly finishing their pints. Sara came behind the bar and stood beside Oisin. Her eyes were flashing, looking almost black next to the flush on her face.

"She didn't slip," Sara said loudly.

No one reacted. It was as if they didn't hear her, though her voice was clear enough. All they did was become busier; Declan raised his voice on the phone, Fiona rewrapped Nieve's wound, the other Aunts ushered the protesting Malachy outside.

"She didn't slip," Sara said again. Oisin, who was now the only one listening to her, couldn't think of anything to say.

Nieve had five stitches put into her arm, after which the doctor whispered to Declan that the wound seemed "deliberately straight."

"Don't be daft," Declan replied.

The Aunts were angry with Sara—whether over Malachy or Nieve's accident, it wasn't clear—and there were murmured insults and glares on both sides. Malachy, after one furiously low-voiced conference with his mother, left for a music festival in Donegal.

The doctor gave Nieve tablets to help her sleep that night. Safe between the covers, alone with his sister at last, Oisin whispered above the sound of rain on the roof.

"Nieve? Did Mama hurt your arm?"

Nieve turned on her side to face him, and though her eyes were sedate, and her breathing drugged and heavy, he could feel the nervous motions of her feet, she was rubbing her arches together under the blanket. She used to do that when they were small, whenever she was too worried to sleep.

"I stopped them," she said. "They were about to do it. But I stopped them." Her voice was toneless, but he could sense another voice underneath it, coiled and vicious.

"But, Nieve," Oisin said, moving his feet to press hers still. The rubbing was driving him mad. "What happened to your wrist?"

She blinked at him—confused and, he thought, a little frightened.

"Oh that," she said, letting out the bark that had lately replaced her melodious laugh. "That was an accident." She began rubbing her feet again, kicking his out of the way.

"You should have seen Malachy's *face*," Nieve said. "He was unrecognizable. It's sex, Oisin. It does something horrid to you." She shivered, and for a moment he felt as he had when Rose showed him Sara's life—he could see through Nieve's eyes, and the world did look horrid. As horrid as the creatures that once sent him blind.

"Let's never, ever do that," Nieve said. "Not with anyone. Promise me."

And Oisin, afraid to answer and blurt out his confession, afraid that she would find him the most revolting of all, pretended to have fallen asleep.

18.

It's the first time in a month that Aisling has entered Gabe's room, and she finds him dissecting a dead dog.

She gasps, and Gabe looks up, his face half hidden by a blue Styrofoam mask. The carcass is stiff, its thin legs jutting upright in the air, and the smell of day-old death, so familiar, makes her gag.

"Whose . . . dog . . . is . . . that?" she says when her throat opens again. Gabe's arms are gloppy up to the elbows, making his latex gloves seem a useless precaution.

"It's a coyote," Gabe says. Above the mask his eyes are fighting between delight at her seeking him out and resentment for the past few weeks of desertion.

"I found it in the woods. I'm trying to determine cause of death before my mom gets home and makes me get rid of it." He nudges his glasses straight with one shoulder. "What do you want?" he adds, a bratty, betrayed note creeping into his voice.

"Gabe, that's . . . horrid," Aisling says. Gabe squints at her.

"You've seen me dissect things before," Gabe says. "You didn't think it was gross before you became a *woman*." He feels a twinge of shame when he sees that her face has gone gray with fear.

"Leave if you're so squeamish," he says, and though the anger has gone out of his voice, she slams the door behind her.

For a moment he considers going after her. But he thinks of the times he's seen her at the store, hanging all over sleazy Danny Mc-Gorey; she always pretends she doesn't even know him. So Gabe goes back to work.

"You *will* eat it," Darragh said to her, and his face went from pale and gaunt to red with frustration. Aisling was beyond words; she could only cry and shake her head.

"Aisling," Darragh said, kneeling next to her. He pried her hands away from her nose and mouth. She tried to breathe without her nostrils, fearing the stench which had already made her heave once.

"I'll only tell you one more time," Darragh said, his voice clipped. "They'll have surgeons waiting to inspect us. If we're ill, we won't be allowed on the ship. We have to walk for three days; if we don't eat now, either we won't make it, or we'll be turned away when we get there. Close your eyes, think of rabbit, and chew."

She glanced toward the headless carcass, hung by its skinny legs over the fire; the smell alone made her want to vomit. She could not even imagine eating it.

Darragh had meant to kill the dog and roast it before she knew what it was. But she had come upon him in the field, kneeling in a puddle of blood, preparing to skin the body, its furry white muzzle slit so deep that the head was almost off. A sheepdog, a fat one, which meant it belonged to one of the landlords. All of the tenants' dogs had starved to death a long time ago.

Dogs had always loved Darragh; it must have come up to him wagging its tail. She closed her eyes, trying not to picture it alive. The worst thing was, in the midst of her disgusted nausea, Aisling was still hungry, so hungry it felt like something was eating her from the inside out.

Darragh held a piece of gray, stringy meat out to her, and she covered her mouth again, backing away.

"Aisling," he said gently. "Please." When he stepped closer she knocked his hand away and the meat fell with a juicy smack onto the floor.

Darragh had never shown anger toward her. Many times she had watched him swallow rage, turn away from impatience, breathe deeply before he spoke. But now he was running after her, grabbing and jerking her arm so hard that she cried out with the pain.

"Do you want to die?" he screamed, and the rage in his voice paralyzed her. He dragged her over to the hearth, ripped a new piece of meat off, burning his fingers.

"Eat it," he said. She clamped her teeth so tight there was a throb in her temples. She wished herself invisible. But Darragh had always been able to see.

His open palm sent heat biting across her cheek. She'd been hit before, by her father, her sisters, and, of course, her mother; the hardest, most powerful hand. But Darragh's hand, which had always been so soft, hurt the worst. It was as if she'd been hit with love itself, and it stung more deeply than hate ever had.

Darragh stood over her for a moment; looking terrified, then turned and ran from the house. Crying and gagging, she knelt down and ate, barely chewing, until her stomach couldn't hold anymore.

When Darragh came home, he ate the rest, and, silently, they lay down to sleep to prepare for the journey ahead.

"Do you want to go without me?" Aisling whispered in the dark.

"Don't be daft," Darragh said. He held on to her tightly, as if trying to still her, though he was the one shaking.

Aisling had gone to see Gabe out of a vague belief that he might make her feel better. Gabe was odd, but he was real, and lately—though she is surrounded by people who can see her—she has been feeling as unreal and invisible as she did when she was a child or a ghost. Only now she is invisible to herself. Not completely, but in pieces, as though her image is wrought with gaping holes. She is trying to fill in the spaces with other people. If she knows what they see when they look at her, perhaps she will be able to see herself.

But Gabe no longer recognizes her. She hurt him by treating him like a child, while she gave all her attention to Danny and the girls. Gabe doesn't know that Danny is now beginning to bore her; that her mind changes so quickly she can't keep up. Gabe knows who he is. Aisling is a different person every ten minutes.

Though it began merely as an experiment, practice for what she imagines doing with Oisin, she still likes kissing Danny. What she likes is all wrapped up in physical details. The taste of his mouth, the taste of her mouth *on* his mouth, the burning sensation of stubble that leaves her chin raw and only wanting to kiss more. She likes how she can manipulate his mouth with the careful pressure of teeth, the tilt of her neck, or the teasing then plunging of her tongue. Kissing, unlike some of the groping they have embarked upon, has never been awkward for them. He is experienced and she is a natural. She smiles a lot, he grins and sighs. They can kiss for hours; it is a process, a story they trade back and forth all night in the dying, spark-filled light of a bonfire.

Their conversations don't go as well. Even when they first met, flirting in the lot of the general store, they looked at each other's mouths more than they listened to them. Danny is not much of a talker, and, at first, she liked this about him. His eyes and his posture told her much more than his words. He seemed to carry, within that lounging, catlike façade, a jumpy fear and deep-staining sadness that colored his view of the world. He reminded her of Oisin, the part of Oisin that had first reminded her of herself. Like he was waiting, somber and a little mistrustful, for someone to return.

Danny had lost his brother. Jake was five years old when he accidentally shot himself with his father's handgun. Danny, who was twelve at the time, had taken the gun out of its locked box to show his friends, and forgotten to put it back. A year later, his mother left them, and now he lives alone with his sloppy, drunken father. Aisling knows all of this not because Danny told her, but because of the little boy, with Danny's huge dark eyes in a thin face, who sometimes watches them kissing on the sand. When Danny gets so stoned that he falls asleep, Aisling replaces his dreams of a bloody, featureless face with the giggling ghost of his brother, filling the silence with the same infectious, deep-rooted laughter that once never failed to make his whole family smile.

Sometimes, when she's been kissing Danny for so long that their eyes have gone lazy, that the smell of pine trees, ocean, and burning oak has become a part of the taste in their mouths, she wants to freeze the moment. Imprint the curve of Danny's cheekbone glowing orange in the firelight, record the look of wonder that sometimes comes over his face. Eventually, though, she always remembers, with a combination of guilt and resentment, that Danny is only a boy, a boy she is using as a surrogate for the man she really wants, a boy she is leaving behind as she grows beyond him.

She would like to stop growing; to savor an age for longer than a few weeks; to hold still long enough that she can step back and see who she is, capture the truest of the multiple girls she has become.

Aisling's bare feet had blistered on the first day, and by the time they stopped for the night, the blisters had burst and begun to bleed. Darragh washed her feet, thick with dust and dried blood, in a small stream by the roadside, then ripped one sleeve off his shirt to use for a bandage.

"You need shoes," he mumbled, tying the strips of cloth around her arches. "Perhaps we'll find some on the way."

In the morning she told him she felt better, and tried not to flinch with every step. She would rather shred her feet than wear shoes pried off of one of the stiff bodies lining the road.

With the sea on their right, and a dozen purple and brown mountains receding in the distance on their left, they trudged on, passing villages that had either died or been abandoned, stepping over the swollen, black-faced bodies that had failed to complete similar journeys. One morning it snowed, just enough to soothe her burning soles. At every crossroads, they met up with others on their way to Galway; once Aisling rode for an hour on a donkey-pulled cart full of emaciated, elderly women. She soon chose to walk again because the smell of death in the hay and blankets was making her ill.

Darragh talked with the men. Those who weren't raging with fever were optimistic. Their landlords had bought their passage and promised them acres of farmland in Canada. They talked of the New

World as if it were a place with no sickness, poverty, or even hunger. Aisling wanted to believe them, but she could see by Darragh's face that he was skeptical.

"Is there really free land in Canada?" she asked him that night, while he rebandaged her feet with his other sleeve.

"No," Darragh said harshly, but he forced a smile when he saw her face. "But there is food."

They arrived in Galway on the fourth day. Aisling had never been to a big town, had never seen so many buildings, people, and horses in one place. Country people were wandering around in rags, begging for food or the price of a boat ticket. But there were rich people as well, handsome men in complicated, unwrinkled clothing, checking the time at the ends of gleaming watch chains, smoking, laughing, and speaking English beneath their perfectly trimmed mustaches. There were women with parasols and huge dresses that looked like they'd been sewn from fields of wild, dark flowers. And there were carts, drawn by healthy horses, carts filled to overflowing with barrels of wheat, crates of vegetables, and limp chickens, live pigs tied squealing to the side slats.

"Darragh," Aisling said. He was trying to lead them through the spaces between people and carts. "There's food here." He tightened his grip on her hand.

"That's for export," he said, looking hungrily at a passing cart. "Not for us."

Then Aisling saw men riding alongside the barrels, holding guns at their shoulders and glaring at the mob.

"I don't understand," said Aisling, and Darragh put his hand on her hair.

"I don't expect you to," he said, and they continued to wind through the streets, heading, along with the crowds, toward the sea.

It is Labor Day weekend, and Deirdre's nieces are packing to go home. When they'd arrived, Aisling had been slightly shorter than Jemma; now she is an inch taller than Colette. They all envy what they think is a normal growth spurt. Aisling watches them pack, accepting their gifts solemnly, as though they are dying rather than going back to school in Boston. Colette bequeaths her the lucky sweater—the blue chenille that has been removed from each of them by various boys at bonfires over the summer. Mags donates her favorite barrette, a red spider that grips her hair with delicate rhinestone legs. Jemma parts, with obvious hesitation, with the summer's fought-over lipstick—a wooden stick sharpened down to its final nub, in a color that has been discontinued. It looks better on Jemma than the rest of them, because of her full, dark lips, but Aisling accepts it anyway. She is comforted by the idea that she is being left with things that have touched all of them—as if the qualities she admires in these girls will be left for her to glean from fabric, plastic, and wood.

In the beginning, she had wanted to be Colette. Small-chested and sleek, self-assured posture, a lazy, confident smile that said she was older, past the stages that her sisters were floundering in. Aisling had tried straightening her spine, maintaining a bored expression, pretended to think of herself as *steady*. But she kept slumping over, giggling with Jemma, blushing under the gazes of boys who Colette thought were immature.

She began to like Mags more then—her tomboy strut, freckled, glowing skin that she never powdered, most likely to say things so shocking that other teens either admired or feared her. She had a loud, sexy voice that drowned out all others; she laughed with a defiant cackle.

Aisling failed quickly at imitating Mags. Her own liquid walk (she moved like she was floating, though she didn't know it) could not be turned into a strut—she jerked and tripped whenever she attempted a tomboy's stride. She was still too cautious to say anything shocking; her old instinct to listen from the sidelines made her quiet in conversation. By the time her mind formed a Mags-like comment, it was too late to articulate it. She was often asked why her mouth was hanging open.

Jemma, Aisling found, was impossible to emulate because of how unconscious her mannerisms were. She was sexy without knowing it, enjoyed being inside her own body so much that it made others want to join her there. The attention she got from boys was a pleasant but not so important surprise to her. She was highly sensitive; the world's pain seemed to seep in alongside her breath, and she had not yet figured out that not everyone felt the pain of others so deeply. When Aisling tried to worry about the world, it seemed too big and alien to empathize with. She worried about herself, about Oisin, and occasionally about her neighbors who were mourning dead loved ones that she could give back to them with a touch. (The Molloy girls never called to the dead; they hadn't known Gabe's father well, and hadn't lost anyone they loved yet.) Aside from ghosts, she couldn't bring herself to cry about people she couldn't *touch*. Jemma could cry for anyone.

As Aisling watches them pack—Colette folding in exact geometric squares, Mags sitting on a suitcase too full to latch, and Jemma, so often distracted that she has barely started—she realizes, not for the first time, that she can't ask them the question that is plaguing her. Don't you ever wonder who you are?

She had believed originally that her uncertainties were a part of youth. But now she thinks that perhaps there is a soul-based confusion in her that does not exist in these girls. They change their fashions, fall in and out of love with boys and ideas, but they know who they are. They have roles, definitions, entire lives in which to hone their personalities. Colette is the oldest and her mission is order. Mags needs to shake things up. Jemma's senses guide her. Like Gabe, or Darragh, they often wonder what they should do, but rarely question who they are while doing it. Aisling thinks that there are two different kinds of people in the world: those who know themselves and others who flounder in a forest of cast-off definitions and dreams. It does not end with childhood. Oisin, she feels, though he's already going gray, is still haunted by who he once was, who he wanted to be, and who he has become.

But Oisin won't talk to her about it. He won't touch her and, no matter what he says, she knows it is a rejection. Doesn't he know she will never be real unless he wants her?

The Molloy girls know about her desire for Oisin (they think she is the daughter of Oisin's friend and are romantic enough to ignore propriety), and they advise her on how to appear sexy, though each of them have different theories. Colette thinks she should tempt and play hard to get, Jemma votes for candlelit confessions. It was Mags who gave Aisling the idea of using Danny to make Oisin jealous while practicing the essentials. She has tried it all, nothing has worked. She suspects Deirdre would have better advice, but can't ask for fear she would be appalled rather than enthusiastic.

Tired of packing, the girls gather on Colette's bed and talk about what to do on their last night together. (There is nothing to do but go to the store and the bonfires, but they always discuss it as if there were options.) Aisling seethes silently with envy for them. This summer was their holiday; they are returning to a life that has a past and future, full of recognizable touchstones. Aisling's past is another world, her present an ungraspable flux, and she may not have a future. Soon she will have to leave. She is being slowly called back to the dead, which is why, she believes, it has become easier to see them. They interrupt her constantly now, asking her to bring them to those they left behind.

She hates these girls mostly because they will go on living. And though these months have been a gift—though she has had the chance to taste the life she lost long ago, it is not enough. It will never be enough.

The surgeon, an unpleasant-looking man with gray hair, had put a hand on her forehead, poked his fingers below her jaw, and opened her mouth, peering inside. He grunted, then performed the same examination on Darragh. Standing a distance away, Aisling noticed how dreadful her brother looked. His face was skeletal and tinged with yellow, his eyes had grown huge and sad, retreating into pits behind his cheekbones. She wondered if she also looked so near to death.

The surgeon passed them on, and they were sent to a sailor sitting at a table laid with a quill, some paper, and a bag of money. Darragh gave him coins from a small sack tied to his waist beneath his tattered shirt. Aisling opened her mouth to ask him where he had found money, but thought of the dog and closed it again. She didn't want to know what Darragh had been forced to do to get them here.

The man counted the coins, dropped them in his bag, then, in English, asked Darragh for their names. Aisling watched him write them down on a list divided into columns.

Quinn, Darragh, age 19, farmer/laborer.
Quinn, Aisling, age 7, orphan.

"Your rations are six pints of water and a pound of meal per day," the man said to Darragh without looking up. "The girl gets one-third that. The water is for drinking, cooking, and washing, so be mean with it."

"Thanks very much," Darragh said through his teeth, pulling Aisling along. They boarded the ship on a rickety walkway, Aisling peering at the waste-clogged water below the planks. She was almost excited, though so hungry that even smiling made her tired.

"*Tír na nÓg,*" she whispered to Darragh, pointing at the name on the front of the ship. "The Land of Eternal Youth." Darragh had told her the story: a white horse in the waves, a woman with hair made of gold, a handsome warrior leaving the world of death behind him.

"Don't be fooled," Darragh said coldly. "They changed the name. In all likelihood this was once a slave ship. We'll be lucky to survive the passage."

Aisling stood on deck, looking out to the bay and the ocean beyond. The sun was shining, the sea air was cold on her cheeks, and she knew they were saved. She tried to remember when Darragh had lost his optimism and become the dour, morbid old man who stood beside her. A few days at sea would bring him back, she thought. Until then, she would have to be the hopeful one.

On the girls' last night, Aisling wears the chenille fooling-around sweater. They arrive at the bonfire late enough that a few girls and a dozen boys are already slugging beer and feigning expressions of refreshment. Danny doesn't come straight to her; it will be twenty minutes before he pretends to accidentally sidle over to her group. Once, Aisling found this exciting and slightly dreadful; waiting to see if he still wanted her. Now she thinks the whole thing is silly, childish. Everyone knows they are a couple, what is the point of ignoring each other when in a hour they'll be lying together on the bed of someone's pickup?

She would really rather spend tonight with the girls, be absorbed into the amoeba of perfume, tan limbs, and giggles, separate from the jealous eyes of boys who watch and wait hopefully. But Colette and Jemma wander away with their own partners, and Mags pairs off with a new boy she's been eyeing since last week, ignoring the betrayed stance of Jimmy Noonan, who had great plans for their last night together. Aisling lets herself be led into the shadows by Danny's thin, sweaty hand.

An hour later, when he asks if he can take her sweater off, she lets him, not because she wants to, but because she's tired of protesting. Until now she has only let him push her shirt up to her chin and grope beneath the bra that he doesn't seem to know how to unfasten. Apparently, someone has coached him recently, because this time he manages to strip them both to the waist. And though the cold air on her naked back, and Danny's skinny but soft chest against her breasts, feels lovely in its own way—a little as if she'd been set free from the ground and is flying—she can't help feeling annoyed. Danny's breathing is panicked and loud and his hands are moving too fast. She has an overwhelming urge to push him away and snap: *Calm down!* She cannot lose herself in this; she's not sure she even likes this boy. And the fact that he doesn't know this, that he is oblivious to her ambivalence in the midst of his wanting, makes her despise him. In a minute she will stop, put her bra and sweater back on, let him hold her hand on the ride home. But for now, she closes her eyes and tries to imagine that Danny's fumbling hands are the scarred, heat-filled palms of Oisin—hands that once bandaged her small, bleeding feet. Just as she knows every line of his hands, he knows exactly how she needs to be touched. Because he is the only one who remembers who she was as a child.

19.

In August, the Aunts decided that Sophie should go to Boston with Declan's family. A month had gone by with no word from her mother, and they were worried about Sophie, who showed signs of becoming one of those floundering small-village girls—drunkenly promiscuous and lacking ambition. (The Aunts were in favor of romance as long as it didn't interfere with self-sufficiency.) America would be a firm slap—it would wake her up and show her that she had choices in the world.

So, after his father went back to sea, Oisin's nights were no longer filled with ghosts. They were still there, hiding like shadows in the corners of his house, but he didn't have the time for them. His dark hours were ruled by women.

Sophie began coming to his room. The couch bed was lumpy, she was cold, she was not used to sleeping alone . . . could she crawl in with him for a while? She would spoon herself against his back, her breasts teasing his shoulder blades, while Oisin lay awake, willing away his erection, trying so hard not to tremble that in the mornings he was exhausted, his muscles jumpy and sore. Sometimes, in her sleep, Sophie would murmur and writhe against him. If he was very careful, he could turn to face her, and her unintentional rubbing would lead him to a brief, lip-biting release, followed by hours of guilt. He started washing his pajama bottoms in the wee hours once again.

Nieve rarely left her room, but he knew she wasn't sleeping. On his trips to the bathroom, Oisin saw the glow of candlelight in the crack under her door, and heard her muttering. Sometimes her voice would rise—"I'm *fine!*" she would sneer—and then fall quiet, as if she had just remembered the late hour. Oisin assumed she was on the phone with one of her friends: no longer the beautiful people, now the moody misfits who smoked and drank in the alcoves of the school. But one night he lifted the hall receiver delicately and heard only a dial tone. He hurried back to his room, embarrassed and slightly afraid. Who was she talking to?

In bed, with Sophie breathing shivers onto his neck, Oisin would hear his sister prowling the kitchen. Drawers opening on rollers, a toaster humming warmth, the soft thuck of the freezer door opening. He knew it was Nieve because Sara didn't eat anymore; she drank so continuously, she couldn't be bothered with solids. Though his mother and Nieve had ceased to cook anything, Sara still went shopping once a week buying only foods that required no preparation. Breakfast cereal, corn chips, ice cream, canned spaghetti, cold cuts, hot dogs. So Oisin and Sophie snacked in spurts, standing by the kitchen sink, rolling up bologna slices and guzzling cans of Coke. Nieve ate at night, when no one was looking, always one type of food in large quantities. In the morning, a whole box of cereal would be gone, or all the ice cream, or a block of orange cheese. If offered food,

Nieve refused with a look of disgusted betrayal, pretending that eating didn't interest her.

Sara drank every night and was passed out by the time they all left for school. By afternoon, when the bus brought them home, she was drunk again. Oisin ignored her. The years of enduring her probing, sweaty hands, her desperate grasping for love, were over. He had another life now. Sophie, a senior at the high school, had created a new reputation for Oisin. Her attention in the halls had caused girls to look at him with wary interest. Often he was the only boy at a picnic table of gum-cracking, hair-brushing senior girls, who touched and teased him and gave free advice on kissing and how to tell if a woman wants to have sex. He was a pet, a mascot, and though he suspected he should feel humiliated, he loved it. For the first time in his life, women were paying attention to him.

And when Sophie started to touch him—when their spooning nights turned into a game of invitation and advance, protest and retreat; when each session in his dark room uncovered a new soft or wet part of Sophie's body—Oisin's remaining concerns for his mother and sister vanished like retreating ghosts.

It was with Sophie that Oisin learned the steps that led up to sex. When he was older, and the women he dated were no longer concerned with keeping him waiting, he would forget that sex had once required an elaborate dance through prerequisite stages. That kissing had once been a parody of what he could not do—mouths growing wider, wetter, his tongue plunging the way he wanted to with his cock. As an adult, every moment blurred into sex; as a boy, every second hinted at it.

Sophie was a virgin. Oisin was surprised and disappointed; he had imagined immediate entrance but what he got was an obstacle course with shifting boundaries. For one week, he and Sophie lay with their shirts off, until tentative touching and kissing led to rolling around in frustration, the sweaty fronts of their pajama bottoms meeting for brief moments of muffled ecstasy. Then came the night where Sophie allowed him to creep his hand past the waistband of her underwear, and he probed for an eternity, the landscape growing more slippery, his wrist numb from the pinch of elastic on the panties she wouldn't let him remove. At first she kissed him consistently, hiding her reactions in his mouth, later she let him watch her face as he pushed his fingers in and out of her. Oisin learned the rules quickly. It was his job to venture forward, hers to let it happen or to stop him. He resented this arrangement, but went along with it. He didn't know what he was doing, this was obvious when he moved too fast or too hard or the wrong way, and she pushed at him with tiny noises of discomfort or protest. Every few times there was something new—less clothing, closer bodies, mouths moving down to kiss new territory. Each night the stages were replayed, until the moment Sophie decided whether they would go on to the next. The session inevitably concluded with Sophie breaking away, then both of them would lie there, sprawled and sweaty, conscious of their breathing, not touching until the tornado of sensations calmed down. After a nap, they would start again from the beginning.

One morning, after a sleepless night during which Sophie had let him come in her mouth for the first time, Oisin, gratefully fetching her a glass of water, encountered Nieve in the kitchen. She was fishing pickles out of a jar with a thin fork. For an instant, he forgot the recent distance between them, and he smiled at Nieve, his face revealing everything, as though he were a little boy again, when nothing was real until he shared it with her.

Nieve glared at him until his happy flush was humiliated into scarlet.

"You disgust me," she whispered, and Oisin was hurt first, then angry, and finally felt something beyond them both.

For his entire life, Oisin had witnessed his parents trading low blows, seen his cousins and his aunts pierce one another with the words they knew would hurt the most. Loved ones seemed so able to zero in on the most vulnerable spot. He and Nieve had been the exception. Now Oisin, normally mute when cornered, felt a sudden, frightening, almost erotic hatred for his sister.

"I'm not the disgusting one," he spat, and walked away. The pickle jar shattered on the doorjamb of his room, and he heard a high, ghostly wail, but by then, nauseous with what he had done, he had already closed the door.

O isin's father came home for a week in November, and the house sparkled briefly with new life. Sara sobered up just enough to cook a real dinner, and treated Declan like an old boyfriend rather than the husband she'd despised for years. Even Nieve seemed better. She came out of her room more, her hair was washed, and she abandoned the oversized sweatshirt of Oisin's that had recently become her uniform—sleeves gnawed into tatters, carrying a sweet, limp smell that had always made Oisin think of turned soil. She even smiled, a bit stiffly, when she first saw her father. Declan couldn't hide his delight. Oisin didn't have the heart to tell him that this wasn't their normal family, that his mother and sister had cleaned up temporarily like asylum patients receiving visitors for the first time in years.

On Saturday night, Declan took Sara out to a party. She dressed in silk; her hair was newly colored, and makeup almost disguised the premature aging caused by gin. Oisin watched her preening in the hallway mirror, and, for an instant, was five years old again. He and Nieve were in footed pajamas, waiting for the baby-sitter, watching their mother slide lipstick onto her smile. Back when they thought it was normal that their parents, who didn't seem to love each other, could be married; when Oisin and Nieve imagined themselves special—the only two people in the world who were truly loyal to each other—because they were twins.

Oisin turned from his mother and almost bumped into Nieve.

"Seeing ghosts?" Nieve whispered. Before she walked away, Oisin saw, beneath the clean hair and new clothes, that something was still wrong. He thought again about his mother's family—the long line of destructive anguish that Rose had shown him. Though Nieve, of course, was stronger than his mother. Still, maybe he would tell his father, tomorrow, after the hangovers had worn off, that Nieve was not snapping back into herself. Though if Oisin couldn't help, what could Declan possibly do?

Oisin went back to his room to wait, listening for his parents' clicking shoes into the night, and for Nieve to close herself in her room. Right now, he wanted them all to disappear, because tonight was the night he'd been waiting for. Sophie had been taking birth control pills, and they were finally going to stop stopping, and have sex.

Tell me you love me," Sophie whispered.

Their last pieces of clothing were off, the mercurial boundaries had faded, he wasn't going to be told to pull away—she was inviting him in. There were only words between him and the tight ecstasy he had once known in a graveyard. The words were easy; he said them over and over.

"Love you," he whispered against her lips, kissing her lightly all over her face and neck. "Loveyou loveyou loveyou," gently, gruffly, beautifully. He sounded so convincing that he shivered along with her.

And there he was. Up against a barrier it was his job to break. It would hurt, there might be blood—they'd read about everything in a book Sophie had borrowed from a friend. She looked terrified, all her wantonness had vanished, and she was holding stiffly onto the sheets, as if she was expecting a surgical knife rather than his cock. Oisin closed his eyes and prepared to plunge. Then the air in the room changed, and he knew they weren't alone. There was a ghost in his room, watching them.

"What's the matter?" Sophie whispered when Oisin crawled off her and sat tensely on the edge of the bed.

"Quiet," Oisin hissed, and then laid his hand on her thigh in an absent apology.

Somebody was crying.

"What now?" Oisin barked at the air. Sophie, who knew about Oisin's gift, but had never seen him looking into the invisible like that, pulled the sheet up to her neck and scurried against the wall.

"Jesus," Oisin addressed the dark. "You have all of eternity, you couldn't wait another fifteen minutes?"

The air in his room was shining, vibrating with the ghostly quality that made life—even sex—seem dead by comparison. The voice was so quiet and mournful, it was sending shivers down Oisin's back. Something like this had happened before. This ghost was not crying for herself. She was crying for him.

"All right, Oisin," Sophie said. "I'm scared now. Make it go away."

"I just have to check something," Oisin mumbled. He pulled on his jeans and told Sophie to stay put, opening the doorway of his room. The kitchen was dark except for beams of snowy light, intersected by the shadow of window grids. He hadn't noticed that it was snowing, but a glance out the window showed him the bushes were already weighed down with three inches. His parents were not home yet; their bedroom door was open, the bed still strewn with Sara's rejected outfits. The crying was fainter now, winding down, which, strangely, made him panic. There was no candle glow from under Nieve's door, but yellow light pierced the hallway from the bathroom doorframe.

"Don't ever disturb a lady in the bathroom," his mother had always said. He remembered how he had once stood in this spot, holding his crotch, jumping from leg to leg in an attempt to dislodge the pressure, waiting for Nieve to open the door. Now he stepped forward and rapped on the peeling panel.

"Nee, you gonna be much longer?" he said. His voice was wobbly.

After a decent interval, he knocked louder and tried the knob. It wasn't locked. He entered slowly, averting his eyes for modesty. He thought he heard a startled intake of breath, and later he would wonder whose it had been.

There was so much blood that at first he saw nothing else. Then he noticed a limp head against the terry-cloth tub rest, an arm sliced open in one long, perfect line, sprawled over the tub edge, dripping into a red pond. A *body* in the tub, the arm lifeless, frozen in an attempt to get out. He closed his eyes for a minute. But, he thought— and this thought would repeat in him all his life—he was still alive, he had to open them again.

As he knelt in the scarlet pond, looking at his sister who was still wearing her white flannel pajamas, gone pink and floating away from her body, the fabric bubbling toward the surface; before he left the house and, with his jeans red and sucked against his shins, ran to where his parents were drunkenly dancing with their neighbors; before he began to shriek like a banshee, so loudly his father had to hit him;

before he was sedated for insisting Nieve was not dead because he hadn't seen her ghost; before he had sex with Sophie, though he felt nothing and she cried the whole time; before all that, Oisin's thoughts were calm and very simple.

He remembered being a little boy, so little that his sister was the only person he could see without tipping his head all the way back. They were at the park, in the sandbox, and Nieve was bleeding. She had scraped her arm on a buried shard of broken glass, and for a moment, before they went to tell their mother, the two of them sat and watched her bleed. They were not scared. It was almost lovely; slow drops formed grainy maroon balls in the sand. Nieve looked at Oisin, and he knew what she was thinking before she said it.

"How come you're not bleeding, too?" she asked.

PART FOUR

Fall

On Raglan Road on an autumn day I saw her first and knew

That her dark hair would weave a snare that I might one day rue;

I saw the danger, yet I walked along the enchanted way,

And I said, let grief be a fallen leaf at the dawning of the day.

PATRICK KAVANAGH

"Raglan Road"

20.

This isn't going to work, she thinks, but she pulls his covers aside anyway. Oisin sleeps on, his back to her, his knees bent like a child curled up against a nightmare. The mattress creaks as she lies down, but he doesn't stir. She pulls herself against him slowly, carefully, curving her knees into the angles behind his, her stomach pressing his lower back, her nose just at the point where his hair leaves off to his neck. She inhales, and there is the smell she loves in his sweatshirts: fire, ink, wax, the cold, sweet odor of dying leaves. Her hand crawls over his hip to cradle his stomach; he is so warm, so solid, so real—she would like to press until his flesh opens up and swallows her whole.

This is not the way she imagined it—tricking him into touching her. But she doesn't have much time left, and it is all she wants.

Her arm makes him stir. He mumbles, sighs, arches his hips so his bottom presses tight to her abdomen. She lowers her hand, and, for an instant, he helps her, his palm guiding her down to the warmest place, where he wants, the part that throbbed against her that one time before he pulled away.

Then he grabs her hand with a different sort of urgency, and she knows he is fully awake.

He shakes off her arm, kicks back the covers, and leaps away from the bed, all in barely enough time for her to take a breath.

"Aisling," he says. "What the hell?" She thought he might be angry, but he merely sounds scared. She pulls the sheet over her head and squeezes her eyes tight. Bad idea, bad idea, she chants to herself, and with each syllable she thumps her head back on the mattress.

"Aisling," Oisin says; he has recovered to a scolding tone. "Get back to your own bed."

"I can't." She peeks out from under the sheet. He is standing in his boxer shorts, hunched over, hands in front of his crotch as if he desperately needs to pee. "I'm not wearing anything," she adds.

"Jesus!" Oisin says, and he runs away, his bare feet slapping the floorboards, the fan-light whirring into life as he closes himself in the bathroom. She hears the moan of pipes and the first splatters of the shower. He is washing her off.

She gets out of bed and canters over to her side of the room, pulling on the first thing she grabs: a flannel, ankle-length night-gown that Oisin gave her, with girlish frills at the neck and cuffs. She hates this nightgown—it twists into a straitjacket while she sleeps.

Oisin stays in the shower for a long time, and when he comes out, wrapped tightly in a fleece robe, she pretends to be asleep. She listens as he stops in the middle of the room, feels him watching her the way he's done every night since she arrived. Lately, she had hoped he was looking at her with longing, but now she knows she's been stupid. He watches her with caution, with awe, with a little resentment, but he is still watching a little girl. He doesn't want her any more than he did in the beginning.

She slips away when dawn comes peeking through the thin frost on his windows.

For the first week, *Tír na nÓg* was a haven of order and discovery. Before the human smells took over, the hold where they slept was sweet with bleeding timber—a memory of the forest that had traveled to England from Canada. Aisling, who had never seen more than a few trees clumped together in one place, imagined Quebec to be a fairyland; they would be shaded there, safe beneath the guarding arms of a forest.

Each morning she woke next to Darragh on a hard, narrow bunk, and together they climbed up to the clean, misty air and the vast freedom of the open water. There was food—disgusting meal cakes burned to the consistency of rock—but food nonetheless, every day, enough to lower her hunger to the level of bearable. Once, a woman gave Darragh some of her secret stash of bacon, saying he had the face of her son who had died. Darragh gave it all to Aisling, who gobbled it before she thought to save him half.

Many were seasick; Aisling often met passengers retching over the sides on her journey around the ship. She was a natural sailor, knowing instinctively how to balance herself in a wave-strewn world. Darragh volunteered as a deckhand, and Aisling was allowed to shadow him, practicing the sailor's knots he showed her with old, shredded strips of rope.

In the evenings, the hold was crowded but joyful. The glow from lanterns created long shadows between the tall bunks and hanging clothing. Different conversations melded into a drone that changed like music as she walked across the floor. She never spoke to anyone, tried to remain invisible, but occasionally a woman would smile at her, a man wink and nod. One boy with a whistle often played tunes before bedtime, and the healthiest passengers danced, the fatigued ones clapping and singing if they could. Aisling often caught Darragh smiling in the old way, and this more than anything convinced her that the worst was over.

Then there was the first storm.

The crew locked the passengers in the hold as the ship screamed and bucked against the sea. No lights were allowed and the darkness was as thick and palpable as the smell. Fear, sweat, and rancid breath was soon eclipsed by tart vomit and the warm, cloying odor of tipped chamber pots. Belongings flew back and forth like cannonballs, cracking against the walls or thudding into flesh, producing screams of agony. Babies wailed until they sounded like they were drowning, choking on their own tears. When they weren't being thrown off their feet, people called for a doctor, for food, for air, until their voices were too hoarse to be heard over the sea. A group of men tried to shoulder their way through the door to the deck, until they heard gunfire and the voices of the crew, promising to shoot anyone who came out.

Darragh used Aisling's knotting rope to tie them both to the vertical planks of their bottom bunk. Aisling, fastened to his lap, drifted in and out of an anxious, cramp-ridden sleep, jolted awake by wailing, screaming seas, and once by a hard object that slammed into her forehead. She felt warm liquid oozing into her eyes and thought at first she'd been hit by a chamber pot, until she realized she was bleeding. Darragh pressed his hand on the wound until the sticky flow subsided. When she had to pee, unable to hold it any longer, she asked Darragh to untie her.

He refused. "I can't let you go," he said. His voice was deeply muffled in the stormy dark. "Do what you need to. It doesn't matter now."

So Aisling let her bladder flow, soaking her skirt and her brother's lap, stimulating a responsive stream from him. She cried silently as they soiled each other, again and again, for ten indistinguishable days, until the sea calmed with a sigh, and they crawled up out of their filthy, sightless world.

Aisling sits in a kaleidoscope of deeply colored leaves. She lights a match, guides it to the tip of the cigarette cushioned in her lips. The tobacco and paper fire up with a comforting sizzle. She pulls with her mouth, a gesture that reminds her of kissing, and inhales, holds, exhales, following a rhythm that temporarily drowns the screaming in her head.

This is why people smoke, she thinks: it makes the unbearable bearable for five minutes. She lights another cigarette on the volcano tip of her last. The packet she stole from Danny is almost finished, she needs to get another from the store. Perhaps she will buy a carton.

Oisin's fort, a lattice of branches strung between two trees, where she first woke to the world, is where she now sleeps. She sleeps all day, falling into a heavy, muffled unconsciousness that she couldn't escape from if she wanted to. She doesn't want to; being awake has become too difficult.

During the few snatches of the day where she actually sits up, her head throbbing with trapped blood, she smokes and thinks about hunger. She hasn't been eating. Purposeful hunger feels much different from the starvation she remembers. Her emptiness now has a soothing quality, it slows her down, puts her to sleep, there is none of the panic over where to forage her next meal. Food is unnecessary. This much she remembers: you are supposed to be tired and hungry just before you die.

Oisin hasn't come for her yet—he is working again, locked in his studio. At night, when she is driven home by the cold (she has grown too accustomed to shelter) she peeks through the window and sees him sketching or carving metal with manic energy. He sleeps on a cot in his studio and is usually back at work by the time she leaves for the fort in the morning. Her footsteps fail to make him glance up. She knows now that despite the emptiness she sensed in him all along, he does not need her. He has his prints, just as Gabe has his experiments, and Darragh had books. Everyone has something, some bit of life they can cling to that is their own. Everyone but her.

She has done this wrong. She wrapped her new life up in hopes for others, when she should have tried to glean something out of herself. People are alone in life, just as in death, and what a waste of time it is to try to change that. She should have built her own cabin in the wilderness, adopted a dog whose needs were easy to meet, written her life story on thick, cream-colored paper. Given up the childish dream of being wanted.

Of course, now that she is determined to be alone, she is constantly interrupted. Gabe comes to see her after school, his bright backpack blindingly modern in her primitive little world. He brings her snacks from his Leonardo da Vinci lunchbox—waxy apples, cookies shaped like buffalo, miniature plastic bins of crackers and cheese. All she wants is cigarettes, but Gabe is not allowed to buy them. She has resorted to stealing Oisin's tobacco, because she lacks the energy to hike to the shop. The cigarettes she rolls are warped and hollow, and the paper unravels before she can smoke the whole thing. Gabe brings her a picture of cancerous lungs from his medical textbook.

"I'm already dead," she says, and he puts the glossy page back in his bag.

Gabe often spends the entire afternoon sitting beside her, oblivious to her glares that are meant to drive him away. If she were still his age, she would trade cruelty for privacy, but now that his head reaches only to her shoulder, she feels a resentful protectiveness. She can't bear to tell him to go right to his face—his features are too soft, too young. This must be how Darragh felt, and Oisin. So she leaves Gabe propped against the tree and crawls into the fort, scrunching so she can fit, and escapes into sleep.

"My mom did that," Gabe says one afternoon as she nuzzles down on her bed of moldy leaves. Aisling pretends not to hear him, but he goes on.

"Slept all the time. After my father died. It's a symptom of depression, though not as common as insomnia." He is using his science voice, a high-pitched parody of the grown-up doctor he will become.

"Eventually you'll have to get up," he says. "Everyone does."

You're so wrong, Aisling thinks as she hears him walk away, swishing his feet in the leaves.

It was sometime during the first storm that fever infected the ship. Once the filth and debris were shoveled out of the hold, and their clothing was washed with seawater, dried to itchy planks on their backs, Aisling could smell it. Putrid and black, the odor of food rotting under soil, of bodies decaying from the inside out. Darragh helped drag the corpses up on deck. Twenty had died during the storm, a few from broken bones and bleeding, others swollen and stiff, like discolored dolls, marked black and purple by a disease they thought they had left behind. The bodies were wrapped in meal sacks

and tossed overboard. Aisling, expecting pleas and prayers, was frightened by the silence, the vacant expressions of those left alive. One
woman rolled herself over the side, cradling the wrapped body of her
child, as casually as if she were shifting position in sleep. Sharks began
to follow the ship, smooth dark bodies, beautiful and menacing in
their speed.

Darragh's newly resurrected smile had vanished. He was back to
planning, his eyes darting around in search of escape. His voice was
flat and demanding as he instructed Aisling: all day, every day it was
possible, they were to remain on deck in the open air. At night, locked
in the hold, Darragh tied a piece of old sailcloth, soaked in seawater,
over Aisling's nose and mouth. Aisling was either stiff and sharply
cold, pacing miserably beside Darragh on the rocking planks of the
deck, or swollen in the dark heat below, gasping for breath through
the damp, heavy mask. Every morning, more corpses were swallowed
by the sea; one day it was the ship's surgeon who was wrapped in a
torn sail and splashed into his grave. Darragh took it upon himself to
show the children whose parents were ill how to wipe their faces, tip
water into their swollen, bleeding mouths.

The sea was gray and endless, each day the horizon so empty, Aisling often imagined they were stagnant in the water. She leaned over
the bow to watch streaking foam, reassuring herself that they were
still moving. Four weeks passed; they were due in Canada but no land
or birds appeared. Meal and water rations were cut by half, and Aisling's stomach began chewing again with hunger.

"How much longer?" the children asked Darragh daily; he had the
most English and was not afraid to question the crew. Darragh repeatedly shook his head. No one knew.

During storms, in the dark cave of screaming, both sea and
human, Darragh whispered the future into Aisling's ear. He told her

of America's seasons; land green only half the year, then leaves like blood and trees that leaked sugar, snow transforming the ground into a cloud-covered sky. She would be allowed to go to school, he would be paid for work, they would own a house built of wood, two stories, with windows as large as doors, their own field of gardens. There would be a library where they could read every book ever written, rather than the same tattered few he'd memorized over the years. When the sea tipped them so far that they strained against the ropes or were crushed beneath falling objects and bodies, Darragh held her tight and chanted her fear away.

"You're all right, I've got you, you're all right, I won't let go."

She felt strangely calm in the chaos. For her whole life, his voice was the only thing she had allowed herself to believe. So, when they were released on deck again and she saw the flush in his face, felt the heat coming off him even in icy wind, and smelled something newly rotten from his skin, she focused on his voice, as though by listening hard enough, she could keep him talking forever.

21.

Deirdre does not believe in the existence of the carefree child. She thinks that all children, no matter how stable their lives, fear and worry with an intensity that they forget as an adult. Deirdre used to think of her own childhood as happy, until she had Gabe and was reminded in painful flashes of the formless anxieties that once infected her girlish mind. Though she was not faced with death until she was in her twenties, as a girl, the anticipation of it often kept her from sleeping. After requesting that she be tucked in so tight she couldn't move, she would lie awake all night, unable to curb morbid fantasies of her parents perishing in fires or car crashes that left her alive but alone. When she entered kindergarten, her parents were baffled by her tantrums; she was transformed from a quietly agreeable child to a screaming banshee with a lunchbox. She never told them that she was afraid they would die while she was at school.

For a while after Brian's accident, Deirdre told herself that in the long run, it would make things easier for Gabe. He would know the worst, and never again have to fear it. She was both right and wrong in her prediction. Her son is twice as anxious and morbid as she was at his age, but he is braver. He takes his fears and channels them into science, still believing, because he is a child, that there is some undiscovered secret to conquering death.

Deirdre sometimes has surprisingly vivid flashes of the man he will be: delicately handsome with an insomniac's brightly bruised eyes, a doctor who will put his patients at ease because his empathy for them is palpable. Women will find him trustworthy but mysterious; he will be stubborn in his opinions and gentle with his children. When she sees this man within the outline of her baby-skinned son, she wonders if the results would be different if Brian hadn't died. Perhaps Gabe would have laughed more, or gone through the rebellious, unreliable phase in which boys indulge when they don't feel so responsible for their parents. She knows and regrets that much of his seriousness comes from his concern for her. This is the hardest part of being a parent: every day, within the personality of her son, she is confronted with the evidence of her mistakes, peering at her beside her good intentions.

Because she tends to be more sentimental about endings than beginnings, fall is Deirdre's favorite season. She loves anything to do with the start of school, cherishes removing her sweaters from huge zippered bags, wishes for a perfume inspired by the odor of fallen leaves. The only thing that mars the perfect chill of this season is the dread of her son's birthday.

Gabe was born on November second, All Souls' Day, the day, according to the Catholic church, the souls in Purgatory come back to earth on their way to Heaven. For Gabe's entire life, someone or something has died on his birthday. The good years are when it is only a cat or a goldfish. Deirdre's parents died one year apart, on the days he turned three and four, his own father on his sixth birthday. Elderly islanders unable to face another Maine winter tend to slip away on the same day Gabe should be celebrating life. Deirdre and Gabe always visit the island graveyard before he opens his gifts, a tradition he refuses to give up. One year, when he was eight, Deirdre tried to throw him a normal boy's party at a sports complex in Portland. When she arrived with a vanful of children, she found the building closed off by police tape—a boy had broken his neck on the trampoline. Gabe, who had been wary about the party from the beginning, never let his mother plan one again.

Since then Deirdre has tried to comfort him (and herself, she admits) with expensive gifts she charges to her credit card, which she spends the rest of the year paying off. Though it is only October, there is already a two-thousand-dollar high-power microscope burning a hole in her bedroom closet. She still pretends to approach November with enthusiasm, not wanting to give in to the natural morbidity that Gabe brings to the occasion.

"How are we planning to celebrate eleven years old?" Deirdre asks casually one afternoon, when Gabe has come home hours late from school. Beneath her cheer, she knows they are both wondering: Who's going to die this year?

Gabe shrugs, glaring at her for broaching the unmentionable. They sit down to supper, chicken and three kinds of squash (Deirdre is also a fan of autumn vegetables). She ignores the warning in Gabe's eyes and charges on.

"We could have Aisling and Oisin over for cake and a movie," she says. "What do you think?"

"Aisling's leaving," Gabe says, intently maneuvering his knife and fork. He always appears to be dissecting his food, rather than merely cutting it.

"Where's she going?" Deirdre asks. For a moment it makes perfect sense. In a year, Aisling has grown to the leaving-home age—where she will want to go away to college or move to the city, start a life of independence.

"Back to the dead," Gabe says, peering into an incision in his chicken.

"Oh," Deirdre says flatly. "Did she tell you that?"

"Nope," says Gabe. "I just know."

"Shit," Deirdre says, before she remembers to treat this gently. She stands up and begins to clear the table: she needs something to slam around.

It's amazing the things you can take for granted, she thinks, running the kitchen tap hot enough to scald her hand. Despite Aisling's creepy, unnatural growth, Deirdre stopped marveling at the bizarreness of it months ago, and lately has assumed her a permanent part of their lives. What was she thinking? That at some age Aisling would level off, then continue to grow normally? Or that she would be an elderly woman before Gabe hit puberty? The truth is, she had stopped thinking, and gotten used to Aisling's presence just as she adjusted to having a baby around after Gabe was born.

"Shit!" Deirdre says again, breaking a glass in the metal sink. Gabe walks up behind her, pats her shoulder in a parody of parental comfort.

"It's okay, Mom," he says. "She got what she wanted. She got to grow up."

Deirdre turns to hug her son, smoothing his wild hair and inhaling his boyish smell—so convoluted it's as though he has been a thousand different places in one day. She pretends to be comforted by him. She cannot bear to voice what he doesn't yet know—that growing up is not something that has a finish line, that you don't receive your adult diploma as soon as you reach your permanent height. There are moments of insight along the way, where you can see yourself at one end of change, but there is always more growth looming in the future.

She thinks methodically and painfully, the way she does at funerals, of all the things Aisling will miss. She'll never have a first apartment, where she would arrange things in a rebellious opposite of Oisin's house, only to reorganize them later when she realizes his way makes her feel more at home. Her first car—does Aisling even know how to drive? Never mind the first time she has sex—what is that compared to the first morning she wakes up next to someone and knows that as soon as she touches him, something will begin? She has not traveled, at least not for pleasure, doesn't know the feeling one has when abroad in foreign countries—that there are dozens of possible lives under her surface which could be set in motion by the sound of a new language or the sight of ancient architecture. Aisling hasn't felt old in her twenties, then known how young she was by the time she hit thirty. Deirdre's husband was twenty-nine when he died, and lately, in her memory, she finds it difficult to take him seriously, as though she'd been married to a boy. Aisling will never know what it's like to look in the mirror and compare herself, not to the girl she once was, but to the young woman she thought she'd be forever.

"You okay?" Deirdre whispers to her son. He nods against her chest, unable to speak. She knows he won't sleep tonight; they will be making cocoa and playing Scrabble at three A.M. When he was an infant, his nighttime crying could always be cured by swaddling him in a blanket so snugly that he couldn't move. She finds it so unfair that it once took only a blanket to insulate him from the world.

"I know you're going to miss her," she says. "I am too."

What she is thinking, but doesn't say, is how much she misses herself as a girl, her husband bright-eyed and twenty-one, her little boy at every age he has left behind. And that someday, when Gabe remembers Aisling, he will miss not only the girl who was his friend, but the boy he was beside her.

The next afternoon, while Gabe is in the woods with Aisling, Deirdre swishes through the unraked leaves that border Oisin's house. He is not at home, and the one-room cottage looks dusty and abandoned. She follows the path to his studio.

She knocks on the glass door and Oisin, leaning over his worktable, looks startled. He stares for a moment, as though trying to remember her face. Then he comes to the door, wiping his inky hands on the thighs of his jeans. The jeans are layered with a history of colorful fingerprints, looking, in a certain light, like claw marks.

"Hello, Deirdre," he says. In his newfound sociability, Oisin has begun addressing people by name. Deirdre has seen the surprise on the faces of islanders who thought Oisin didn't even know them. This courtesy reminds her of Ireland (she honeymooned there with Brian), where even the B&B owners would use their names while chatting over breakfast. She and Brian had to memorize everyone's name to avoid the embarrassment of giving them what sounded like a bald American greeting.

"Aisling's leaving," Deirdre says abruptly, making Oisin flinch. This is the way Gabe looks in the morning if she tries to strike up any sort of conversation: unprepared and a little frightened by her energy.

"Uh-huh," Oisin says, taking a step back from her. "Do you want some coffee?" He closes the door behind him and follows her deter-mined footsteps back to the house.

In his filthy kitchen, Oisin brews burned-smelling coffee grounds. Deirdre puts sugar in her empty mug while he's not looking—she likes coffee to taste like sweetly flavored milk, and this embarrasses her around black-coffee drinkers like Oisin.

"Until I was fifteen," Oisin began, pouring black liquid into her sugar, "I could see ghosts. They were always there, as real as the living—more real, in some ways. It was my grandmother who told me the stories of what I was seeing. Before she died, she told me about something I'd never experienced. Some ghosts, she said, go beyond a simple visit—they actually return to the world in flesh. They are so restless about an unresolved aspect of their life that they force themselves back into the pain of the world. They are re-born on All Souls' Day. They die again a year later, regardless of whether or not they want to stay; I suppose there are limits to everything.

"So, yes, I know Aisling is leaving. I guess I've known all along, though I didn't admit it. You see, my grandmother never told me what would happen if a *child* returned—I never expected the growing."

Oisin pauses when he sees the way Deirdre is looking at him. "What's the matter?" he asks.

"Sorry," she says. "This sounds stupid, but I never imagined you as part of a family."

Oisin smiles. "Oh, I was part of a huge, loud, Irish Catholic mob, much like everyone on this island. I still am, I suppose, though I'm not in touch with them, and the principal characters are all gone."

Deirdre's questions are in her eyes, and Oisin tells her the rest in an emotionless voice, as though the man who once told nothing about himself has been practicing this speech about his history.

"My twin sister, Nieve, killed herself when we were fifteen. After that, my mother left us, divorced my dad and ran off with his brother. Dad drank himself to death by the time I entered art school. Mom and Uncle Malachy died in a car accident in Italy when I was twenty. I never met my mother's family, but I inherited some of their guilt money—her father had cut her off for a time, but after her death, sought me out and added me to his will. I still have aunts, uncles, and cousins in Ireland, but I stopped talking to them. I didn't want to be a part of a family to whom such things happened."

Oisin's voice changes and, for a moment, she can hear sadness alongside the facts.

"I didn't want to be part of *anything* for so long." He looks at Deirdre and tries to smile. "How's that for a dysfunctional family?" he says.

"I've known worse," Deirdre says, and the truth of this statement strikes her with both humor and hopelessness.

"If you know Aisling's leaving," she says, "why is she moping in the woods while you're locked in your studio?"

"I need to finish something," Oisin says, avoiding her eyes while he clears their cups.

"It can't wait?" Deirdre says, pushing her chair back. She always stands when she's about to raise her voice.

"Look," Oisin says, thunking the cups down. "This is more complicated than you know."

"That girl has placed every hope she has in you, and you don't want the responsibility. I know that much." Deirdre's yelling now, and glad to see she has made him angry. She would like to throw him bodily from the house, march him into the woods until he is face-to-face with all he has tried to avoid. Doesn't he know that every minute counts? That waiting is often the same as missing a lifetime?

When Deirdre was twenty-two, a month before she married Brian, she experienced a moment she looks back on as a split in the road of her life. Walking past an apartment building in Portland, she saw a man balanced inside the first-floor window. He was dressed in carpenter's pants, painting the molding with a thin, gloppy brush. He stopped painting, looked at her, and smiled.

Though Deirdre has had her fair share of glances from men, for some reason she was pulled body and soul into that smile, and every possibility it contained. But she'd been walking so swiftly, she was out of his sight before the smile and the feeling it gave her even registered. She'd had no time to acknowledge him. She paused after half a block and then walked on, chiding herself for making too much out of a smidgen of flattery.

But later, and repeatedly for the next twelve years, she thought of that man and fantasized about what her life would have been had she acknowledged him. She does not regret marrying Brian, and could not bear a life without Gabe. But she has come to think of that moment as a chance at love, one of those chances that appear only a handful of times in life, if you're lucky. She has only ever felt that with Brian, and, though she hates to admit it, briefly with Oisin. She often wonders who she would be if she had stopped by that open window and smiled back at an alternative future.

She wants to tell Oisin this story, tell him she'd been wrong when she said to be careful with Aisling, beg him to give the girl everything he can in her last month, regardless of what seems right and wrong. She wants to say that possibilities die more often, and more completely, than people. But Oisin speaks first.

"Does everything always turn out the way you want it to?" he says. "The way you think it should?"

"Of course not," Deirdre says. "That's my point . . ."

"Just trust me," he says. Then he laughs at the look she lets escape from her face.

"Okay, that's asking too much," he says. "*Pretend* you trust me."

And though it's the oddest request he has made so far, she nods and leaves Oisin alone with his life.

22.

Gabe trudges toward her, carrying a bright blue sleeping bag. Aisling rolls her eyes, hiding her happiness. Solitude has begun to bore her—she has been waiting for him all day.

He has also brought a thermos of tea and his travel Scrabble set—a small case which opens to reveal tiny, individual plastic beds for the letters.

Aisling accepts the gravel-colored camping mug without a thank-you, refuses milk and sugar, and drinks the liquid until her throat is hot and bitter. They play three games without speaking.

"Do you think Oisin will come for you soon?" Gabe says. As twilight approaches, he folds away the game.

Aisling's memory rises and swirls: Oisin wiping her feet, laying her dinner out, giving her baby aspirin and ginger ale. When did he back away?

"My mom says if you wait for people to read your mind, most of them will hear only your silence." Gabe even sounds like Deirdre.

The carousel of memories goes round again: Aisling, small and dirty, in a house full of angry women, trying to be invisible while waiting for the right moment to reappear.

"Which is why I have to tell you something," Gabe says. His cheeks are redder than the cold could make them. He shoves the empty thermos and the game into his backpack.

"When I'm old enough to have my first love, I'm going to re-member you," Gabe says. "Is that okay?"

"Sure," Aisling says, and she smiles. She thinks briefly about kiss-ing him, in the gentle, lingering, innocent way she once imagined Oisin kissing her. But she changes her mind while looking at his mouth. His lips are far too small to fit against her own.

"See you tomorrow," Gabe says, slipping his arms through the straps of his pack. She watches him walk away with his jaunty, tireless gait. He leaves her the sleeping bag.

When she sleeps again, she dreams of Darragh, but he is not the brother she remembers. This Darragh is a boy, a boy with Gabe's round, smooth cheeks and knobby shoulders he hasn't grown into. A boy who has never been kissed. In the dream, she is taller than him. He looks up at her with eyes that spiral with want. He is hungry.

Darragh's feet swell first. Too large to strain into shoes, grotesquely marred with purple spots.

"Not enough exercise," he says to Aisling, limping along the deck hiding his flinch. Aisling has seen enough sickly swelling to recognize it, but she pretends to believe him.

When he coughs there is a rattling that sounds like he is coming apart inside. At night, Aisling feigns sleep while he vomits or groans out foul diarrhea in the chamber pot. Every morning he looks more like an elderly man—his fever-bright eyes swallowed in his bony, rough-skinned face.

Aisling begins to pray. She's never been in the habit—unlike Darragh, who folds his hands every night. She has always worried that if she began to ask God for help, she would ask too much. Her life is full of want. So she's held back, saving her prayers like precious coins, for when she needs them the most.

"Don't take Darragh," she chants silently in the darkness, as he retches beside her. "You may have everyone else, but allow me to keep him."

When she sleeps, she drifts off to the rhythm of her own prayer, which often takes the form of one word repeated over and over again: *Please.*

But he gets worse. The swelling moves up his legs and he begins to stay belowdecks all day.

"A wee rest will cure me," he says to Aisling, but she knows he can no longer walk. She cooks their meal cakes herself, brings him the little brackish water they are allowed. Darragh makes her eat his share of the food.

"I'm not hungry anymore," he says cheerfully, as though this is a good sign.

For the first time in her life, Aisling looks beyond Darragh for help. But she sees that the other passengers are thin, vacant, and useless. Every one of them is tending someone who is ill. The few women look as angry as she remembers her mother, the men have frightened, unfocused eyes. Most of those on their feet are children, looking as ragged and desperate as she feels.

Aisling goes in search of James, a young British sailor that Darragh sometimes smokes with. She climbs up to the foredeck and slips silently into a group of large, odorous men. One peers at her, spits, and gruffly demands she go back where she belongs.

"I'm looking for James," Aisling says in the barely audible voice she uses with everyone but Darragh. The other men look uncomfortable, and the one who speaks is blushing.

"He's dead," the man says, his voice losing a level of gruffness.

Aisling asks for medicine, but all they give her is an extra ration of water. She saves it for Darragh. He is thirsty all the time now.

Another storm attacks the ship and Aisling tends her brother in darkness. She blindly wipes him with a dry, tattered shirt, saving the water to tip against his mouth. The heat coming off him is so strong, she imagines he is baking a hard, black shell like their meal cakes. When he isn't coughing or vomiting, he hoarsely chants plans, but they no longer include him; they are instructions for Aisling alone.

"It will be winter there," he says, as Aisling cries quietly, her tears dripping cold on his burning arm. "Snow and ice, you must have shoes and a woolen cloak. Try to avoid an orphanage. Find a family who has lost their children; if they still have their own, they won't treat an orphan as well. Someone on the ship, or an Irish family in Canada. Tell them you're five, not seven. If you can't find anyone, beg for coins on the street, steal food if you have to. Never, no matter what you are offered, go off with a man alone. Accept help from women, but never from a man. Promise me."

Aisling vows, though she is sure Darragh is confused. Doesn't he remember how cruel women can be?

"Perhaps you should take that boy with you," Darragh says. Aisling doesn't know who he is talking about.

"Which boy?" she says, touching his cheek. His face has swelled during the storm; she can't see it, but she feels the difference in the dark.

"The black boy," Darragh says, his voice disembodied in the void. "Over there, chained to the wall."

"There's no light in here to see a boy," Aisling says. "And they haven't chained anyone since that man was caught stealing whiskey."

"He's right there," Darragh says, thrashing in his bunk. "A slave who was left behind. He's trying to tell me something, but he doesn't know our language. Listen."

Aisling hears only the moaning strain of the ship's walls and the shrieks of the hundreds packed in with them. She soothes her brother, gives him the last dribble of water, whispers yes, she will take care of the black boy. When he finally sleeps, she lies shaking beside him. What frightens her more than anything, more than sickness, darkness, or even Darragh's dying, is the fact that his mind, which she has depended on for so long, is already focused on a world she cannot see.

Darragh died four days before the storm did, and by the time the hold was unbarred, his face was black and bloated, monstrous, and there was no odor left of himself, only decay. Aisling watched as the men dragged bodies on deck, wrapping them in sacks and old sails. As bodies were shifted along the line of sailors, she lost track of which bundle contained her brother. She watched as each stiff parcel was tossed over the side and sucked into the water. It would be so easy, she thought, to be with Darragh again. Two small, graceful movements: up and over.

But somehow, before she knew it, the day passed with her still on the deck. Stars appeared, clustering in the twilight, and she went alone to their bunk, wondering why she was still alive.

In the end, Aisling goes to him. Sleep fails her, she lies for hours with eyes that refuse to droop, her limbs twitching, crying for movement. Part of her is angry that she is not the sort of person who can lie down and give up.

She finds Oisin in the kitchen, preparing dinner. He is whistling, basting eggplant slices on the broiler. She can see what his recent work has done to him—he looks thinner, tired, empty. But he smiles when he sees her, his eyes crinkling in the way that has recently begun to lodge her breath just below her throat.

"Hello, Aisling," he says, wiping his oily, ink-stained hands on his sweatshirt. "Hungry?"

"I . . . yes." Aisling fumbles, trying not to stare. Had he even noticed her absence every day for a week? But the urge to storm away and punish him dissolves in her suddenly ravenous appetite.

They eat in silence, olive oil and salmon juices shining on their lips in the low light of the kitchen. Oisin pours her a glass of wine— her first—and she savors the velvet tartness that clings to her tongue. She crosses her legs, remembering when she first sat here, swinging her feet inches above the linoleum. Oisin is having trouble looking at her.

"I'm sorry about the other night," Aisling blurts out. "I know you think of me as a little girl."

Oisin is grinning, but trying to hide it behind his napkin. She remembers her first day, when she blurted things to him with the same urgency, hoping to reel him in before he had a chance to step away.

"I'm not blind," Oisin says. "I know you're not a little girl." He stands up, begins to clear the remains of their meal. He drops a pile of bone-and-skin-covered dishes in the sink.

"Come on," he says. "I have something to show you."

She follows him outside into the twilight—indigo air painted with the black arms of trees—and down the path to his studio.

Oisin flicks the light switch and the ceiling pops and brightens bar by bar. On the long wall where he usually tacks sketches and prints in progress hangs the largest piece she's ever seen. Taller than her, covering almost the entire wall, is a collage of women. Women and girls, faces and body parts, so jumbled that at points they seem to be crawling out of one another; women emerging from the cocoons of girls. The print is in color, the edges where he must have used separate plates are undetectable.

It is the most beautiful and intricate piece he has ever done, and she hates it. This is too many women to stand in front of. No wonder he never came for her.

"What do you think?" Oisin says, and Aisling pretends to smile.

"It's beautiful," she says, but she's not even looking at it anymore. Everything is blurred beyond a membrane of tears.

"It's you," Oisin whispers, and she blinks. She steps closer.

At first she thinks he means that he's included her in the collage. She searches for a little girl, and finds her along the edge, tangled hair, eyes like saucers of gold, a bramble scratch across her cheek. Then she sees other hers. Bloody feet in a basin. A body too tall for the overalls that pinch at her crotch. A smile caught halfway between sets of teeth, jagged new stubs looking huge and indelicate next to perfectly formed pearls. Handprints in solid blue, three pale lines dissecting the flesh.

She is everywhere, covering the wall with a thousand different faces. Has she really been all these girls? Laughing with every muscle of her face, hiding blemishes behind shanks of hair, gazing upward with a mouth begging for a kiss. Mixed in are moods she'd felt but never seen: Aisling pouting, raging in anger, trying to hide a teasing smile. The best one—so unexpected—shows her as a mature, sensual young woman, a woman you could not imagine had ever been a starving little girl.

This is what he can give her, she thinks. What he knows how to do. He didn't come after her, he doesn't want her as much as he wants safety in his own self. But with metal, ink, and paper, he can make her visible, sculpt her into reality, render her immortal. The wall whispers: *I have seen you all along.*

She turns to face Oisin, he is leaning on the edge of the table, rubbing the ink off his hands into little worms of discolored skin. She goes to him slowly, takes his hand, waiting for his flinch. But he stays still as she traces the ruined palm—burn marks and scars and a life line sliced away into three irreconcilable pieces. She strokes these lines as if she can soothe the life itself, and she feels Nieve behind her, lurking, Nieve who has always been there, though Aisling has refused to let her out. If she gives Oisin his sister back, there will be nothing left that he needs from her.

"When Nieve died," Oisin begins, and Aisling can feel the sorrow from both of the twins, running through her like she is a tunnel connecting them. "I wouldn't let them bury her. I didn't believe she was dead. Not just because I couldn't see her ghost, though that was part of it. I didn't understand how she could die and leave me living when . . ." Oisin's voice breaks.

Aisling finishes for him.

"When she was the stronger one," she says.

Then Oisin is holding her. Etched thick and sorrowful between them are the bodies of two ghosts.

23.

Here is the most important seduction of Oisin's life (perhaps—he shudders—the only important one), and he does not know where to begin.

After planning the moment for so long, he is paralyzed with indecisive anxiety. In the last few days he has remembered hundreds of first kisses, the eyes of women running past him like an interminable film, eyes brimming with invitation, some at first sight, others he needed to coax along. Once there was nothing he enjoyed more than a woman glancing furtively at his mouth. He could read in that glance what was expected of him: tentative probing or passionate onslaught. There were women who wanted to be kissed without hesitation, women who found the pause just before the touch of lips more arousing than the kiss itself. Though he has disappointed countless women, his first kiss has never let them down.

For months Aisling has gazed at his mouth and silently begged for kisses. Closed-mouthed and innocent, deep and bruising, her desires change every time she looks at him. Sometimes she seems to be asking for every kiss he has ever given, all at once, and it confounds him with an insecure desperation to please that he hasn't felt since he was a boy.

This has never happened to him before—this feeling that each moment holds within it the possibility of touching her, partnered with a fear that he never will. He lives beneath a layer of electricity, imagines he gives off noxious fumes. He smiles to himself too much, jolts awake from a manic concoction of terror and delight. He is forty-two years old and afraid this malady is his first crush.

He is sleeping when it happens.

He has drifted off while sketching in bed, surrounded by tossed-aside drawings of Aisling dozing, one leg pulled up, her arms cradling her head. When he feels the press of her lips, he rises without drowsiness; he cannot remember feeling so fully awake in all his life.

He sits up and kisses her back, so carefully, every movement of his mouth as reverent as though it is the last. He holds her jaw lightly with his hands so he can feel the tremble there. His first thought is an insecure one—she tastes so new, he is sure that his own tongue must have the flavor of decay. But when he leans back to look at her, she runs her tongue swiftly across her own mouth, as if savoring the taste of him.

"Are you awake?" she asks, looking worried.

"Definitely." Oisin smiles. He pulls her toward him, lifts and rolls her over so they are lying side by side, sliding and crushing sketching paper, images of her mouth, limbs, and eyes mirroring the flesh she presses against him. He peels off her T-shirt, letting himself gaze at the body he's tried so long to avoid staring at. She is so perfect that he half imagines, as he leans in toward her, that he will move straight through her like a mirage.

"Tell me about her," Aisling says, her whisper making her breasts move beneath Oisin's lips. He looks up at her.

"No, don't stop," she says. "But tell me about Nieve."

He pauses, pondering this request. Oisin has always been known for his silent concentration in bed, so silent that women often ask him questions, needing to hear his voice as proof that he is with them body and mind. He has never answered before.

"She was beautiful," he says, pausing as Aisling arches against his mouth. "In the perfect way some ghosts are—the way you are—as though every molecule of her was shining."

Aisling pushes him onto his back, begins to kiss downward with concentration, new portions of his body are appearing to her for the first time.

"We didn't look like twins," Oisin says, catching his breath when she discovers the spot just below his ribs. "Everything attractive about her was awkward on me. I had terrible skin and chronic pinkeye. I was infected with ugliness."

A lift of his hips and she has pulled away his boxers. She kisses the insides of his thighs and smiles up at him as though she's discovered what she's been looking for.

"Oh." Oisin sighs, arching his neck and sinking further into the bed. Though he knows it should seem odd, it feels more than natural, almost necessary, to tell her the rest as she pulls him in and out of her mouth.

"The morning after she died, my face was different in the mirror. My skin was clear, no scars. My eyes were completely open for the first time ever, blue and clean. I'd never seen anything so horrible, it was like looking at myself dead, like I was the ghost. I screamed until my father knocked down the bathroom door and hit me."

Aisling's mouth is growing to accommodate him; the more he

swells, the wetter and longer she becomes. He is beginning to imagine she could fit him body and soul in there.

"I went back to the graveyard after the funeral," Oisin says through ragged breath. "I dug until my fingernails were shredded and bleeding, and when the watchman pulled me away, I scratched at my new face until I was sure it was ruined. But it never scarred. I wanted my sister back, I waited for her ghost, but she left only her beauty behind. Whenever I looked at myself in the mirror, I was reminded that I let her die."

And Oisin, who has always swallowed the voice of his pleasure, is crying Aisling's name as he comes, unable to hold anything within him. For the first time, he does not feel as if he's disappearing or on the verge of death as he empties into her, but rather like he is being rendered visible, whole, beneath the pressure of her hands and mouth.

For a moment, she won't let go, rocking back and forth with the retreating waves of his orgasm. When she crawls up, covering him with her weight, her chin resting on her hands just at the point where his heart is still racing, he sees that she is crying. He puts his hand out to catch a tear, then tastes it, as salty and warm as if he were swallowing himself.

"Do you think I let Darragh die?" Aisling says.

"Of course not," Oisin says. He pulls her up so their faces are level. "For God's sake, you were seven years old."

"And you," Aisling says, kissing him gently, "you were only a boy."

"What's that supposed to mean?" Oisin says. He hears her sentence in the voices of every woman who has ever dismissed him as a male.

"No, Oisin," she says, as though she can decipher the fear that has stiffened him. "You were a *child*."

He takes hold of her face as he kisses her, teasing, deep, hungry, gentle, every kiss she wants at once—it is possible after all. Never has he kissed quite like this. It's as though his mouth has eyes, as though it is finally seeing after a lifetime of blind, distracted pressure. This, he realizes, is what all those women wanted, that he was never able to give. A kiss from his soul.

"Are you going to tell me who taught you to do that?" he says, biting gently at her lower lip.

"You did," she whispers, and he feels her voice move like a current through his body.

"I was planning on seducing *you*," he says, and she blushes.

"Go ahead," she whispers.

"It seems I'm still a boy," he says. "Or at least I've recovered the libido of one."

"What does that mean?" she says.

"It means I don't need a nap before doing this," he says, moving down and spreading her thighs open with tiny kisses.

"Finally, something good," Aisling says, sighing, "about being young."

For a week they can't do anything without their mouths moving together like wet magnets. The house and studio are littered with half-finished nudes of Aisling, abandoned because he can't stand not to be touching her. Meals are cooked and then left to congeal uneaten as they fall back into bed. Oisin hasn't smoked a cigarette in days, all he needs in his mouth is her. They continue to talk while making love, words accompany the thrust of fingers, tongues, and hips, bitter stories ringing out amid cries of pleasure. They trade the position of lying on top of the other, Oisin wanting as much as Aisling the weight that seems to center him in the world. When they finally sleep, he does not let go of her, holds tight rather than turning to curl into himself as he has always done. Not since he was a child with Nieve has he slept holding on to someone else. He has abandoned the notion of leading Aisling along. He is the young one now.

Once, after a morning of breakfasting on each other, when their bodies have taken on the combined scent of the two of them, until they can barely tell where one leaves off and the other begins, Aisling sighs and says, "I knew it would be like this."

Oisin, feeling as though he is about to burst, to cry and scream and say everything he's ever held back in his life, hides the sorrow in his eyes by kissing her deeply.

"I didn't," he whispers. "I never knew."

And though he has christened every millimeter of her skin with his mouth, though he has sucked and probed with his tongue until she is shivering and stretching her arms out—trying to grab hold of her climax, though he has felt again the caress of her throat as she swallows him whole, he has not had the courage to enter her. He fears the thing he wants the most. He is delaying the inevitable, for he believes that when he finally pushes inside her, she will disappear like the ghost in the graveyard when he was fourteen. At their closest moment, he will reach out and she will no longer be there.

24.

Aisling is no longer a teenager. When she looks in the mirror after a sleepless night with Oisin, she finds tiny lines underneath her eyes, sketched in the shape of a smile. After she sleeps, the lines are gone again, but she knows, if she stayed, they would become deeper, permanent, carved into her face, the way Oisin's life has left evidence on his skin.

Her eyes have lost their frantic look. The gold of her iris has changed color—it is slightly deeper, tarnished, mirroring the new calm that has grown within her. The want in her eyes has been smothered by satisfaction. Oisin either hasn't noticed or refuses to acknowledge it, because suddenly he is trying to give her the world.

He has finished the print, working in small snatches while she is asleep. He's added new images from her stories—a girl tied to the stormy deck of a ship, a small face sleeping trustfully next to the form of her brother. And, in the center, there is a portrait that both fascinates and embarrasses her. It is the way she looks during orgasm, reaching upward with her arms, her breasts peeking up from the shadow of night which surrounds her, her bright eyes looking as though she has finally grabbed hold of whatever was out of her reach. Life, perhaps; love.

Oisin is the frantic one now, obsessed with what Aisling is missing. He spends an entire afternoon at the library printing out on-line travel guides. One minute he wants to take her to Paris, the next Rome or New York, Africa, India, or back to Ireland. There are too many places to choose from. Aisling only smiles and kisses him back into bed. She doesn't want to go anywhere, she didn't come back to see the world, but he refuses to understand this. He takes her to the Portland cinema, where they watch three movies in a row, until her eyes ache from following mammoth faces. He buys a pile of heavy books and spends days flipping her through the history of art. She pays dutiful attention until colors and textures have melted to meaninglessness in her mind.

One morning, rather than wake her with kissing, Oisin throws her clothes on the bed and urges her to hurry. They take the six A.M. ferry and drive Oisin's car to Boston, Aisling jerking from her doze whenever Oisin announces their progress with highway signs. They enter the city on a huge, rusty green bridge, cars sliding across lanes like clumsy ice-skaters.

Oisin loses his way, and for an hour they drive in between buildings and construction sites while he swears under his breath.

"Why don't you ask someone?" Aisling says.

"I'm not *lost*," Oisin says. "It's these stupid detour signs."

She feigns sleep as he honks his way right and left; she can't bear to look at his desperate, foolishly angry face.

When they finally find the museum, Aisling is so carsick the paintings look blurry. There is a special van Gogh exhibit, "The Early

Years," and Oisin holds her hand, to keep her from moving too quickly through the carpeted rooms.

"Van Gogh," she whispers to him, "was he the one that cut off his ear?"

"Good," Oisin says. "You remembered that from the book."

"Mmmhmm," Aisling says, nodding. Her eyes are on a red-bearded man, a dirty bandage marring his profile, who is trying to touch up a painting with a brush that slips straight through the canvas. "The early years," the ghost hisses at Aisling when she walks by. "Why not show my nursery drawings and complete the humiliation?"

Another room displays clay and woven pots much like the ones her mother once used, and a mummy child a thousand years dead, smothered in cracked brown cloth. Aisling imagines herself as an artifact—eternally seven years old, propped beneath protective glass. She wonders if, after she leaves, Oisin will keep her clothing, arrange it in the cluttered museum of his closet.

After the modern art exhibit, Aisling is so hungry she has a headache. Oisin suggests a train ride (she knows he's afraid of getting lost again in the car), so they pack themselves into a green tram full of people who stare openmouthed at each other, but pretend not to. They emerge from a stuffy, popcorn-smelling station to cement stairs as large as a field, which lead down to a marketplace. Here the street is cobbled and lined with wagons, which rather than vegetables or meat carcasses, hold brightly colored trinkets and clothing painted with sentences and skylines. Oisin is frantically pointing out what he thinks is new to her, not knowing that TV at Gabe's house has shown her most of this world already. If she stops to look at something, Oisin buys it, so she tries to keep her eyes to the ground.

She grows quieter as the day wears on, begins to hate the camera-laden crowds, is disturbed by the number of graveyards they pass along the guided Freedom Trail tour. Eventually, it is all she can do not to scream every time Oisin points something out to her.

After a lunch of greasy snacks collected from vendors in a cardboard box, they walk along the water to the aquarium. The woman at the ticket booth asks if they are interested in a membership.

"No, thank you," Aisling says. "I'm dying, and my last request is to see fish in captivity." After a pause, the woman decides she is joking, and smiles stiffly, stamping their hands with fluorescent dolphins.

"Very funny," Oisin says. "Look," he says, determined to remain cheerful, "a jellyfish exhibit."

They circle a huge tank, their shoes slapping damp cement, white portions of their clothing glowing like moon fragments under blue lights. Lazy sharks slide up behind them in the glass, and whenever she starts, Oisin takes it as a sign that she's being entertained. When they reach the top, and Aisling looks downward into a spiral of fish and plant-covered rock, she has a brief urge to toss herself in. But she holds on to the railing, knowing Oisin would only jump in behind her.

She feels the fight swelling during dinner; when they finally sit down, Oisin can no longer avoid the pouty silence she's been wearing all day. They eat furiously, glaring at their lobsters as if they are the cause of the tension. Their window overlooks a harbor of brown water and gliding boats.

"I thought we'd stay here tonight," Oisin says. "Head for New York in the morning." Aisling excuses herself, escaping for five silent minutes to the formal bathroom.

After dinner, they walk along the docks; Oisin has stopped speaking, too. The quiet without his tour guide platitudes is as piercing as a scream.

"What is your problem?" Oisin finally asks, without preamble, as though continuing a speech he began in his head.

"I don't have a problem," Aisling says, picking at the braided ropes with her fingernails.

"You've been sulking all day," he says, stepping in front of her so she is forced to look at him. "I'm doing this for you, you know. I'm trying like hell . . ."

"I see what you're trying to do," she says. "I know what you want from me."

"What *I* want?" Oisin yells. "Since when has this been about me? It's what you want, what you've been begging me for with those big eyes all along: take me in, give me a life—and now that I'm trying to do it, you don't even want it anymore. Jesus! I am so tired of trying to read your mind."

Oisin is pacing the wooden planks of the quay, and she is reminded suddenly of Darragh, leading her with false bravado onto the deck of a ship that would be his coffin.

"You can't cram the whole world into two weeks," Aisling says, raising her voice to meet his yell. "This is never what I wanted. You're trying to make up for the last year by showing me paintings and fish and buying me T-shirts. I didn't ask you to make up for anything. And neither did Nieve."

"Now that you've reached the age of twenty you know everything?" Oisin says nastily. "This has nothing to do with Nieve."

"You're lying," Aisling says, and her voice has gone soft again. "It has everything to do with Nieve, and I've known it all along."

Oisin looks so dejected, so much like Gabe and Darragh, who tried and failed to save her, that she is suddenly ashamed of fighting with him. She moves forward and takes him in her arms, and they hold on tightly, as if trying to protect each other from cruel words that have been sent by someone else.

"There is so much more," Oisin says. "You have no idea how

much. You think you're grown-up, but you've barely begun. I can't bear to think of what you'll miss."

"What have you missed?" she whispers, holding on to the red-sweatered buoy of his chest. Either he doesn't hear this or he can't answer it. He merely hugs her tighter.

She wants to tell him that all the things she once wanted have been pushed aside by what she has: his breath in the darkness next to her, an image of the woman she could have been, and Darragh waiting for her in the shadows. All that is left is what she can give to Oisin.

But he is begging.

"Please," he says. "Tell me something I can do for you. Anything."

"Okay," she soothes. "Take me out there."

He follows her eyes to where the clear twilit sky meets dark water, where ships large and small sound their horns in greeting as they pass by one another on separate journeys.

25.

Oisin had wanted to rent a yacht, but what he navigated through Boston Harbor was a sturdy but decrepit-looking thirty-foot sailboat. It was the name that had decided Aisling—*Tír na nÓg*—spelled out in chipping Gaelic letters across the stern. The owner was a third-generation Irishman from Southie; a large man dressed in chest-high fishing waders, who, despite the ease of his smile, reminded Oisin of his father. By the end of his life, Declan had absorbed a smidgen of this man's South Boston accent, hard and drawling, the voice of sailors calling to each other across a stormy deck.

"Do I sound like that?" Oisin whispered to Aisling, while the man disappeared into a wharf hut to prepare the paperwork.

"How do you mean?" she said. Her cheeks were red in the early winter wind, but he reached out to touch one, thinking it would be warm. It was.

"Do I have an accent?" he said, and she smiled.

"You do," she said. "An American one."

"I knew we should have traveled." Oisin sighed.

He had been nervous at first about handling the rigging, but everything came back to him. Now he could be twelve again, with his father and Malachy in the waters off Galway. He weaves them through the harbor and out to open sea, where he catches a wind that propels them along the surface of the water.

"Faster!" Aisling yells, lifting her face to the spray of sea. He tightens the sail, and, with the added speed, she is laughing like a child. Her delight infects Oisin until they are both doubled over with rib pain. When they catch their breath, Oisin embraces her from behind, noticing how she knows to spread her legs to keep her balance.

"When I used to sail with my father," he said, speaking softly with his cheek pressed to her ear, "I saw ghost cities, tiny and perfectly formed, lost but still thriving beneath the sea."

He can feel her smile, the swell of her cheek that pushes his own slightly away.

"Are they still there?" he says. She nods, and for a few moments they watch the surface of the water, indigo and unfathomably deep in the twilight.

"Thank you," Oisin whispers, his mouth on her neck, tasting her like a tiny morsel of some delicacy.

"For what?" She laughs. "You rented the boat."

"For choosing me," he says, and she turns in his arms, her brow raised in suspicion. He thinks briefly that if she lived, she might carry that look with her like a scar: initial distrust whenever she is offered love. Or perhaps she would learn to discard it, come to believe instantly and without difficulty that she is desired, the way she is trying to right now.

The hold of this boat is stifling, not with illness and fear, but with the thick-fingered odor of bodies in joy. There is barely enough room for the berth, and they are both already bruised from the low ceiling and close walls. Aisling likes their little cabin—a world large enough only for her, Oisin, and the pleasure that runs between them.

They are slick with an ocean of sweat. Oisin pauses, as he always does, for an interval she has learned to enjoy. Their bodies continue to pulse, and they gasp, diluting passion with air—a slowing down that holds within it the promise of beginning again. But tonight, Aisling does not want to stretch or breathe or kiss long and steady like legs winding down from a sprint.

"Don't stop," she whispers, and Oisin stiffens with his biggest fear. He moves on top of her, hovering, his elbows at her shoulders, his hands buried in her hair. She lifts her hips, and for a timeless instant they are still, the tip of Oisin soft, round, and warm, like a kiss at the entrance to her soul.

"I won't let go," she whispers, and he glides down and in, filling her. Her first shock is the depth, and then it is both familiar and strange, this habitation, this knowledge that her body does not end at its edges, that somewhere inside she has always cradled the form of this sadly beautiful man. As they move, rocking together as naturally as the anchored hull in the sea, Aisling imagines that she can feel, not only the solid heat of him inside her, but the exact sensation of entering herself, wet and endless, from the outside.

There is more," he says to her later, his ear pressed between her breasts to hear the thudding of her heart as it floats down from ecstasy.

"More than that?" she says, lifting his face.

"You can spend a lifetime learning about sex," he says. Aisling glances at the nautical clock on the wall.

"We don't have that long." She smiles, pulling him forward, so he can fill her again. "Show me now."

Are you afraid?" Oisin says. They have been below for what seems like weeks, but now they are back on deck, wrapped in each other and a blanket, watching the moon light a road from sky to water.

"No," Aisling says instantly, as though she has been thinking and answering that exact question to herself.

"You didn't like it before," Oisin says. "With the dead." He is trying to keep his voice casual; he is in danger of issuing threats, whines, shameless begging.

"I was hiding before. Now it will be different."

"How do you know?"

She shrugs. "I think death is like life. You've choices."

"That's comforting," Oisin sneers. He can imagine his soul lurking around the edges of death, refusing to join the others, who insult him with their happiness.

"You're not like that anymore," Aisling says, and he loves her for her certainty: it allows him to imagine himself a different man.

"All I know for sure is that Darragh is there." She points to the silver membrane of the water.

He tightens his hold on her. "I have to say this," he begins.

"Oh, Oisin," she says with sorrow.

"There is nothing I want more than for you to stay here with me."

Aisling turns to face him. He runs his fingers through her hair, wondering how he ever could have resented the strands that knitted themselves into his things. He will go home and collect them, wind them around himself, create a cocoon, and never leave.

"What am I supposed to do now?" Oisin says. The thought of returning to his life before her is unbearable. He cannot go back to that empty house, to tools and papers lying forlorn and useless in his studio. To the silence of Purgatory.

"I thought that would be obvious, even to you," she says, kissing the tremble from his mouth. "Live."

"Ha!" Oisin says, but it comes out like a contemplative, agreeable sigh rather than the ridiculing bark he intended.

"There *is* something else you want," Aisling says. "Something I can give you."

"Oh, yeah?" Oisin says. He hates the pouting tone of his voice. "What?"

"Nieve."

For his entire life, Oisin's nightmares have been the same. Like a print plate, the plot of his dreams was carved long ago, and the only variety is in the colors. In every dream, Oisin is wandering through a labyrinth of rooms—Irish cottages attached to Southie brownstones, opening on corridors from high school that lead to hostels in Europe. He is usually looking for Nieve, he needs to warn her—the labyrinth is on fire or someone is stalking her. But everyone he meets—his classmates, his aunts, women he's slept with, Moira from the shop, his father—shrugs his questions and warnings off even if he screams. In Oisin's nightmares, no one will listen to him.

He knows this is not another dream because of the smells. Baby shampoo, eye ointment, the filmy odor of fabric softener that clings to their sheets. He can tell he is in his old bed, the way it was when they still shared a room, pillows arranged at the touching ends of twin mattresses. He is afraid to open his eyes, afraid he will reduce this reality to memory. But a small hand is jostling him.

"You're not *sleeping*, are you?" a voice says, a voice he thought he remembered, but now realizes he lost deep inside himself a long time ago. He opens his eyes, half expecting the crusty resistance his lashes had in childhood.

"Nieve." She is sitting cross-legged at her pillow, in her yellow pajamas, gauzy summer fabric with a scattering of tiny roses. Her hair, fresh from a bath they have taken together, is dark and wet except for the fringes of air-dried gold at her ears. Oisin inhales again: the scent of himself as a man is gone. All that is there is the smell that once came from the both of them—two small, clean bodies. They are no more than seven years old.

"Nieve?" he says again, anxious, unsure whether to begin with questions or explanations.

She takes him by the hand and leads him out the door.

They glide through dozens of rooms, passing ghosts who give him a wave or a smile. "Oisin," they say with a nod, as though they haven't noticed he's been gone for decades. Some of them are grotesque, the manner of their death still clinging to their souls.

"Look how brave you were," Nieve whispers, and before he can protest—*I was never brave*—she pulls him out another door.

The night is softly damp outside their father's pub. Malachy emerges with a rush of smoke and laughter. He heads toward the beach, and Nieve and Oisin follow, Oisin's hand grown clammy in his sister's grasp.

A woman waits for him by the water. Her face is in shadow, but Oisin thinks the long, glinting hair is Sara's. She steps forward, winding her arms around Malachy's neck. Oisin can see that her hands are trembling.

"What are you doing?" Malachy says, but he doesn't let go. "Ah, Nieve. Stop."

Oisin turns to his sister with a confused smile.

There are two Nieves. The seven-year-old ghost beside him and his fifteen-year-old sister, beautiful, manic, and determined, stretching her whole self upward so that she can capture Malachy's mouth with a kiss it has taken years to prepare.

Time moves with unmerciful speed. Suddenly Sara is there on the beach, there are screams from two female voices and muffled pleading from Malachy, the sound of a slap, then glass breaking, and all Oisin can see is blood. Blood on his mother and his sister, and that is not the worst. The worst is the smiles on their faces—his mother's superior and satisfied, Nieve's full of pride in the pain that leaks from her arm. Then he hears Sara's voice, sober and mean in the sea air.

"You'll need to cut deeper than that," she says.

Through it all, as the past bleeds in front of him, Oisin stands shaking by the water, holding his sister's face against his chest, because the only thing he understands is that she must not see any of it.

Then they are back in their childhood bedroom, pinned between clean covers.

"I should have stopped you," Oisin whispers. The sentence repeats, then warps in his mind. Could I have stopped you?

"Shh," she says, annoyed. "It's my turn to tell a story."

"There is a land beneath the sea," she whispers; and he remembers this feeling in his stomach, the expectation that they will be scolded for talking past their bedtime. "It is called Tír na nÓg, the Country of the Young, because age and death have never found it. Only one man who has gone there has ever returned—Oisin, brave leader of the Fianna.

"When the princess Nieve first saw Oisin, she was instantly in love. 'Come with me to the Land of Eternal Youth,' she said, 'where my father is king, where you will never grow old or discouraged, and where no one ever dies.'

"Oisin, who was no fool, knelt before her. 'Why you should love a man as common as me, I'll never know. You are the shining one, the sweetest and the comeliest, my star and my choice above all the women in the world.'

"Nieve warned him that, to come with her, he must give up his world and all that he cherished within it. But Oisin, unconcerned in his love, climbed on her horse and did not look back for three hundred years.

"When he finally became homesick for Ireland, his princess tried to discourage him. 'There is nothing left for you there,' she said, but his eyes still wandered beyond her. He planned a visit, and Nieve cautioned him not to get off her horse or mortal life would seize him away.

" 'Come with me,' Oisin said to the princess. He already knew he would step down from the horse.

" 'I cannot,' she said. But this was a lie. She could have gone with him, could have entered his world as he had hers, could have made it so they never lost each other. But she was afraid. She had none of Oisin's bravery—she had never needed it in her world.

"Oisin mounted her horse, and as she watched him move away, she whispered her love into a breeze that would tickle his neck for the rest of his journey.

" 'It is you who are the shining one,' she breathed. 'You who are my star and whom I love above all who live in these worlds.' "

With the end of her story, Nieve yawns, and as if that is all, as if there is not a lifetime of things to explain, she settles her damp head on the pillow, stretching her arms in his direction, the way she once did every night before drifting off to sleep.

That's the wrong story, he wants to say, wants to scream until his voice ages her to a point where she can understand. *I didn't leave you. I was never brave.*

But instead he looks at her hands, already limp with sleep, and her wrists, pale and smooth and exposed, with no trace yet of the fear that will slice them.

He feels a boy's sleepiness—the pure, earned exhaustion that comes at the end of a full day, with nothing to jerk it awake until the promise of another in the morning. He lays his head down, reaches up to touch his sister's waiting hands.

"Miss you, Nee," he mumbles, or is it "Love you"? He is too tired to be sure.

"You too, Ossie," she says, and the last thing he thinks before he drifts away is that she sounds older than she ever was.

While Oisin sleeps, his brow relaxed but still etched with the three furrows of his lives, Aisling wraps herself in the sheet, leaving the blanket to keep him warm. She climbs on deck without looking back. She does not need to memorize his face, it is more familiar than her own.

Darragh is waiting, leaning against the railing, looking at her with more pride and less fear than she remembers. She steps up to face him. They are exactly the same age.

The two movements, up and over, are not as simple and weightless as she thought they'd be. A part of her, the part that is worried about Oisin waking to empty darkness, makes her clumsy. The falling is easier; she is graceful after she gives up the option of turning back. Her fear for Oisin flutters away with the love-stained sheet.

He will be alone. But only until he returns to shore.

EPILOGUE:
THE LIVING

In travel guides of Maine, tucked between sea maps studded with tiny islands, Tiranogue is a recommended excursion, especially in early winter. The island is noted for its Irish-American inhabitants and their odd accent, which still holds traces of the lilt that arrived on famine ships long ago. But there is a particular tradition, taken from an ancient one, though only practiced there for the last fifty years, for which Tiranogue is famous. The celebration of All Souls' Day.

Every year on the second of November, just before twilight, the islanders gather in the graveyard and place lighted candles on the stones of the dead. No grave is left unlit; families long extinct are divvied up among the living. Gabe Molloy, with the help of his grandchildren, lights three candles on one stone, engraved with the names of his mother, his father, and his stepfather, Oisin MacDara, whose epitaph reads simply *Loving Husband and Guardian*.

Then the islanders stand, children in front, around the grave of

Jack Seward, the fisherman who lost his life saving a shipful of souls. A name has been added beneath his, *Aisling Quinn*, though there are no dates to confine it.

Here Gabe tells the children the story of how their island was saved by a tragedy. He describes a ship, filled with young people who were cold, hungry, and sick, that ran aground in a winter storm. He tells of one girl, who wanted to live so badly she tied herself to the vessel, and how she was rescued, only to pass quietly away on solid land.

The story does not frighten these children. They have heard it every year of their lives. They already know that the young can die.

It is the rest of the tale that burrows like a seed in their little minds. The part where the girl comes back, tries to fit a lifetime into four short seasons, and finds love in the foreign place where she died. Whether they believe in the truth of Gabe Molloy's story or not (the very young do, the older ones try), they come away feeling that the possibility, at least, is real. They look into the twilight, beckoning visitors.

Then a child is chosen, an honor every young islander covets, to recite the words that are chiseled into the back of the Seward stone.

> *The angels are bending*
> *Above your white bed;*
> *They weary of tending*
> *The souls of the dead.*

> *God smiles in high heaven*
> *To see you so good;*
> *The old planets seven*
> *Grow gay with His mood.*

I kiss you and kiss you,
With arms round my own;
Ah, how shall I miss you,
When, dear, you have grown.

If you are a visitor, led there by a travel book, worn out from what seems such a long life, perhaps, while you watch this performance, you will yearn for your childhood home.

In that immeasurable instant where day fades to night, it is possible to believe that such a country exists—Tír na nÓg: a land created, exclusively and reverently, for the young.

AUTHOR'S NOTE

In the Country of the Young is a work of fiction; Tiranogue Island and its inhabitants are figments of my imagination. However, my imagination was inspired by history.

It is estimated that during the Irish potato famine, from 1846 to 1851, one million people died and two million more emigrated, mostly to North America. The "coffin ships" that carried these immigrants were overcrowded and unsanitary, and typhoid killed many both during and after the journey. In 1851, one of these vessels ran aground off Nantucket Island, and the passengers were rescued by local whaling men.

The following books were the most helpful in my research of the famine and Irish folklore:

A Famine Diary by Gerald Keegan; *The Famine Ships* by Edward Laxton; *Life Before the Famine* by Ignatius Murphy; *Patient Endurance: The Great Famine in Connemara* by Kathleen Villiers Tuthill; *1847 Famine Ship Diary* by Robert Whyte; *The Celtic Twilight* and *Writings on Irish Folklore, Legend and Myth* by William Butler Yeats; *Visions and Beliefs in the West of Ireland* by Lady Gregory; and *The Year in Ireland: Irish Calendar Customs* by Kevin Danaher.

I send a special thank-you across the sea to Desmond Kenny of Kenny's Bookshop, Galway, who supplies me with Irish books no matter where I am in the world.

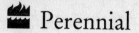 Perennial

Books by Lisa Carey:

IN THE COUNTRY OF THE YOUNG
ISBN 0-06-093774-2 (paperback)

On a stormy November night in 1848, a ship carrying Irish immigrants to America's shores ran aground twenty miles off the coast of Maine. Many were saved, and settled on the small island of Tiranogue, but some were not—including a young girl whom died crying out the name of her brother. In the present day, the artist Oisin MacDara lives in self-imposed exile on Tiranogue, haunted by memories of the twin sister who died tragically when he was a boy. Then on a quiet All Hallows' Eve, a restless spirit is beckoned into his home by a candle flickering in the window: the ghost of the girl whose brief life ended in that fateful shipwreck. For an empty man chained by painful memories, nothing will ever be the same again.

"Breathtaking...One of those rare books whose every scene is gripping, every mood and moment and minor character compellingly drawn, every new page an epiphany." — *Washington Post*

THE MERMAIDS SINGING
ISBN 0-380-81559-1 (paperback)

There is an island off the coast of Ireland called Inis Murúch — the Island of the Mermaids — a world where myth is more powerful than truth, and where the powers of family and love can overcome even death. Here the lives of three generations of Irish-American women are woven together: Clíona, who left Inis Murúch as a young woman; her fierce and beautiful daughter Grace, resentful when her mother decides it is time for them to return to the island; and little Gráinne, the daughter Grace steals away when she can take the confines of her mother's homeland no longer. The voices of these three women are woven together in an unforgettable tale of love and resentment between mothers and daughters and of the heartbreak of being torn between worlds.

"Mingling myth and motherhood, and jumping generations and continents...Lisa Carey has created a magical first novel." — *Boston Globe*